PLAYING WITH THE BOSS

MCKENZIE BROTHERS #1

LEXI BUCHANAN

HFCA Publishing House
Ireland

www.lexibuchanan.net

First Published 2013
This Edition 2024

Editor: Sirena Van Schaik
BETA Readers: HM Bendana, Kristy Louise Garbutt, Suella Holland, Marsha Thalleen, Gabriela Tortolano and Nadine Winningham

SYNOPSIS

Five handsome brothers prepare to meet their match!

Michael McKenzie, CEO of McKenzie Holdings, has a horrible habit of prioritizing work over everything else—until a chance encounter in an elevator changes his perspective.

Lily Redmond is on her first day of work, and she is unsure whether she should be startled or thrilled that her new boss is the sexy businessman she met on the way into the office.

If Lily's boyfriend David takes the initiative to ask for forgiveness, will Michael fight for what he feels is rightfully his, or will Michael and Lily both want to live happily ever after?

1

Lily

I LAY NAKED ON THE BED, IGNORING THE PANG OF disappointment when I heard David shuffling around in the bathroom. No doubt he was in there cleaning up after our sex session - at least that's what I'd call it. David had been having sex with me for the past five months, which consisted of a few open-mouthed kisses, a few licks and nibbles on my breasts, and a brief moment when he would insert a finger inside of me before he pushed himself home, leaving a trail of sweat and moans down my neck. Within seconds of entering me, he would shudder and release into the condom. I lay there feeling empty and unsatisfied, wondering what I'd done to deserve this.

David and I had been together since high school, about seven years. We were both seventeen when he moved to my town, and within a week of him starting school, we were inseparable.

He was my first kiss, my first date, and my first lover. Sighing, I turned and stared at the photos of our life together on the nightstand. We lived together while attending the same college and then moved to the same city after graduation. We even worked for the same company until two weeks ago, when I lost my job along with two hundred other employees. David was still working there, and for the past week he'd been making comments about my unemployment status, as if it was my fault that I didn't have a job.

Secretly, I'd been looking for another job because I was starting to want something else. I'd actually felt relief when the company let me go. For the first time in a long time, I was free, and there was nothing David could do about it. At least that's what I thought.

David, however, thought differently. My life had a constant soundtrack of how it was my fault. David told me almost daily that if I hadn't been "gathering wool" during department meetings, the boss wouldn't have noticed and I wouldn't have been on the "let go" list.

Ugh. I looked at the photo of us at the company retreat five months ago. I'd noticed a change in him then. When our sex life had turned into a one-man sprint. Up until then, we'd had what I'd call a "normal" sex life. Not always full of passion, but there was always mutual enjoyment.

Well, I could honestly say that I hadn't had an orgasm since then, and I really didn't think David cared. Not only had it started to annoy me, I found it troubling. We were still together years after all our friends had told us we wouldn't last, but I was beginning to think maybe they were right.

David was my lifeline, the only family I had since my parents died in a car accident five years ago. I didn't have any siblings to get me through it, and I clung to David even more than before. He was my security blanket. I came to this conclusion after talking to a psychiatrist for three years after their deaths, without David's knowledge.

The faucet in the bathroom turned off, warning me that David would be out soon. I glanced at the clock and knew now would be the best time to tell him that I was starting a new job at McKenzie Holdings headquarters. I hadn't told anyone about this job, simply because I wanted something that was mine and mine alone, at least for a while. The way David had been lately, he would have had a lot to say about it, not to mention the fact that the company was owned by Michael, Sebastian, Ruben, Lucien and Ramon McKenzie. Sebastian McKenzie was always in the paper with one starlet or another. Michael, the second oldest, was only ever in the paper when the company was mentioned and there was never a photo. Ruben and Lucien made the paper, but not as often as their brother Sebastian.

I'd never met the brothers; a Mr. Roberts had interviewed me for the job and I'd taken an instant liking to him. I smiled when I thought of him; his gray hair, slight paunch, and smiling eyes reminded me of my grandfather, who had died when I was about eleven years old. I'd signed the contract right then and there, and I was going to be Mr. Robert's assistant, which, I had to say, I was really looking forward to.

I quickly looked at the clock and groaned. I really needed to get out of bed, shower and get dressed, but David was hogging the bathroom. I'd just have to hurry after he left for work. I certainly didn't want to share.

The bathroom door opened, so I quickly covered myself with the blanket and pretended to be asleep again. Talking to him was the last thing I wanted to do.

Peering through my lashes, I watched as David fastened his watch to his wrist and tucked his wallet into the inside pocket of his suit jacket. Then, without so much as a glance at me, he picked up his keys from the nightstand before walking out of the bedroom. I held my breath and watched the bedroom door as I listened to him shuffle down the hall, loathing every sound he made. A few minutes later, I heard the front door to the apartment open and close, and the lock click into place. No goodbye from the door, no quick kiss on the forehead. It was as if I'd ceased to exist the moment he pushed his body away from mine.

I slowly came to the conclusion that our relationship was over. Tears stung my eyes at the thought. Part of me just wanted to lie in bed all day and cry; another part of me was relieved that I was ready to take the steps to end it. The only problem I had was that if - or should I say when - I left, I wouldn't have anywhere to go or enough money to put down a deposit on another apartment. I would have to save every dollar I could from now on and bide my time.

With a sigh, I pushed the covers away and climbed out of bed. I stretched my sore muscles and walked into the bathroom, grimacing at the mess he'd made in the sink. I rinsed the sink while staring at my pale complexion in the mirror above. Usually my skin tone was more olive due to my dark hair, but not today. I brushed my teeth before stepping into the hot shower and scrubbing David's touch off my skin.

With a towel wrapped around me and my hair still wet and dripping down my back, I stood and looked in my closet, not sure what to wear. Was I going for the professional look? Or the professional hot chick look? I decided to go for the in-between. The professional girl who could become a sultry vixen at night. I smiled to myself as I took my navy blue suit off the hanger, then laid it on the bed while I searched for the white blouse I liked to wear with it. When I found it hiding in the back of the closet, I pulled it out and placed it on the bed with my other clothes. I quickly put on my white lace underwear.

I fastened the blouse and pulled up the skirt, which was tailored to my curvy figure and came to rest a few inches above my knees. Not too short to be inappropriate for the office and not too long to make me look older than my twenty-four years.

Another rummage through my closet and I found the matching blue heels that made my legs look longer than they were. I stepped back and looked at myself in the mirror - I looked hot, especially with my hair pulled back in a mess on top of my head. David always thought it made me look sexy. Not anymore.

I took a deep breath, shook my head of unpleasant thoughts, and walked out of the apartment and to my new job.

Michael

Gripping my cell in one hand, I found myself clenching my teeth as my temper began to rise. Sebastian would deliberately ignore my attempts to contact him because he'd be thinking with a different part of his anatomy.

I'd been trying to reach my brother for two days

since I returned home. Oh, I knew he was safe. I also knew he was having a good time with a woman he'd picked up at the hotel bar during the conference in San Diego.

The woman had been eyeing me until she'd spotted Sebastian. Was I bothered? No. My brothers loved nothing more than to poke fun at me for keeping my private life just what it was...private.

No, I wasn't a monk, although I had been for the last few years. I didn't advertise what I was up to because the minute I was seen with anyone, the press would have a field day. The last time the press took a picture of me with a woman was six years ago, and the woman in the picture was my wife, Viv, just before she died.

I tossed my cell phone on the breakfast bar as I walked through the kitchen looking for a bagel. My brothers had once tried to set me up with a chef, as if that would ever happen, to get me to eat better. It hadn't worked because I loved my private space and no one was allowed in unless invited.

I found a bagel in the breadbox, sliced it, and popped it in the toaster. Pouring myself a coffee, I crossed my ankles and leaned against the cabinets. The day was going to be busy. I had a meeting at eleven and countless other things to do. Fortunately, my new assistant would be arriving first thing.

Dale Roberts had assured me that my new assistant, whom I had yet to meet, would be perfect and wouldn't let me down. Lily Redmond. She had no idea that her new position was as my assistant. Dale had interviewed her for me and had deliberately given her the impression that the position was with him. At least that way I'd get someone who knew how to use a computer instead of how to put polish on her nails.

Every time I interviewed someone, the interview had a habit of going downhill quickly as the young woman in question seemed more interested in me and my brothers than the actual job, which was damn frustrating.

Dale had run a background check on Lily. He had checked the reference she had provided from her previous employer. As far as he could see, she had been laid off due to company downsizing. Only it didn't add up. Her resume was spotless, her references even more so. Looking at her work history, she shouldn't have been fired, especially when her boyfriend was kept on.

The coffee tasted bitter as I watched the red coils in the toaster. Something didn't add up, and that was why I had asked a friend of a friend who worked at the company to dig deep and see what he could find out about why she was really let go. Something was wrong, and I would bet my last dollar that it had something to do with the boyfriend.

My bagel popped out of the toaster and I decided to put some cream cheese on it for a change instead of my usual butter. With the cheese spread on top, I took a seat in the breakfast nook just off the kitchen, which I preferred because of the amazing view of the garden and the mountains beyond.

Once in a while, I'd sit here and wish I had a woman to share it with-not often, but occasionally. I'd been alone since Viv died. She'd died on her way to meet our divorce attorneys, by which time whatever love I once had for her, if that's what it was, had died. We'd been married for three years, and in those three years I'd lost count of how many men she'd been with. I probably only knew about half of them. She'd completely skewed my perception of relationships and made me a skeptic. When you're alone, you can't get hurt, but sometimes it sucks.

It had taken me a long time to believe that she was the one with the problem, not me. I owed that revelation to my brothers, after they knocked some sense into me. Literally.

After breakfast, I quickly washed and dried the few pots and pans, collected my keys, and walked out to be greeted by my driver, George. I genuinely enjoyed driving, or more specifically, I enjoyed sitting on my Harley and letting it run wild. Unfortunately, the office was no place for my Harley, and it drove me crazy to drive into town with all the traffic and try to find parking. Instead, George drove me to the office, left me there, and parked at a nearby hotel where he spent the day drinking coffee, flirting with Janet, one of the receptionists, and waiting for me to call him for a ride. He also took advantage of the free wifi and hooked up his laptop.

"Morning, George," I said in greeting.

"Morning, Mr. McKenzie."

Once I got in the car, I sat back and tried to relax. Normally I would read the paper on the way into town, but Sebastian was on the front page, so I decided to pass. I had no objection to my brothers sowing their wild oats, but having Sebastian in the news every time he did it pissed me off.

I'd been so lost in my own thoughts for the last twenty minutes that when I looked out the window, George had already pulled up in front of the McKenzie building. "See you later, George," I said warmly as I opened the door. "Have a nice day," I told him as I got out of the car.

He blushed slightly and nodded in response. I fought the urge to chuckle. Even though he was a cool professional, Janet always had him hot under the collar. After the first week, I refused to let him get in and out of the car every time I needed to open the door.

It had taken a while to get used to being driven around, but I wasn't lazy enough to let the door open for me. I watched as he drove away and made a U-turn to get to the hotel. How the hell he never caused an accident with that move, I'll never know.

As I walked into the lobby, John, the security guard,

looked up and nodded in my direction, his crisp uniform always spotless and his radio on his hip. I continued on to the elevators. John was flirting with a woman at the front desk, which caused me to slow my pace. She was what Sebastian would call a "babe," with her long legs, tight skirt, and equally tight jacket over firm breasts. The heels she wore made her stand in a slightly provocative manner. Whisps of dark hair fell around her neck.

I swallowed at the sight of her and shook my head. She's just another girl trying to get the McKenzie brothers' attention. I walked on, and as I waited for the elevator, I turned and saw the receptionist walking toward me with her head down. She had no idea that I was standing there watching her.

When the doors opened, I stepped inside and held them open for the mystery woman. Her scent wafted toward me as she approached, and my dick instantly went hard. Shit, this was not good. I'd never reacted so quickly to a woman's scent before.

She looked up, and when her blue eyes met mine, they widened dramatically. She stopped mid-step and looked up at me. I hesitated, but managed to look away from her intense focus. "Your carriage awaits," I said brusquely.

Damn, I felt like I had been hit over the head. I watched her carefully, noting how her throat moved as she swallowed and then took a deep breath. Her jaw tensed and she stepped into the elevator. Was I affecting her as much as she was affecting me?

I felt quite uncomfortable. My cock throbbed and I wanted to believe it was due to lack of use rather than the attractive woman standing next to me.

Yes, keep telling yourself that.

2

Lily

SURPRISED. EXCITED. THRILLED. YES, THAT WAS PROBABLY the best word for it. Nothing else could explain the quickening of my pulse when my eyes met the man's at the elevator. My heart had stopped and my stomach was quivering as I stepped into the small space and tried to make room for the man. Never in my life had I reacted so strongly to a man.

As I stood in the elevator, the doors closed, leaving me trapped inside with the sexy man. I quickly leaned forward, pushed the button for the floor I wanted, and felt the heat flow from his body to mine. My stomach was still quivering and I was pretty sure my panties were soaked. He watched me carefully through the mirror on the doors, while I watched him out of the corner of my eye.

What was happening to me? David was acting like a jerk, but we were still in a relationship. At least I thought we were. I had no reason to be attracted to a stranger.

The man who had decided to give me his full attention, sending a rush of heat down my body as he glanced over me - I didn't think my panties could get any wetter.

"I haven't seen you before," he said, or was that a question? I wasn't really sure, but my toes practically curled up at the deep tone of his voice.

I finally managed to pull my tongue back into my mouth to utter a weak, "I'm new."

He didn't move his gaze. "I take it you work in the building?" I asked, trying to hide my embarrassment. I wasn't used to being the object of such a penetrating gaze. His eyes twinkled.

"You could say that. You didn't tell me your name?"

What did that mean? Either he worked here or he did not. "You didn't ask me my name." Oh God, was I just flirting with him?

"I'd like to know your name, if you don't mind telling me," he replied, a cocky grin playing at the corners of his full mouth. He's smooth. I'll give him that.

I groaned inwardly. This guy was really making a fool of me. I knew it would be a really bad idea to touch him, but I held out my hand anyway. "Lily Redmond."

He seemed to freeze for a single second before he straightened and took my hand. He wrapped his fingers around mine. The heat of his touch radiated through me, igniting a fire deep in my core.

I looked up, my hands still clenched in his. His eyes had darkened and there was a pulse at the side of his neck. Mmm, I wouldn't mind using my tongue in that area. I licked my lips, and his blue eyes darkened slightly as they followed the movement of my tongue.

He coughed, released my hand and stepped away. He was equally moved by me, as the bulge he was trying to hide in his pants showed. This realization made me hotter - and wetter. "I'm Michael McKenzie."

Those words poured cold water on me. He's my boss! Shit!

I hadn't even arrived at the office before I was flirting with my boss, or rather one of them.

"Michael McKenzie, as in McKenzie Holdings. My boss?" The words slipped out of my mouth almost incoherently.

"Yes, that's me." He looked about as happy as I was. I quickly tried to compose myself, hoping he didn't notice the panic in my eyes. This was definitely going to be an interesting day at work.

"Oh." The elevator beeped and the doors opened with excruciating slowness to the floor of McKenzie Brothers Executive Offices. The floor where Mr. Roberts had asked me to meet him.

I was rather disappointed that he was one of my superiors. I was really interested in getting to know him better, and I did not mean through sex. He was a very attractive man, tall with broad shoulders, a slender body, and the most stunning blue eyes. As he looked at me, I could feel a hunger in him. I wasn't sure what it was, but there was something there, something substantial and more than just attraction. I ran my fingertips together as they hung at my side, trying to grasp what I was feeling - it was almost as if we had a bond.

I heard a throat clearing and pulled myself together enough to step out of the elevator in front of Michael McKenzie to greet Mr. Roberts. He looked from me to his boss with curiosity in his eyes.

"Ah, Lily. You've met Michael McKenzie," he asked, his eyes fixed on me.

"Yes, we have met. Let's go to my office," Michael replied for me. Mr. Roberts jerked in surprise, shock written all over his face. The clipped tone made me wonder if he was going to fire me the moment I walked into the office. Michael gave me a quick scan before making his way to the glass door, which I assumed led to the inner sanctum.

I followed Michael and Mr. Roberts down the hall, trying not to tip over in my heels. The carpet was so thick my heels sank in like a sponge. The offices were luxurious, with no expense spared on the executive floor. I wondered what the other floors looked like. The art on the walls was vibrant. I wasn't sure where all the documents were stored because the furniture seemed minimal yet expensive.

I wasn't sure if I was ready to work for McKenzie or if McKenzie was ready for me to work for him. My personal office would probably be a complete disaster within a week - I wasn't the neatest person.

Following Michael into his office was like walking into the lion's den.

Michael had set his briefcase on the table and pulled out a few documents before setting it on the floor.

"Dale, these are the documents you left here yesterday. I've signed them, so you're good to go. Thanks for taking care of Lily, but I'll take it from here," he said to Mr. Roberts, who seemed flustered.

"Okay, Michael." Mr. Roberts turned to me and smiled reassuringly. "I'll talk to you later, Lily." He quickly walked out of the office, leaving me alone with the extremely attractive Michael McKenzie.

Michael

As I led Lily and Dale to my office, I tried to control my libido and my disappointment. I cursed myself silently and tried to keep a calm pace. I was an idiot for not recognizing who she was. I knew I had a new assistant because Dale had convinced me she was terrific and the best choice. After seeing the look on Dale's face when he realized we'd already met, I wondered if Dale had an ulterior motive for hiring Lily.

I hurried across my office to my desk, quickly retrieved the papers for Dale, and placed my briefcase near the coat rack. I looked at them briefly before taking a seat, adjusting myself slightly to hide my desire. My brothers, especially Sebastian, would be thrilled to know how I was reacting to my new assistant. I disliked reacting to women because it made me feel out of control, when I needed to be fully in control.

After Dale left, there was a heavy silence between us. She shifted in her seat, smoothing out the creases in her skirt. Her eyes darted around the room as she fidgeted, indicating that she was nervous. That was hardly surprising, given the fire that pulsed between us in the elevator. When she realized who I was, the heat in her eyes drained away, as if she had been drenched with water. But the change was so subtle that I would have missed it if I hadn't been paying so much attention to her. It wasn't fake. She really didn't know who I was. My assistant was the only woman in the world who really didn't.

"Lily." Her name slipped off my tongue and I loved the way it did. Her eyes met mine and locked, driving me crazy with need. "Dale interviewed you for his assistant position, but the open position was actually mine. I've had some problems interviewing in the past, so I decided to delegate the task to Dale. I apologize for the lack of honesty, but I hope you will stay."

I could see the wheels turning in her head. "Why do you have problems with interviews?"

I certainly wasn't expecting a question back; most people just agreed with me. "When I interviewed before, the interviewer knew my identity. They ended up being more interested in my siblings and me than in the job. It's not only embarrassing, it's annoying. Whereas in the elevator, you had no idea who I was. It was... refreshing."

I rearranged some papers on my desk to regain control of the meeting. I never shared. I just expected everyone to follow without question. Lily was refreshing.

"As my assistant, I expect every deadline to be met. I don't expect you to rush around running personal errands for me. If I stumble and ask, say no."

She laughed. "Okay. I'll have no problem saying no."

The sound of her laughter reached my dick as I saw her luscious lips curl into a huge grin, and all I wanted to do was take her over to my desk and seal our lips together.

I cleared the lump in my throat that I knew was lust and stood up, hoping she wouldn't look below my belt. "Please follow me, Lily, and I will show you to your desk. The reference we received for you was excellent, and they praised your computer skills, which I am sure will be an asset in this position."

Lily placed her purse on the desk and turned to face me. Her cheeks were flushed and her breathing was uneven. I wondered if she found the intimacy challenging as well.

"Okay, then. Here is the password for the computer. When you log in, please change it to something only you know, but please tell me. Don't write it down."

Standing so close to her made my body ready for action, so I informed her, "The coffee is over there, and it should be fresh. Sylvia at reception makes it every day. The work is over here," I placed my palm on the rapidly growing pile of papers, "which I think will keep you busy for most of the day. So I'll leave you to it for now."

Turning, I strolled over to the coffee maker and poured myself a cup before returning to my office.

"Mr. McKenzie?"

I didn't notice her approach, and when I turned around she was so close I had to fight myself not to back away. "Yes?"

She seemed flustered. "Thank you for not giving me my marching orders earlier," she exclaimed, swinging her arms.

Why would I do that? "You did nothing wrong." I couldn't take my eyes off her, noticing they were practically violet.

"I mean for...um...well...flirting," she blurted out.

Flirting. My heart raced - she was flirting with me. I hadn't imagined it.

"Okay." I turned and walked back to my office, closing the door behind me. Once inside, I leaned back against it and let out a sigh of relief. I was really screwed. Maybe it was a good thing that my womanizing brother Sebastian was in San Diego.

I got out of bed this morning, unconcerned about anyone but myself, uninterested in anyone. I walked into my office building only to be struck by lightning.

My cell phone started ringing on my desk, jolting me out of my daydream. Realizing who it was, I leaned over and answered it.

"Lucien?" He was my older brother, and the most serious. He had been as horrible a womanizer as Sebastian until his car accident five years ago, but now he was almost a recluse.

"What's Sebastian up to now?" He asked as a kind of greeting.

I sat down firmly in my chair. "Your guess is as good as mine. I haven't spoken to him in two days and it's not for lack of trying." I leaned back in my chair and turned ninety degrees to face the window and the Lexington skyline, watching the clouds roll in and block the sun.

"Tell him I need help out here.... He'll come."

"Are you sure?" Sebastian had never followed instructions, which always irritated our mother.

"Yes. Send someone to find him and put him on the next plane to me."

Shit.

I hung up as the phone was already beeping in my ear. Lucien had always struggled with manners, but after his accident they were nonexistent.

After a few minutes of thought, I texted Roger from the San Diego office and asked him to find Sebastian and contact me when he was with him.

3

____

Lily

As the door clicked shut behind Michael's departing back, I sighed with relief. It was hardly the ideal way to start a new job - flirting with your boss.

I didn't understand my reaction to Michael. Sure, he was attractive. But I had met handsome men before without giving them a second glance. I think my behavior was primarily motivated by loneliness. I put my face in my hands and sighed. I had flirted with him and then tried to apologize!

With the computer turned on and prompting me for a password, I entered the information Michael had provided and presto, I was connected to the system. After a cursory glance at the tasks that needed my attention, I walked over and poured myself a cup of coffee.

Mmm, it was absolutely wonderful, much better than I usually make.

Back at my desk, David came to mind. I didn't know what to do with him. It was hard. We had been together forever, and until recently he had always been there for me. Something was definitely going on with him, and if I didn't know better, I'd say he was having an affair.

"Hello, you must be Lily?"

I snapped out of my thoughts and looked up at a petite blonde wearing heels higher than mine. "Yes, that's me." I held out my hand, hoping for a name. I didn't have to wait long.

"I'm Sylvia. I work at the front desk. I've only been here three weeks." She shook my hand before pouring herself a cup of coffee.

She was beautiful, with a slender figure and extra-large assets that any man would want. Sylvia's sparkling blue eyes shone with joy, and her blonde hair was pulled back at the nape of her neck with a beautiful purple diamond, yet she still looked like she belonged in college.

"I guess I can thank you for the coffee? It's delicious." I took another sip.

"Do you want me to keep making it? Or would you like to prepare it when you arrive?"

"Oh, please keep making it. If you don't mind."

"I don't mind." She sipped her coffee. "So is the gossip

true? That you had no idea the work was with Michael McKenzie?" she murmured.

Sylvia definitely liked to gossip. "Dale Roberts interviewed me, and I don't remember if he told me who the job was with. I was very nervous." That should be enough, I hoped. I wasn't one for gossip.

Sylvia looked at me for a few seconds before shifting gears. "Do you have a boyfriend?"

I laughed.

She was curious and charming. She grinned.

"I think I have a boyfriend named David. We've been going out for seven years. I don't have any family and my previous job laid me off a few weeks ago along with about 200 others." I leaned back in my chair, took another sip of coffee, and watched her process what I had just said. I discovered that the best line of defense was to put everything out on the table. Rumors became less likely once everything was out in the open.

"So you're not going after Michael?" She paused. I frowned. "Almost all the girls want him, but he never shows any interest. In fact, rumor has it that he hasn't been interested since his wife died six years ago. I think that's what Jacky said. In fact, Jacky claimed that she thought there was something between you two when you got off the elevator.

Embarrassed, I felt heat rush to my face. At least I hadn't imagined the fire between us. I started to shuffle papers around my desk, hoping Sylvia would get the hint and leave so I could finish some work. She did.

Finally alone, I focused on my task. In no time, I had completed the task that had been placed on the desk. Not knowing what else to do, I got up and was ready to go to Michael's office when a woman dressed in exaggerated 'everything', including make-up, entered the room. I tried not to stare, but it was extremely difficult. I could not believe it was all real, especially the hair. She was quite a sight.

I cleared my throat. "Can I help you?"

"You're not my type," she scoffed. "Is Michael around? Now he is my type."

Oh my God, don't tell me he had sex with her. It shouldn't have bothered me, but it did. A lot.

"I'll check. What's your name?"

"Brandi."

How original.

"Have a seat and I'll see if he has time to see you." I made my way to Michael's office, hoping I was mistaken. With a quick knock on his door, I entered.

He grinned at me and my heart stopped. "There's a woman outside to see you." He seemed perplexed. "Brandi," I replied, and he raised an eyebrow in question. "She made it sound like you knew her, if you, uh, know what I mean."

Standing, he clenched his jaw and walked toward

me. I took a step back, feeling the cool roughness of the wood against my back. Unsure if I should open the door and flee, I lifted my chin as he leaned into me, my back pressed against the door. His body radiated heat, but he did not touch me. Instead, he stood close enough for me to inhale his musky scent. Butterflies filled my stomach.

"I don't know any Brandi in or out of the sheets," he said softly as he took the final step to close the space between us.

His erection pushed into my stomach. I just wanted to reach out and touch it. When he replied that he didn't know her, I felt a weight lift from my heart.

I looked into his eyes and the heat flashing in them made it clear that he wanted me as much as I wanted him. His erection jerked against me. My breathing became labored as I reached out and touched his chest. He shivered. This was not a good idea. I reminded him, "Brandi," hoping to break the spell.

He took a deep breath and moved away from me. "Open the door. Let's see what she wants."

All I wanted to do was throw myself into his arms. I opened the door and when he saw Brandi, he gave me a quick look before returning to her.

"Hi Brandi. I'm Michael McKenzie. How can I help you?"

Maybe he didn't really know her. She didn't act like she knew him either.

"I'm looking for Sebastian. Do you know where he is?"

Michael became uncomfortable at the mention of his brother. "I'm looking for Sebastian myself and he hasn't contacted me yet."

She got up and started walking away. "Please tell him that Brandi is looking for him."

"Will do."

He exhaled loudly and turned to me. He ran his hands through his hair. "Please don't ask."

"Okay." I walked back behind my desk and took a seat. "I finished the work that was on the desk."

"You have?" He sounded surprised. "There was a lot to do."

I smiled at him. "I'm a fast worker."

"Give me five minutes, then follow me to my office." After watching me for a minute, he turned and walked into his office, closing the door behind him without saying anything.

Michael

I loosened my tie as the door closed behind me. I felt flushed, uncomfortable, and aroused. I was seconds away from slamming my mouth on Lily's. As I approached her, I became rock hard, wanting nothing more than to lock my door and wrap her in my arms, lift up her skirt and see how wet she was for me. Then I'd fuck her senseless. I'd bet my left nut she was wet and as excited as I was.

God. I got some much-needed air and went to my desk, where I sat down before Lily walked in and discovered the boner I was trying to hide.

I leaned back in my chair and looked out the window. What the hell am I doing? I wondered. She lived with her boyfriend. She was my assistant and seemed competent, so I did not want to lose her. The reasons not to get involved were screaming at me. I knew I'd have to get used to a cold shower because I'd keep my zipper up no matter how much I wanted Lily's hands inside.

Why her? I had never reacted to Viv the way I did to Lily. Oh, I had lusted after Viv and made the mistake of thinking it was love. Not a mistake I wanted to repeat. But what was it about Lily that made me hard as a rock the moment she looked at me and ready to orgasm the second she touched me? I had a feeling she was going to drive me completely crazy.

Lily. I had to tell Lily about the eleven o'clock meeting. Even though it wasn't my goal, I felt obligated to do so to prevent her from being surprised by her boyfriend's presence.

I was actually glad that he would be at the meeting so

I could see the competition. Shit, I was not in the competition. Yeah, right. You keep telling yourself that.

A tentative knock on my door snapped me out of my thoughts. "Come in, Lily." She opened the door and ventured in slowly, apprehensive but lovely. I stood and walked to the sofa. "Let's sit here while we discuss the meeting at eleven."

"Okay. Where shall I leave these letters for you?" she asked.

"Just put them on the corner of the desk." I sat down in the chair by the side of the sofa, hoping that not crowding her would make her feel comfortable.

I watched her move across the floor and noticed the blush on her cheekbones. She was sitting on the sofa, close but not too close.

I couldn't even remember what I wanted to talk to her about. I leaned forward, bringing my thoughts and myself together. "The meeting's with Oakfield Architectural Design." Her wide eyes met mine. "They're one of three firms selected to bid on McKenzie Holdings' new development outside of town. Is that going to be a problem?"

She seemed more nervous than usual as I studied her intently, and she remained silent.

"I know who your boyfriend is because we do background checks on all prospective companies. Lily, David is one of the Oakfield representatives who will be attending the meeting."

She looked everywhere but at me. "Lily?" She gave me a quick look before concentrating on her clenched fists. "Please talk to me."

"He doesn't know I started working here. I never told him about the interview, the job offer, or the fact that I started here today. I guess I just wanted something for myself. He can be quite outspoken, and I was really looking forward to working here, so I decided to keep quiet rather than have him chastise me." She finished with a shrug.

"Okay," I replied, although I wasn't sure what to say to her. Hadn't she talked to her boyfriend? "How do you want to handle this?"

She nervously tucked her tangled hair behind her ear.

"I need you at the meeting, Lily. If I could spare you, I would." I barely managed to keep myself from falling at her feet. God, if one of my brothers were here right now, they'd be laughing at me for acting like a fool over a woman I'd just met.

"Don't worry, Michael. Can I call you Michael, or do you prefer Mr. McKenzie?"

"Michael when we're alone, but you should probably use Mr. McKenzie in the presence of others."

"Okay. We're all adults, and David's always the professional, so hopefully he won't be mad at me, at least until tonight," she replied, trying to laugh it off.

Why on earth would her so-called boyfriend be

angry that she had a job? A job that paid well. He was an idiot.

"Lily, if he makes you nervous at the meeting, I'll be right next to you."

She nodded.

"Okay, Oakfield is leading the bidding now. I'll tell you that I prefer one of the other companies, but my brothers are very happy with Oakfield. The purpose of today's meeting is to review some designs that we have requested from all three companies. I'm going to review them and hear what they have to say, but I'm not going to make a decision until I meet with my brothers. I will ask you to take notes, but don't write everything down. I'll let you know when I need something written down, okay?"

"Yeah, that sounds easy enough." She smiled and I lost my train of thought. "Is everything okay?" she asked, nervous because I had been staring at her.

"Am I making you nervous, Lily?" I couldn't believe I was asking her that. My mouth had to reattach itself to my brain. I held out my hand. "That was out of line. Let's get this meeting over with." I was also out of line earlier when I pinned her to the door. She had every right to scream sexual harassment, but she felt too good for me to care.

We stood and I grabbed her elbow; she shivered as my fingers closed around it. "Lily." She looked at me, and I saw what my proximity meant to her.

She hesitantly pulled away and started for the door. "I'm just going to grab a notebook and some pens," she whispered over her shoulder, closing the door behind her.

I was an adult acting like a teenager with his first crush. I really needed to pull myself together.

4

Lily

I slumped heavily into my desk chair, not sure if my legs could hold me up much longer. I wasn't sure how I was going to get out of Michael's office. The reaction to my boss was not good, but regardless of who he was, I was still in a relationship with David, even if he was acting like a first-class jerk. The problem was that I couldn't deny my intense feelings for Michael, no matter how hard I tried.

"Ready?"

I hadn't even heard him leave his office. I stood up quickly, grabbed my notepad and pencils from my desk, and joined him. "Ready as I'll ever be."

We walked side by side down the hallway that I

assumed led to the conference room. I could smell him: all man and cologne. Nothing was sexier.

As we rounded the corner, Michael opened the door for me. I froze as I walked into the conference room and saw David sitting there. His face went from a bland, welcoming smile to confusion and anger. Michael bumped into me, knocking me off balance, and his arm snaked around my waist to keep me from falling on my face.

The feeling of being held against Michael, feeling his arousal against my backside, was delightful. But when I turned to ask him to release me, our faces were only inches apart. His eyes bored into mine with an intensity that sent shivers down my spine, and I couldn't help but lean in closer, feeling the heat between us intensify. The air crackled with anticipation as I waited for his next move. "Let me go," I whispered.

He squeezed my waist before carefully untangling himself and leading me further into the room. David was sitting next to two of his colleagues, John and Peter. David stared speechlessly. "Hello, David. John, Peter."

Michael grabbed my elbow and pushed me into the chair to his right. David remained speechless.

"I hope the fact that Lily is now my assistant doesn't cause any complications. I know Lily had nothing to do with your proposal, so there shouldn't be any conflict of interest," Michael informed them.

David narrowed his eyes at Michael's hand on my

elbow, then focused his cold gaze on my face. I resisted the impulse to look down; my nostrils burned with anger. He had no right to look at me like that. I lost my job; why shouldn't I look for another one? Okay, maybe I should have told him, but I didn't want a lecture, which is exactly what I would have gotten.

"How long have you been here, Lily?"

I recognized the tone. He was angry. "I started here this morning."

His eyes narrowed. "So while we were being intimate this morning, you didn't think to tell me?"

Heat burned my face and guilt rushed through me. How could he? In front of others.

"Enough." Jumping, my gaze shifted to Michael, his fist clenched against the table he had just slammed into. He seemed as angry as David. "Are you going to make a bid or not?" Michael demanded.

During the confrontation, Peter cleared his throat and gave David a warning look before shuffling his papers. Then he began the lecture in a reedy tone. I tried to concentrate on what Peter was saying, but only the points Michael had instructed me to note seemed to sink in. Instead, I thought and focused on David.

He spent the whole presentation staring at me, giving sporadic feedback on the idea and acting like he was in charge of everything. He was an ass. Why did I only see this now? How the hell could someone who cared about someone else blurt out something 'intimate'?

Michael noticed my anxiety and slid his hand under the table. His strong fingers massaged my hand before intertwining it with mine. I held on tightly and stroked his thumb. It wasn't right, but it felt good. It was soothing, but my blood was still boiling.

He clasped my hand and then released it, running the backs of his fingers down my leg and hip before bringing his hand back over the table.

He looked at me, his eyes burning. "Can you make a note of this?" He smiled, realizing what he had done to me.

With a shake of my hand, I began to put pen to paper, but I couldn't remember what had been said. My mind had been on Michael, not the meeting. He understood my position and reiterated what he wanted noted.

We didn't touch for the rest of the meeting, which went smoothly, and David seemed to have stopped being a jerk. I still couldn't believe he'd told everyone that we'd been intimate that morning, something I wished Michael hadn't known about. Admittedly, I should have corrected him and reminded David that he was the one getting intimate while I was just lying there accepting him.

John handed Michael copies of the papers and sketches he was keeping for his meeting with his brothers while I stood there hoping for a quick exit. I looked at Michael and understood that he had too much to carry back to his office.

"It's okay, Lily. You can go back if you want. I can come back and get the rest," he explained.

I couldn't do that. I wanted to stay close to him. It was amazing to have him touch me during the meeting, and I wanted to feel his hands on me again.

"It's okay. I'll stay and help." He frowned over my shoulder. I looked around and saw David lingering at the end of the table.

"Lily, can I have a word with you before I leave?"

There was tension in the room and I could tell it was between Michael and David. I turned to Michael. "I'll just be a minute." He grimaced and seemed about to say something, which made me hesitate before turning my attention back to David. "Let's go over here." I walked away, leaving him to follow.

"What the hell are you doing here, Lily?" he hissed, his voice cold.

"I needed a job. I applied and got it. It's a great company to work for, and you should be happy that I got another job so quickly. It pays more, too."

"Well, I'm not happy. Why don't you just let me work while you take care of the apartment?"

My eyebrows furrowed. "I can't live on fresh air, David." I was astonished. He wasn't upset because I'd kept the job a secret, but because I wasn't unemployed and free to take care of the apartment or whatever.

"I would give you housekeeping," he added in a tight, controlled tone, which was generally a clue that he was upset.

As I straightened my spine, anger bubbled up inside me. "I'm too old to get an allowance, and what the hell was that about being intimate?" I asked angrily, poking him in the chest with my finger.

"McKenzie was looking at you, so I wanted him to know who you woke up with this morning."

"You're an ass. Since he knows I live with you, I guess he expected me to wake up with you this morning. That was totally inappropriate."

"Lily. We need to get back to the office." Michael called. Thank God. I really didn't want to be anywhere near David.

"Okay. I'm done here."

I was about to go back to the table to get my stuff and some of Michael's documents when David grabbed my arm.

"I'll see you at home, Lily. Don't forget, we're meeting Daniel and Val tonight," he said, loud enough for the whole room to hear.

Michael looked like he was going to lose it. I moved my arm away. "Whatever."

I followed Michael out of the conference room. I knew the conflict was far from over.

Michael

What the hell did Lily see in that bastard? I'd never felt like hitting someone like I did with him. Throughout the meeting, he stared at Lily, making her uncomfortable. I wanted her to know that she was supported, so I slipped my hand under the table and ended up holding her hand, which felt great. She touched my thumb gently and tantalizingly. While I couldn't concentrate on the meeting, I imagined her warm hands moving up my crotch. Of course, the contact and the fantasy made me feel a strong throb in my pants.

It had been over five hours since we had met and I already wanted her all to myself. I felt possessive of her. Back in the conference room, all I wanted to do was punch the bastard and tell him she was mine. I wanted to grab her and claim her with my mouth so they both understood to whom she belonged. I wanted to keep David away from her.

Damn it, I had lost all reason. I should have listened to Ramon's rant the other night about how I needed to get laid. It had been a long time, and maybe if I hadn't been so horny, I could have acted like a CEO instead of a hormonal teenager.

"Are these all right?" Lily asked.

I nodded, painfully aware of her movements as she arranged the materials on the conference table in my office.

"Do you think you could type up the notes this afternoon?" I smiled at her, hoping she'd smile back. She did, and her whole face lit up. She was adorable.

"No problem." She raised her hands and wiggled her fingers. "Super fast fingers here."

I chuckled as I watched her walk away, and before she closed the door, she winked. Damn!

She had left a lot of paperwork on my desk, but instead of going through it, I left it and checked my email to see if Sebastian had sent anything. Nothing. I picked up my phone and dialed his number, and he answered.

"Sebastian, where the hell are you?" I ran my fingers through my hair.

"I'm still in San Diego, and our friend Roger is standing guard. What the hell is going on?"

I smiled. He didn't sound too happy. "Lucien called. He wants you to go to Denver. Don't ask me why; I have no idea. He just wanted me to get you on a plane. Now that you've been found, Roger will take you to the airport so you can calm the baby down."

He huffed with laughter. "Did you not just call our older brother a baby? It was an excellent one. Just wait till I tell him."

I groaned.

Lucien used to be a lot like Sebastian, but things changed after he was involved in a car accident. He had now fled to Colorado to avoid the outside world. Lucien visited but enjoyed his own space.

"Just go, Seb. Make sure he's okay, and if possible, bring him home for the picnic in a few weeks."

"Shit. I completely forgot. Okay, I'll do it."

After I disconnected, I tried not to think about Lucien and how broken my brother was, and instead began to go over the spreadsheets Dale had provided for me yesterday. That proved easier said than done, thanks to the image of Lily in my mind.

The thought of her going home to that jerk made me angry. I had no right to react the way I did, but I couldn't help it. The attraction was instant and I was sure she felt the same way. I wasn't wrong. Something about her attracted me, and for the first time, the prospect of more than a one-night stand did not make me nervous. I knew that once Lily came to me, I would never let her go because she was mine.

With a deep breath, I forced myself to focus on the task at hand. I needed to distract myself with work. Before I started sorting through the documents, I saved the spreadsheets I needed to work on to a thumb drive so I could work on them at home. I turned to the conference table and began sorting through Oakfield's documents and sketches.

Lily came in an hour later, arms full of paper. "What

do you have there?" I inquired, walking over and taking some of them from her.

"A cup of coffee," she handed me. "The typed notes, documents a courier brought over, and the mail I found unopened in a filing cabinet I didn't even know existed," she added frantically as she sorted them into neat piles on my desk.

"Wow, you've been busy." I took a sip of coffee, which felt good sliding down my parched throat.

"I don't like sitting around doing nothing." She smiled at me. "Looks like you've been busy too."

I laughed as I glanced toward the conference table and the amount of paper spread across it.

"Your brother called."

Those three words stopped me in the middle of my drink. "Which one?"

"The one who likes to flirt."

"Sebastian," I groaned in a strained voice. "What did he say to you?"

She placed a gentle hand on my arm and offered a warm smile. "He wanted to know who I was. But I drew the line when he asked about my dress size." She chuckled with amusement.

Shit. "You should stay away from Sebastian. He goes through women like bread."

"That's a new one," she giggled again, and I realized I liked the sound. "Don't worry, I'm not interested in your brother."

She had me spellbound, standing so close to me. I reached out with my hand and caressed her face. She moved into my hand and kissed my palm. With a tiny shake of my hand, I put down my cup and came closer. I held her hand and intertwined our fingers.

My cock was about to explode and wouldn't stop twitching. God, one touch and I'd be done.

"Michael, what's happening?" She whispered.

I took a much-needed breath, removed my hand from her face, and rested my forehead against hers. "I'm not sure... But you need to go home. Now." The hardest thing I'd ever done was to take a step away from her. "I'll see you tomorrow, Lily."

Watching the woman I wanted more than anything walk out of my office, knowing she was going home to some jerk who didn't deserve her, hurt me more than it should.

5

Lily

WHAT WAS HAPPENING TO ME? ALL I WANTED TO DO WAS stay in the office with Michael. He tugged at my heartstrings. He looked so lonely. I was torn, and guilt made me reluctant to enter my apartment complex. Not only did I enjoy working with Michael, but I looked forward to seeing him again tomorrow. Now all I had to worry about was David.

David. What the hell happened to our relationship? It drove me crazy trying to pinpoint when things started to change. I couldn't say it was sudden, but rather a long, steady decline.

Five months ago, we spent the weekend at his boss's house with some other employees who were working on a particular contract. The weekend had gone well, but since then our relationship had begun to deterio-rate. Now I cringed when he approached me, which was not good.

I put my head on my apartment door for a moment, afraid of what I would find when I opened it.

With a sigh, I put the key in the lock and opened the door, only to be met with black silence.

Standing in the apartment, I closed and secured the door before walking down the narrow hallway into the living room and coming to a stop when I saw what was waiting for me. I was completely speechless.

David was sitting in the chair, his hand encircling his heavy cock. He was naked.

"How about giving me that sexy mouth?" I had never seen him like that and I could feel my cheeks burning with embarrassment.

As I stood in shock, he accelerated his fist and his breathing changed.

"David." I honestly didn't know what to say or do. What are you doing?"

"Hell, babe." He laughed. "I'm almost done. Will you come over here and blow me?"

"Like hell. Your fist seems to be doing the job just fine." I went to the bedroom, grabbed my yoga pants and a shirt, and locked myself in the bathroom, feeling very proud of myself.

I turned on the shower and immediately got

undressed. I climbed in before I succumbed to the tears that had been threatening for weeks.

My mother always said that a good cry was a great relief and improved one's attitude. I hoped that was true.

I couldn't get over stepping in and watching him jerk off. I didn't think he could ever surprise me. But he had.

My mind went back to that tender moment in Michael's office. I'd wanted him so much and still did. My body burned for him and I had known him for less than 24 hours. His shaft seemed much bigger than David's and I looked at it as I left his office. Michael was fully aroused, judging by the large bulge in his pants. Now, if Michael had been naked in the chair asking for my lips, I would have had no problem with that. So why did I have a problem doing it for David? Guilt washed over me until I remembered that David had pulled away first.

After my shower, I stepped out to dry off. I threw the towel in the hamper and pulled on my clothes. Sitting on the side of the bathtub, I thought about how to handle the situation with David that had left me astonished and ashamed.

We were supposed to meet some friends, Daniel and Val, at our usual wine bar in about three hours, which was the last thing I needed tonight. I'd rather crawl into bed and wake up tomorrow when it was time to go to work.

Michael

I watched Lily leave my office and then the building. It had been difficult. She'd definitely gotten under my skin. That was why I was still in pain, or rather my dick was. Oh, I saw Lily look down and see how aroused I was. I had also noticed a blush on her cheeks just before she closed my office door. With a sigh, I ran my fingers over my desire and took a breath. I was tempted to give myself the satisfaction I desired, but true relief would only come when I was buried between Lily's legs.

Before I could do anything, I had to take care of a few things. I immediately picked up my phone and called George.

"Mr. McKenzie?" he answered.

"I'll be ready in five minutes, George." I ran my hands through my hair as I looked out the window into the early evening dusk.

"I just left the hotel, so I'll be there soon." He hung up.

I tried to straighten up a little; I hadn't realized I was so rumpled. I rolled up my shirt sleeves, fastened the top two buttons at my neck, fixed my tie, and grabbed my suit jacket. I checked that everything was turned off, grabbed my things, and turned off the lights before locking the office doors.

Standing in the elevator, I grinned as I remembered my morning ride in the same elevator. The ride changed my perspective on what I wanted out of life. Lily.

I grumbled and exited the elevator, making my way outside to find George standing by the side of the car with a broad grin on his face. His face did not change as I approached. When I realized that his body was there, but his mind was clearly elsewhere. I grinned, "I take it you had a good day."

"Oh yes!" He blushed. "I mean, an interesting day."

"You're not the only one who had one of those days." He raised an eyebrow in curiosity. "Don't ask."

I sat back in the car and watched George drive out of town and toward my house. It felt remarkably private, even though it was only a twenty-minute drive from the McKenzie building downtown. I designed it myself, had McKenzie Holdings build it, and moved in as soon as it was finished. That was four years ago.

It was my home, my space, and no one was allowed in unless invited. Needless to say, I never had a woman inside the walls except for my mother.

My home was a large rustic log cabin on the outside, but it was anything but rustic on the inside. I valued my comforts, and if they included every modern convenience, such as my huge flat-screen TV, which I'd occasionally sit in front of with my brothers to watch a game or two, so be it.

George opened the door for me, which made me

wonder-he must have been exhausted from his day because he knew not to open it.

"We're home now, and I figured since you've been sitting in the back while I've been parked for five minutes, you might need a reminder on how to open the door."

Maybe he wasn't the only one confused. "Okay, thanks for that, George. I'm a little distracted."

He looked at my face and a light appeared in his eyes. "Ah, a woman. You've never had a woman distract you before. Anyone I know?"

"No. She's my new assistant." I let out a growl.

George seemed startled. "Oh."

I exhaled. "Exactly."

"I see the problem." He chuckled and got back in the car. George lived on my land in a small two-bedroom cabin about a ten-minute walk from the main house. It was all part of his job as my chauffeur. Over the years, though, he'd become part of the family. He didn't know it, but the cabin was his, regardless of his employment.

I walked into my house and left everything on the table in the foyer, including my jacket and tie, before entering "the cave," as my mother called it. Every wall was lined with bookshelves, and a massive mahogany desk in the center was equipped with the latest technology. Off to the side was a discreet but sophisticated bar. That's what I really needed right now: alcohol.

I sat at my computer in the dark, drinking whiskey and wondering what Lily was up to. I wondered if her jerk of a boyfriend was trying to rekindle his relationship with her or if he was still being disrespectful. I wanted nothing more than for Lily to be with me, which was absurd considering I'd only known her for a day. I found myself looking forward to tomorrow for reasons other than work.

My phone started ringing just as I was about to take a shot of whiskey. I answered the third ring, holding the glass in my left hand. "McKenzie."

"Mr. McKenzie, it's Derek," the voice trembled with anxiety.

I leaned forward in anticipation - Derek was the man I'd asked to find out why Lily had lost her job. "I know who you are. Have you discovered anything?"

"I overheard a conversation this morning that gave me some insight into why Lily was dismissed. At lunch, David and another man named Peter were discussing Lily. Apparently, they met with you and realized that she was now working for you. David seemed angry, but the other guy asked why he should be worried since he was "banging the boss's daughter".

Fuck. I hadn't expected that. "Are you sure?"

"David made some ugly comments about her and Lily, so sure. From what he said, it seemed that way, and I think the boss's daughter had something to do with Lily's departure."

"Thank you, Derek. You have been a great help. I will send you the money this evening."

"Thank you, Mr. McKenzie. Have a good night."

I slammed the phone down on the desk and drank my whiskey before tossing the empty glass into the unlit fireplace. What a terrible mess. Was I going to tell Lily, or was she going to find out on her own? If I told her, I could console her, as long as she didn't shoot the messenger. If she found out on her own, she might contact me on her own. What a terrible position to be in.

The sooner she got away from him, the better. The thought of them together was driving me crazy.

The harsh ring of the phone interrupted my thoughts. "Yeah," I grumbled, annoyed.

"What the hell's wrong with you?" Lucien asked.

"Nothing. What is it? Has Sebastian arrived yet?" I leaned back in my chair, experiencing the lethargy that typically comes after a glass of whiskey.

"Yes, he's here. I just wanted to let you know that he's arrived. Why are you trying to get rid of me?"

I laughed. Trust Lucien to see through me. "No reason, just one of those days." I paused. "Don't forget the McKenzie picnic in a couple of weeks," I added.

"Don't worry, I'll be there," he sighed. "If I have to."

"You must," I replied. If I hadn't forced him to come, he would have stayed in Denver.

"All right, Michael. I'll see you in two weeks, so don't do anything I wouldn't do." He laughed.

I hung up the phone, only to hear it ring again two minutes later.

"Ruben, what now?"

"Well, you sound like you're in a good mood." Ruben laughed, his voice hollow over the phone.

"Look, I've had a shitty day, so just get on with it."

"Okay, I called to see if you wanted to come to the club tonight for a few drinks. You need to get laid."

I let out a growl. "If I want to get laid, I can find my own woman. But I could use a distraction."

"So you'll come down then?"

My eyes swept the room. I needed a distraction, otherwise I'd be thinking about Lily all night. A few drinks with my brother might be the perfect distraction. I nodded and replied, "Yeah."

I hung up. If I didn't know better, I'd assume he was up to something. Fists could fly if he had a woman ready and waiting. I only wanted one woman.

Lily.

6

Lily

SITTING ON THE EDGE OF THE TUB, I LOOKED DOWN AT MY freshly painted toes. The bright red color reminded me of cherries and I wondered if Michael would like them. Heat coursed through my body as I thought of him, forcing me to look at the bathroom door. Ice water ran through my veins at the mere thought of David.

I glanced around the bathroom where I'd been hiding for forty-five minutes, terrified of what I would find when I came out. My stomach groaned in protest. I was starving and needed something to eat. Sighing, I tossed the nail polish back into the drawer and stood by the door, hesitating as I listened for him. "Please let him leave," I whispered. The last thing I needed was to see him after the show. I mean, what could I say to him?

Okay, I can do this. Putting on a brave face, I opened the bathroom door, only to be assaulted by the aroma of butter chicken.I followed the delicious smell into the kitchen and found David standing over the stove, fully clothed - thank God - with an apron tied around his waist, stirring what I presumed to be butter chicken. The only thing David seemed to be able to cook.

He turned and caught me watching him. "I thought you were going to stay in there all night."

I laughed. "I wasn't sure what I'd be walking into after..." My voice trailed off as I waved my hands in the direction of the living room, "You know."

His jaw tensed as he looked at me for the longest time before turning back to the stove. "I've been horny all day after seeing you all businesslike at McKenzie's."

My mouth dropped. Was he serious? He was pissed as hell.

"Are you sure about that? Because that wasn't the impression I got earlier."

Sitting at the kitchen table, I waited for him to answer. He'd heard me-his shoulders stiffened for a moment. I watched him serve the chicken and rice, and after he put my plate on the table, he took a seat across from me.

He poured us both a glass of wine and looked at me, offering a toast. "To your new job."

Okay, I could play along. "To my new job." I agreed,

putting my wine back on the table as he continued to watch me.

He leaned back in his chair. "Look, I reacted badly today at McKenzie's." His eyes searched mine. "It was just a shock to see you there with Michael McKenzie. The guy couldn't take his eyes off you, which made me uncomfortable."

I smiled as I put a piece of chicken in my mouth and tasted it. Despite some obvious flaws, David could make delicious butter chicken. I sat quietly, savoring the food as I chewed on his words, unsure of how to respond. "David, you were a jerk and acted rather unprofessionally. You can't expect me to sit at home all day and do nothing. I've always worked, even in college. I can't believe you didn't expect me to find another job." I looked at him for a few moments before continuing to eat. I was incredibly hungry, which was not surprising considering I had skipped lunch.

He sighed and put his fork back on his plate. "Okay, I was mad because I couldn't believe you didn't tell me you were working there. Not only that, but when you stopped in the doorway and your boss walked into you, there was no need for him to put his hands on you the way he did."

He was right, but I didn't want to admit it. "Look, I'm sorry I didn't tell you about the job." He raised an eyebrow at me, urging me to continue, but all I wanted to do was eat, go to bed, and forget about going out later. "I didn't tell you because I didn't want a lecture from you. There, I've said it." After I finished eating, I pushed my plate away and glared at him, waiting for his reaction.

He shifted in his chair and looked into his wine. "I'm sorry too, Lily. I really am. I've had a lot on my mind lately and I guess I took it out on you. Will you forgive me? We've been together a long time and I don't want to lose you."

What could I say? I really didn't want to be in this relationship anymore, and I hoped he didn't either. I wasn't sure I was brave enough to say anything yet, especially since I had nowhere else to go, which was a poor excuse.

"What happened when I got home? You've never done anything like that before," I asked, feeling quite embarrassed, and judging by the blush on his face, so was he.

"I thought if you saw me doing it, you might be more interested. I thought you would find it hot."

Stunned, I just stared at him. "I think I should go and get ready to go out, although I would rather go to bed. I'm really tired after my first day at work." I just wanted to get this conversation over with.

"We could let Daniel and Val go and stay here if you want. I don't mind an early night."

That wasn't what I wanted. I didn't want him to

touch me, to be honest. "No, I'm looking forward to seeing Val."

"Okay." He didn't seem too bothered by my rejection, so I got up and put my dishes in the sink on my way out of the kitchen.

"We're still meeting them at the wine bar, right?" I called back to him on my way to the bedroom.

"Club Kenza. It only opened last week, but Daniel called this morning and said Val managed to get four priority tickets. I hope you don't mind going to a club instead of a bar," David said as he started to follow me into the bedroom.

"No, that's fine." At least I'd be able to get lost in the music for a while instead of having to make small talk with David in the wine bar.

Michael

I just wanted to have a couple of beers tonight, so I threw on some jeans and a long-sleeved t-shirt with my leather jacket, then dragged my Harley out of the garage and roared into town to Ruben's new business venture, Club Kenza.

When I talked to Ruben on the phone earlier, it sounded like he had something up his sleeve that worried me. I had hoped he would take me seriously when I said I was not interested, but he mentioned getting laid. The last thing I wanted to do tonight was fight off a woman Ruben thought I'd like. The only woman I wanted was out with her boyfriend.

I parked the bike right in front of the club, knowing that Keith, the security guard at the door, would be keeping a close eye on it.

I got off the bike and shook Keith's hand as I walked through the door he had opened for me. As soon as I stepped inside, I was drawn to the beat of what the DJ was playing. Everyone seemed to be having a good time, judging by the gyrating and screaming. It wasn't bad, especially for a club. I preferred quieter music with less screaming.

The music was just what I needed to bring the headache I had been having most of the day to the forefront. I knew this was a really bad idea, and just as I was about to go find my brother to tell him I was going home, he found me with a woman on his arm.

I wanted to kill him.

"Michael, I was wondering when you were going to get here. I want you to meet Michelle."

I reached out to shake her hand and found her in my arms. What the hell? Ruben made a quick escape.

"Hello Michael. Your brother tells me you're in need of some female company."

"Well, I'm afraid my brother was misinformed," I

replied, trying to pull myself away from her. God, she was like a damn octopus. "Look, Michelle, I'm sure you're a nice young lady, but I really just want to be alone tonight."

She started to cry. What the hell?

Ruben was in deep shit when I got my hands on him.

I could be polite for a short while and then hopefully someone more willing would come along and take her off my hands. I gave her a reassuring smile and said, "Let's go find a table and have a drink." She perked up at that, apparently able to turn the waterworks on and off whenever she wanted.

I grabbed her elbow and led her through the crowd of dancers to a table before placing our drink order.

How the hell did I get into these situations? Or more to the point, why did my brothers put me in these situations? I thought going to Ruben's club tonight would change my mood from irritated because Lily was with someone else to calm. I needed to relax. I wasn't sure how much tension I could handle before I snapped and took Lily to my desk. Unfortunately, any notion of simply enjoying myself vanished thanks to my ass of a brother trying to fix me up. Being stranded with Michelle really pissed me off. It was not her fault, so the least I could do was be polite. I really wish I hadn't ventured out there.

One of the waitresses brought our drinks and set them on the table. I knocked back the whiskey and then drank half the beer. Michelle just sat and watched me while she sipped her wine and snacked on the peanuts that had been left on the table.

"What do you do, Michael?"

"Construction," I replied dryly. This wasn't a date, so date questions didn't apply. Hopefully she would get the hint and look for someone else.

"So you build things, like on a construction site?"

I sat forward and looked at her for a minute. She was really pretty. She had a slim build, blonde hair, blue eyes, and big breasts that she kept pushing up with her arms. Any more pushing up and they'd fall out of her dress.

"Michelle, I don't mean to be a bastard, but this isn't a date. My brother thought I needed a woman, but I don't. In fact, I have one. She's just not available right now. I'll buy you something to eat if you're hungry, but after that I'll be on my own." I emphasized the last word, "I want you to know that."

"She's a lucky woman."

"Yeah."

I leaned back in my chair and watched the dance floor as I finished my beer. Ruben had done an excellent job with this place. McKenzie's had completed the restoration, and I had told him he was crazy for wanting to do it, but now I knew better. Sebastian had told me that the place was packed every night, with people lining up outside to get in. The club had only been open for a week, but maybe this would continue.

A quick glance back at Michelle assured me that she was more than busy.

"Why don't you go over and say hello?" I suggested, hoping she'd take the hint.

She got up and, without another word, stomped off in the direction of the two guys who had been eyeing her.

I picked up another beer, but before I could take a sip, my eyes made contact with the object of my desire. As I put the beer back on the table, I watched her every move.

David had his arm around her waist while talking to another guy, but Lily didn't look happy. I really wanted to go over and talk to her, make her smile. She looked so sad, yet gorgeous.

She was wearing a pair of silver heels with a very short dress that showed most of her legs. The dress was a mix of silver and black with long sleeves. It was sexy as hell.

My blood started to boil and so did my temper. She was mine and he had no right to put his hands on her. Fuck. She was living with that bastard. I breathed heavily and tried to control my jealousy.

She was the most beautiful woman in the room, and she was getting quite a few looks from the guys who had spotted her.

I watched as her group moved further into the room and toward the bar. That's when I saw the back of her dress. I almost choked on my beer. The dress was backless, ending just above her ass. My cock pressed desperately against my zipper, eager to play. I'd be lucky if I could stand. Although I had no intention of leaving until I talked to her or touched her.

I picked up my beer, leaned back against the chair and watched her through the crowd.

Lily

Going out with Val and Daniel had been a good idea because they were a distraction. I really liked Val, although Daniel was a bit of an idiot. David liked him and usually talked Daniel's ear off, which usually left me alone to do my own thing to a certain extent. But not tonight.

I had put on a new dress that I'd been dying to wear, and for the first time in, like, forever, I'd gone braless. A huge mistake. David became very amorous, which I could have done without. Since we left the apartment, he did nothing but touch me, while I spent my time trying to get out of his grasp without making it obvious. It was probably the most he had touched me in five months.

Val kept looking at me strangely. I tried to pull away from David to talk to her, but he insisted that I wasn't going anywhere alone. If he didn't let go of me soon, he'd get a stiletto in his foot.

The sounds of the club pulsed around us and the crush of bodies proved how hot this place was. Even though it was new, everyone wanted to be here. I loved it right away and knew I would be back. The only downside to being here was that David didn't dance and wouldn't let me. He was afraid the other guys would get the wrong idea. The only guy I wanted to get the right idea was Michael and he wasn't here.

It hadn't even been twenty-four hours since we first met and I was already longing to see him - to be in front of him. He tied me up in so many knots. The guy had better come with a warning, because hell, with one look from him, I had soaked my panties.

"Lily, are you okay?" Val asked me.

"I'm fine. Just tired. Had a hard day at work."

Her eyes almost popped out of her head. "I thought...I mean..."

"I started a new job at McKenzie Holdings today."

"You did?"

Why did she sound so stunned? What the hell had David said to Daniel? I needed a minute alone.

"I'm going to find the bathroom," I told David as I turned away from the group.

"I'll come with you, Lily," David said, grabbing my elbow.

"No. You. Will. Not." I snapped through clenched teeth. "I'm perfectly capable of going to the bathroom by myself."

He jumped at my tone and his eyes widened. I had startled him. I turned away from him, hiding a smile, and stormed towards the facilities, or at least the direction I expected them to be.

I came to a stop near the bar, not knowing which way to turn.

"Can I help you? You look lost."

Turning around, I was stunned to find myself standing in front of a guy who looked practically identical to Michael.

"Ruben," Michael growled as he approached without taking his eyes off of mine.

"I take it you two know each other?" Ruben asked, pointing out the obvious. He held out his hand to me, drawing my attention away from Michael. "In case you didn't get it, I'm Ruben, his brother." He pointed at Michael.

"I'm Lily." I shook his hand as Michael came closer.

"Don't you have something to do?" Michael grumbled at his brother.

Ruben laughed and slapped Michael on the back before walking in the opposite direction, but kept looking over his shoulder at both of us.

Michael stood so close to me that I could feel the warmth of his body. He put his hands on my hips. "Dance with me, Lily. Let me hold you for a little while."

My heart pounded wildly, sending a pulse right between my legs. I'd never felt so hot.

"We'll dance in the dark, over there. No one will see us."

I nodded.

He let go of my hips and took my hand, leading me to the back of the dance floor, which was dark as night.

After releasing my hand, I felt cold for a second before he wrapped his arms around me from behind. "If I'm in front of you, I won't be able to stop myself from taking your lips," he murmured in my ear, his breath tickling my neck.

I longed to turn my head and kiss his lips. My nipples were pebbled and my thong was saturated in seconds. He was wrapped so tightly around me. I could feel his passion pounding against me.

My hands reached for his and we intertwined our fingers. As he rubbed his cock between my ass cheeks, it felt hard as a rock. I pushed back against him.

"Lily," he grumbled, taking a deep breath, "if you keep this up, I'm going to come like a teenager. I want you badly."

"I want you too." I lifted our fused hands to my breasts. "Feel what you do to me."

He rubbed his fingers in circles over my aching

nipples. I groaned and pressed my ass against him. I put my hands behind me and reached for his hips. I dug my nails in and pulled him against me. We moved to the beat of the music as if we were the only two people in the room. It was the most erotic dance I'd ever experienced.

"Lily, we really have to stop," he said again, slipping a hand between us, into the gap at the side of my dress, and caressing my waist. His fingers crept gently up to my breast and cradled it in his palm. He gently stroked my nipple with his fingers and thumb. My whole body felt alive and on fire.

"Michael, oh God." I laid my head back on his shoulder and reached up to run my fingers through the hair at the nape of his neck. I felt him shiver against me. I turned my head and looked into his eyes. I could barely breathe. I wanted him between my legs. I needed him between my legs.

"Lily," he moaned. "What are you doing to me?" He leaned down and nuzzled my neck. I couldn't control the shiver that ran through my body. He moved his other hand and began to lift my dress.

"Michael," Ruben said from behind us.

"Fuck... Ruben, go away."

"The guy she came with is looking for her."

He grabbed me even tighter. "Okay."

We were both breathing hard, our chests heaving up

and down. Michael pulled his fingers out of my dress and turned me to face him. "You're a lot more than my assistant, Lily. I know we've only just met, but I don't want you to think I'm taking advantage of you, because that's far from the case. I want you so much it's killing me."

I took his face between my hands, brought his head down and pressed my lips to his. He growled. I wanted to melt into him. Where I found the strength to pull away, I'd never know.

I smiled up at him. "I want you too, Michael. But maybe it's for the best that we were interrupted." I dropped my hands from his face.

"Lily, there you are," David said. I stepped back as he approached my side, Daniel and Val behind him. "Oh, Michael McKenzie, I didn't know you were here." He looked from me to Michael and back again.

"My brother, Ruben, owns the place," Michael told him.

I was surprised because I didn't know that; not that we'd had time to talk about it, we'd been more interested in touching.

David put his arm around me and stared at Michael, clearly marking his territory.

"We're leaving," David announced.

"See you tomorrow, Michael," I said, not wanting to leave him.

As David started to drag me out of there, I reached

out and briefly squeezed Michael's hand. I seriously thought he was going to pull me out of David's arms.

"Lily, why were you standing in the dark talking to him?" David asked as soon as we got outside.

"I got lost looking for the bathroom and his brother came to my rescue when Michael showed up. He's my boss; I wasn't going to ignore him."

David had a strange look on his face that I couldn't decipher. "If you say so."

We got into the taxi, which Daniel could always find within minutes. As I sat back in the car, I wondered if David had noticed Michael and I dancing together. If he did, he wouldn't say anything until we got home, so I'd know within an hour. I realized that I didn't really care if he saw us.

Michael made me feel desirable and really hot. He just had to look at me to make me tingle from head to toe, and that was after only knowing him for a short time.

I couldn't wait for work tomorrow so I could be closer to him again.

Michael

Finding myself at the office earlier than usual, I stepped into the elevator with more enthusiasm than usual at the thought of seeing Lily again, but as the doors closed, I glanced at myself in the mirrored wall and realized I looked like crap; I'd missed bits when I'd had a quick shave, and my eyes looked heavy as if they were about to close.

My dreams had been filled with Lily, keeping me tossing and turning all night, not to mention my cock, hard as hell, desperate to sink between Lily's thighs. Even after I'd relieved myself, my body still felt riddled with tension.

Sliding my hand down the front of my pants, I tried to rearrange my throbbing shaft into a more comfortable position without giving security a show through the CCTV hookup.

As the elevator doors opened, I quickly made sure my jacket covered my erection and stepped out.

Standing in the reception area, I took in my surroundings without being seen. My brothers and I had worked extremely hard over the past ten years to achieve what we had. Our father had loaned us the initial funds, and thanks to Lucien's gamble, we became McKenzie Holdings. We then moved into one of the new buildings we were contracted to build, occupying four floors of prime office space.

For the first time in six years, I was hopeful that I would have someone to share all this with and stand by my side. Someone I could trust.

With a sigh, I walked down the hall and saw a light on in the office. I pushed open the door and my heart stopped. Lily. God, she was beautiful. She was wearing a red suit that seemed to fit her just as well as the one she had worn the day before. I wondered what she was wearing on her feet and if her shoes were red or black to match her blouse.

She lifted her head and looked at me; a smile that did not quite reach her eyes made my heart jump. Something was wrong.

"Give me two minutes, Lily." I dashed into my office and placed my things on my desk, taking off my jacket and draping it over my chair.

As I walked back to the outer office, I looked over at Lily, who was pretending to work on the computer, and went to the coffee machine to get us both a cup. "Would you like cream and sugar?"

She looked startled. "Yes, please." She got up and walked toward me.

I had to count to ten to keep from wrapping her in my arms. She was sexy as hell in her outfit and red heels. Holy hell!

"Lily, come into my office, please." She took her coffee from me. I could feel her right behind me, and the soft scent she wore wafted toward me as I fought the impulse to take her in my arms. Instead, as we entered the office, I took her elbow and led her to the sofa.

I sat down next to her and turned to face her. "What's wrong?" I asked.

She frowned.

"Lily, something's happened. The spark has gone out of your eyes. Please talk to me. Did David see us together last night?"

She looked at me for a moment before her gaze shifted to her hands, which were limp in her lap. She leaned back in her chair. "If he saw us, he didn't say anything." She exhaled and returned my gaze. "Last night David apologized for being a jerk earlier in the day. He said he was surprised I hadn't told him I worked here. I guess I should have told him." She exhaled. "He made me dinner and said he didn't want to lose me." She gave a wry smile. "You look tired," she observed, lifting her hand to caress my face, her thumb stroking under my right eye.

We both froze. My cock came to attention and my heart raced. I took Lily's hand, brought it to my mouth, and kissed her palm. She shivered.

With my eyes still on her, I watched her swallow and couldn't take my eyes off her mouth. Just as I started to lean in to taste those lips, there was a loud knock on my door. We jumped apart as Ruben burst in. He started to speak, but abruptly closed his mouth and looked between us.

I found my voice. "Lily, you remember my brother Ruben from last night. Ruben, you remember Lily, she's my new assistant."

He walked over to us and took Lily's hand. Instead of shaking it, he planted a kiss on her knuckles, and I almost jumped out of my seat to knock his lips away.

"That's enough," I growled, and they both gave me a startled look. "Lily, why don't you finish what you were doing before I got here?"

"Okay," she said to me before looking back at Ruben, "It's nice to see you again Ruben," Lily said on her way to the door.

"Oh, the pleasure is all mine," he said in a seductive tone.

As she closed my office door behind her, I turned to my brother, who had the biggest grin I'd ever seen on his face. "Don't start flirting with her," I warned him.

He started laughing and sat down in the chair as I collapsed back into the sofa. "Wow, brother. You're so fucked." I frowned at Ruben's choice of words. "I can't wait to tell the boys." Meaning our three brothers. Shit.

"There's nothing to tell. I have a new assistant whose boyfriend is a jerk and cheating on her with his boss's daughter. Which she doesn't know, so keep that to yourself. I just wanted to comfort her.

Ruben was still grinning at me. "So if she doesn't know, why does she need comforting? And why were you practically making love to her on the dance floor last night?"

I let out a sigh. "For some reason, she hadn't told him about the job here. He was one of the Oakfield representatives at the meeting yesterday. He was furious, to say the least. He apologized to her last night and I don't think she was impressed." I stayed away from the 'making love' statement.

"Yeah, well, tell yourself whatever you want, but there was a hell of a lot of chemistry between the two of you when I walked in. It's a wonder I didn't get burned."

I'd had enough of Ruben. "I assume you're here for a reason. What is it?"

"So abrupt, brother. You wouldn't happen to be trying to get rid of me so you can get back to your pretty assistant?" He laughed.

"Let's get something straight: she's my assistant, which means she's off limits to anyone with the last name McKenzie. Are we clear?" I stood facing him, unable to keep the scowl off my face.

"Crystal."

Then why was he still smirking?

He cleared his throat and moved to the large window in my office. Ruben was smaller than the rest of us, but he proved that size didn't matter on the mat. We all had to do boxing and karate as kids, which Ruben excelled at, and he would kick our butts, much to his delight. I could see that something was bothering him, and it must be really important for him to come to me.

"Ruben?" He turned to look at me.

"I shouldn't have come." He started for the door.

"Ruben, wait. You obviously have something to say or ask, so just get it over with." I ran my fingers through my hair and waited.

He stopped and looked back at me. "It can wait. I'll see you soon."

This was really strange. Maybe Ramon knew what was wrong with him. They spent more time together than the rest of us. I couldn't even remember Ruben being so... troubled.

8

Lily

As I sat down at my desk, I was stunned at how quickly I'd grown attached to Michael. He was about to kiss me when his brother came into the office.

His brother resembled him, as I had noticed last night, but Ruben was an inch or two shorter and reminded me of a boxer; his nose was crooked, indicating that it had been broken before. His dark hair seemed to be the same color as his eyes, which were filled with glee when he saw Michael and me on the sofa.

Maybe that was a good thing. I had to be more professional with him and remember that he was my boss. Besides, I was still dating David, and I needed to work things out with him sooner rather than later. I should've remembered that last night. What a mess.

I had to distract myself with work, because Michael was not the right kind of distraction. Every time I thought of him, I became aroused.

I sat up straighter in my chair and typed the password back into the computer. I needed to finish the spreadsheet Michael had asked for yesterday.

"Hi Lily. I'm Jacky."

Looking up from my screen, I saw a petite woman of about thirty walk into the room. She was dressed in a dark navy suit that complemented her olive complexion and green eyes. Oh, the one chatting with Sylvia. "Hi, Jacky. It's nice to meet you."

She sauntered into the office and took a seat on the opposite side of my desk.

"So, Sylvia tells me that you live with your boyfriend. Is that true?"

I sighed. "Yes, it is. Why?" I picked up the mouse and started clicking things on the computer to look busy. Something about her bothered me, and the last thing I wanted was to spend too much time with her.

"It means you're not going after Michael." I frowned at her. "Michael is mine," she offered bluntly, a possessive note in her voice.

In your dreams, he's mine. Where the hell did that come from?

"Does Michael know that?" I couldn't resist asking her.

"Not yet, but he will." Her smile was full of confidence as she winked at me.

Michael's office door opened, causing Jacky to suddenly sit up and puff out her chest, only to see Ruben walk out. She deflated.

Ruben walked over to my desk and sat down on the end of it, facing me. "Ruben, do you know Jacky?"

"I don't think we've met," he replied, taking her hand in his and kissing her knuckles.

She primped again. I rolled my eyes, which Ruben caught and grinned.

"Do you work for me, Jacky?" he asked.

"Yes, I do." She fluffed her hair and started to work it up, his attention all on her.

"Then don't you think you should get back to it?" She froze, then jumped out of her chair and practically ran out of the office. Ruben then turned his attention to me.

"What? Are you telling me to get back to it now?" I offered him a grin.

"Better not, considering what you were about to do when I arrived." I blushed and he roared with laughter.

Michael's door opened and we turned to find him standing in the doorway. He was leaning against the doorframe with an annoyed look on his face. "Are you still here?"

Ruben winked at me before turning back to his brother. "I was about to leave until your secretary decided to flirt with me. How could I resist beauty like that?"

I laughed, but Michael didn't look impressed. "She's busy, leave her alone."

Ruben stood up and saluted his brother. He turned and winked at me, then left the office. I couldn't help but laugh. My laugh followed him out the door.

Glancing over at Michael, the laughter caught in my throat at the heat in his eyes. He stood there as if soaking up my very being before taking a step back and closing the door without saying anything. Strange.

I turned my attention back to my computer, finishing the spreadsheet and stretching in my seat to work out the knot that was forming in my shoulders. Halfway through the stretch, Dale Roberts walked into the office.

"Hello, Lily. How is Michael treating you?" he asked, grabbing a cup of coffee.

"Fine. I'm really enjoying the job so far." Which was actually true.

When his coffee was poured, he walked over to me and took the empty seat on the other side of my desk. It seemed like musical chairs today.

"I want to apologize for not telling you in the interview who you would actually be working for." He blushed slightly.

"Oh, Mr. Roberts, please don't worry about it. I'm

happy here, so don't worry," I replied, giving him a reas-suring smile.

"Call me Dale, and I'm glad you get along with Michael. He really is all bark, so when he starts, put your foot down." He took a sip of coffee and I tried to decide what he was telling me in his roundabout way.

"Dale, do we have a meeting?" Michael asked. I hadn't even heard his door open.

Dale stood up and looked at Michael. "No, I just thought I would stop by and say hello to your beautiful assistant."

"Well, my beautiful assistant is needed in my office," he said, smiling at me.

Dale looked between the two of us before walking out without another word.

Michael

Shit. I really have to control my attraction to Lily. Presenting her with a stupid smile in front of Dale was not the best idea. I saw red when I walked out of my office and noticed Ruben flirting with her. When I saw Dale in her office, I was ready to barge in and claim her. He was at least her grandfather's age.

I followed Lily back into my office, this time

directing her to the conference table. I took a seat across from her so there was no chance of me touching her. "Lily, about last night..."

"Michael, it's okay. Let's just forget about it," she said nervously, cutting me off.

I opened my mouth and closed it when I saw the confusion in her eyes. It stung that she wanted me to forget it when that wasn't what I wanted to say. In fact, if she expected me to forget having her in my arms, she would be disappointed. "No. I won't forget." My voice was thick with emotion.

She met my eyes.

"I won't forget it, Lily, but I'll respect your obvious desire to carry on as normal. But I won't forget holding you in my arms or how you felt in them."

"Neither will I," she whispered, closing her eyes, but I caught a glimpse of longing before she did. "Can we just focus on work, at least for now?" She looked at me, and I knew I'd give her the world if she asked.

"All right." I cleared my throat. "We need to finalize the arrangements for the staff picnic in two weeks at my parents' ranch house. You're invited, by the way."

Her face lit up. "That sounds like fun. Does everyone in your company get an invitation?"

"Just the head office. The other divisions have their own all over the country, and either I or one of my brothers goes. The picnics are family oriented and always have a children's entertainer," I explained to her, silently wishing I had a child to share the day with.

"It sounds like you really take care of your employees." A broad grin spread across her face. She was breathtaking. Just watching her made me lose my train of thought.

"Michael?"

I sat down and looked at her again! "Sorry, where were we? Oh, yes. Yes, we do take care of our employees. After all, we wouldn't be where we are without them." I could see the approval in her eyes that made me feel so damn big.

"That's great." She wrapped a strand of hair around her finger.

"Who are you bringing?" I asked before I could stop myself.

She looked unsure. "I don't know."

I really wanted her to be there as my partner.

Getting up, I walked around the table and offered her the piece of paper in my hand. "This is a list of companies with contact numbers and a list of their commitments for the day. They need to be followed up on to make sure there are no last minute problems."

"Okay, I'll get right on it." She pushed slightly away from the table and stood up.

"Just one more thing. Can you dress casually tomorrow? I'll take you to my parents' house. You'll get a better feel for how everything will be set up that day."

She snapped her head around to face me. The action caused the clip holding her hair on top of her head to fly away. All I could see were the dark curls flowing down her back. Without thinking, I moved closer and reached out, my fingers running the length of her hair. Her gasp brought my attention back to her face. Her face was flushed and her eyes were filled with passion.

I held her gaze and slipped my hands under the hair at the nape of her neck before resting her head against my chest. She placed her hands on my hips and held me tight, sending a shiver through me at the contact.

"Lily," I breathed heavily, wanting to kiss her so badly. But I couldn't, not until she was free of David.

"Michael." She rested her cheek against my chest. "Why does this feel so right?" she whispered.

I ran one of my hands down her back to her buttocks and pressed her against me so she knew exactly how I responded to her. My cock throbbed in my pants and as I pulled her even tighter against me, the beast jumped with pleasure.

I took a few deep breaths and rested my chin on the top of her head. We stayed like that for a long time. "I don't want to let you go."

She moved her head to look at me and lifted one of her hands and placed it on my face in a caress. "You're my boss, Michael."

After about a minute, I leaned down and planted a kiss on her forehead before stepping back. I walked to the end of the conference table to retrieve her clip, then handed it to her. "That's not why I didn't kiss you, and you know it."

She backed away toward the door with the papers in her arms.

"I know," she whispered, her voice thick with emotion.

I heard the door click back into place as Lily walked away. I sat back down at my desk and stared into space. She was driving me crazy, and it was only a matter of time before I gave in to my desires and consumed her. I hoped she would quickly get rid of the garbage she called her boyfriend. I had never been more in love with a woman than I was with Lily, and knowing that she was still with him made me a jealous idiot.

Tomorrow we will spend most of the day together at my parents' ranch. The trip was unnecessary; it was just an excuse to spend more time with her. I believed that with my mother around, I'd be forced to keep my hands to myself; at least that was the plan. My only hope was that Ruben and Ramon had other plans and I wouldn't be around to flirt with them. Ruben at least. Ramon was the more quiet member of the family. Ramon's life was much more private than mine.

9

———

Lily

SITTING IN THE CAR WITH MICHAEL MADE MY HEART race. George drove us to the McKenzie ranch and I was apprehensive. I was nervous because I was about to meet Michael's parents. As I looked out the window, I saw Michael's reflection in the mirror. He hadn't taken his eyes off me yet, which made me hot and flustered.

Ever since David and I came home from the club, all I could think about was Michael. While David was complaining about his boss's daughter being a pain in the ass, Michael had my full attention. I sat lost in my own thoughts for over an hour and David had no idea he'd lost me seconds after he opened his mouth. To be honest, David had lost me years ago, and I had only recently realized it.

I turned to face Michael and brushed against the hand on the back of my seat. I couldn't take my eyes off him. He was stretched out on the seat next to me, wearing faded jeans and a long-sleeved t-shirt. He looked good enough to eat. My heart quickened and I licked my lips. His eyes grew darker as he followed the movement of my tongue.

I took a deep breath and met his gaze again. "Michael," I said hoarsely.

"Lily," he replied, just as huskily, but with a crooked smile.

"Are you going to tell me about your family? Who will I be meeting today?" I turned in my seat to face him.

He reached down and took my hand, then slid his fingers through mine.

I held on tight.

"You're going to meet my mother, Pippa, and my father, Elias, and maybe my brother, Ramon. Of course, you've already met Ruben. Sebastian is in Denver with our other brother, Lucien, so you won't meet them until the picnic."

We were still holding hands, and Michael began to stroke my thumb. "Is your mother Spanish? There are a few Spanish names in the family, although McKenzie isn't a Spanish name." I shifted into a more comfortable position and moved closer to Michael, placing our joined hands in my lap.

"My grandmother was Spanish and my grandfather

was American, hence the name McKenzie. My mother is Spanish, although her name is Pippa. Both of her parents were from Barcelona."

"So you're a big Spanish family? I bet five boys drove your poor mother up the wall when you were younger."

"You could say that." He laughed. "We still do." Michael lifted my hand and planted a kiss on my knuckles, moving our joined hands to his lap. "Tell me about Lily."

I offered him a small smile. "What do you want to know?"

"Everything."

The car ride was making me sleepy, so I rested my head against the back of the seat, and when I turned to look at Michael, my heart stuttered. He was staring at me with so much longing in his eyes.

I gave him a wry smile. "I'm twenty-four years old, and I spent most of my youth in Vermont before going to college. I met David during my senior year of high school, and we have been together ever since. My parents died during my sophomore year of college, and David was there to hold me together." I stared at our clasped hands. "Before I lost my job, I was looking for another one, but I hadn't told David because I was afraid to tell him." I turned to face Michael again. "That's what brought me to you," I said quietly.

He took a breath and let go of my hand, only to put his arm around me and pull me to his chest. My arm slipped to his side and his hand rested on my hip. "We only have about forty minutes before we reach the ranch; let me pretend you're mine."

I couldn't help the shudder that came over me at his words and his closeness. I wanted to crawl on top of him and feel his hardness between my legs, but instead I lowered my head and kissed his chest, making him shiver. I moved closer and put my other hand on his stomach. He reached up and covered my hand with his. I wanted to stay like this forever. For the first time in years I felt protected and appreciated. He moaned and pulled me closer.

Michael

Lily was asleep. I sat back in the car and held her close, which made me hard as hell. She belonged in my arms and in my life. She was mine. I just wanted her to realize that. George kept glancing at us through the rearview mirror. He was curious, and I didn't blame him. It was the first time he'd seen me with a woman in six years.

I was up to something with Lily, but I wasn't sure what. I was too protective of her, which was why I was dreading Ruben and Ramon's arrival at the ranch today. Especially Ruben, who would flirt with her just to irritate me. I couldn't figure out what was going on with Ramon, but I knew I didn't have to worry about him flirting with her. From what I saw and heard from my brothers, he was friendly, but not flirting or dating. Something was off, and when I had more time, I wanted to find out what it was.

George drove through the entrance to the ranch, giving me five more minutes to hold Lily in my arms. I wasn't ready to let her go.

I ran my fingertips over the small hairs on the back of her neck. Her long curls were pulled back into a ponytail that made her look younger than she was. It made her look fragile, and all I wanted to do was carry her into my cave and keep her safe from the world. She was wearing faded, low-cut jeans and a purple t-shirt under her tan, soft leather jacket, just like me. I removed my hand from over hers and cupped the back of Lily's head. I squeezed her lightly, savoring the last few minutes of holding her tenderly, not wanting to wake her.

We came to a stop to the right of the house, where my father had made us park so our mother could see the wildlife coming out of the woods and onto the front lawn.

"Give us a few minutes, George," I whispered.

I couldn't take my eyes off the woman in my arms. I heard George leave and close the door behind him. He went over to watch my mother, giving me more time with Lily.

For a few minutes, I just sat back and caressed her face before running my fingers through her ponytail, which felt like silk. "Lily, we're here. You need to wake up." I continued to stroke her face with one hand and rubbed her hip with the other. "Lily, sweatheart. Wake up."

She began to move out of my arms as she slowly woke, and I let her go a little reluctantly.

"I can't believe I fell asleep." She looked at me and started to blush. I moved closer and cupped her face in my hands. "You make me feel safe," she admitted.

"You can sleep in my arms anytime. I like having you there. If my mother hadn't been hovering on the porch, I would have let you sleep all afternoon if it meant I could hold you."

"Michael," her voice broke. Tears had begun to trickle down her cheeks, so I quickly wiped them away with my thumbs.

"Hey, I didn't mean to make you cry." I had to hold her. I removed my hands from her face and grabbed her waist, lifting her onto my lap. She turned to me and wrapped her arms around my neck while mine went around her waist. She buried her face in my neck, causing me to tighten my grip on her.

She felt damn good wrapped around me. The only problem was the erection I couldn't hide. There was no way she could miss how aroused I was with it pressed up between the tops of her thighs.

"You didn't make me cry." She pulled away slightly and wiped her eyes with the tissue I handed her. "I can't hide my attraction to you. It kills me to know that you want me too, but that we can't be together yet."

"I guess it's kind of obvious that I want you. I can't hide my excitement as well as you can," I told her, grinning and watching her blush even more.

She smiled and moved away from my lap, quickly dabbing at her eyes. She picked up her purse from the floor. "Do you feel ready to move? Because I think we'll be safer out there than in here." She glanced down at my lap, then back up at my face, and I actually felt myself blush. Shit, that was a first.

Clearing my throat, I hopped out of the car and held out my hand to Lily. She grabbed it and tucked her fingers between mine as I pulled it out, just in time to see my mom rush up to us. Lily leaned against me for a moment. "You can't see my excitement, but my panties are soaked," she muttered, leaving me breathless by the car as she approached to greet my mother.

What the hell was that? Where on earth did sexy tease Lily come from? Never in a million years would I have expected her to say something like that. The erection I was trying to diminish had rebounded and was pressing against my zipper. I wouldn't be surprised if I had zipper marks on my cock. Thank God my T-shirt covered the evidence.

If it hadn't been for my mother's presence, I would have tumbled her back into the car to find out just how wet she was for me. What a fucking turn-on, knowing she had soaked her panties for me. God, my cock twitched with excitement. I really needed to get my body under control. I was thirty-six, for Christ's sake, not twenty.

I took a deep breath and walked over to my mother and Lily.

10

Lily

MICHAEL'S MOTHER WAS BEAUTIFUL AND LOOKED nothing like I had imagined. For some reason, I expected her to be tall like Michael and Ruben, but I was wrong. Pippa stood about five and a half feet tall, with thick black hair pulled back at the nape of her neck. She was so thin that it was surprising to learn that she had given birth to five muscular men. I hadn't met Michael's other siblings, but I believe they were all similarly built.

As I stood there talking to Pippa, all I could think about was the state Michael must have been in after the comment about my panties. I had no idea how that came out of my mouth. I was shy, or at least I thought I was.

Had I been waiting all this time for him to come along and bring out the wickedness in me?

Michael sauntered toward us as I watched him, and I felt a blush rise up my neck and into my cheeks as I met his sizzling gaze. Hell, my nipples stood at attention.

"He's a handsome man, my Michael. He's been alone for a long time and needs someone to look after him, someone to make him happy," Pippa told me when she noticed the direction of my gaze.

I turned to her and found her grinning at me. I laughed. "Yes, he is."

Michael walked up and, after hugging his mother, stood next to me with his hand on my back. I wanted to lean over and hold him. His mother glanced quickly between us.

"Michael, take Lily into the house to the kitchen for a cold drink before you show her around the ranch. Your brothers want to meet her." I heard Michael groan as his mother turned back to the house and started up the stairs, expecting us to follow.

"What's wrong?" I looked up at him and saw the frown on his face.

"My brothers." He sighed. "Come on, let's get this over with."

"They can't be that bad. Besides, I've already met Ruben."

"He's the problem."

With our fingers intertwined, he gave me a light tug

to get me to follow him. "Michael, no matter how much your brother flirts with me, it's you that holds my interest. You have nothing to worry about."

He stopped and looked at me for the longest time. "You're not mine yet, are you? I want you, Lily, make no mistake about that, and it drives me crazy to think of you naked with that bastard."

I was stunned. I knew he wanted me, but not as much as his speech suggested. I didn't hold back and told him the truth. "We no longer have sex; he has it with me, and for a long time it was more of a one-man show. He hasn't touched me since I met you." I sighed and almost burst into tears, but I had to be honest because I could see the misery on his face as he imagined me with David. I had to breathe. "We'd better go inside." I tried to change the subject and headed for the same entrance as his mother. I turned my attention back to Michael, who had not moved.

As I walked toward him, I stopped and met his gaze. "Michael, I want you too, so much it hurts, but we can't. You're my boss and I'm still with David. I probably won't be for much longer, but I can't be with you while I'm supposed to be with him. I don't work that way."

"I apologize, Lily. You know I want you. I haven't been able to get you out of my mind since we met in the elevator. Whatever I do, you're there." He sighed and turned to run his fingers through his hair. "My mother keeps looking outside. We better go inside. I won't wait forever, and sooner or later you'll be with me, whether I'm your boss or not." He approached me, took my hand, kissed my palm and wrapped it around his before pulling me onto the porch to enter the ranch house.

I knew what I wanted, but how could I get it? If I left David, I'd have nowhere to live, and if I stayed with him, I'd lose Michael. I'd known David for seven years and Michael for almost three days, yet I felt more at home and able to be my true self with Michael.

"Lily, how nice to see you again," Ruben said with a grin in Michael's direction. He took my hand and kissed my knuckles. When he released me, he winked. He really was a flirt and obviously loved to tease his brother.

"Good to see you again, Ruben," I said. I noticed another man standing near the opposite door. He noticed me watching him and walked over, offering me his hand to shake.

"Lily, this is our youngest brother, Ramon," Michael introduced.

"Ramon, it's a pleasure to meet you."

They were all very handsome men, although Ramon looked to be the youngest. The dark hair and eyes were the same as Ruben's, but he had a slimmer build than his brothers.

"The pleasure is all mine. Where have you been hiding them, Michael?" he asked with a devilish grin on his face.

I glanced at Michael and saw him smile at his brother, but it didn't quite reach his eyes.

"I haven't hidden them anywhere, and you, my brother, can look elsewhere," Michael growled, not the least bit impressed by Ramon's flirting.

Ignoring Michael, Ramon chuckled and winked at me.

Hell, his brothers were handsome men and they loved to flirt.

Pippa cleared her throat and stood next to Ramon. "Why don't you take Lily to see the puppies in the barn while we get lunch started?" she suggested, trying to diffuse the tension that had been created by Ramon's comment.

Not knowing what was going on, I walked over to Michael while holding his gaze and slipping my hand into his. He gripped my hand tightly.

"I think it's a good idea. I love animals." I gave Michael a tug that seemed to bring him back to himself and led him out of the kitchen without saying anything more.

Until then, I had no idea he felt that way about me. There was no way I could have mistaken the jealousy and possessiveness he'd just displayed in front of his mother and two brothers. I needed him to calm down first, and then, hopefully, we could talk.

It only took 48 hours for me to realize that I wanted a future with Michael. I'd never thought about the future like I did now. During my time with David, I never considered the possibility. But I was still with him. I had to end my relationship with him before I could start anything with Michael, even though I assumed it had already begun.

Michael

I was totally screwed. When Ramon flirted with her in the kitchen, I almost lost it. I thought I would lose it with Ruben, but not with Ramon. I saw the worried look on everyone's face and I couldn't do anything about it. All I could see was Lily with someone else and I wanted to hurt her.

Lily pulled me toward the barn with her hand wrapped tightly around mine. Given my recent behavior, what was I supposed to say to her? I had no idea. I also owed Ramon an apology, though I'd rather leave that one alone. Damn, he never flirted.

I had to say something. "Lily, wait." I pulled her to a stop and she turned to look at me.

She had tears in her eyes. "God, I'm so sorry for being an idiot. A very jealous one at that. I don't know why the hell I'm acting like this. I've never felt possessive of a woman before, or anything for that matter." I ran my fingers through my hair with my other hand, hoping she would respond.

"I have to go home to David tonight. I can't handle you being so possessive. Part of me loves the fact that you feel possessive, but another part... well, it scares me. I'm not free yet, you know." She looked back at the house before meeting my gaze. "Do you think we can try to get through the rest of the day without you actually causing any physical harm?" She grinned.

Relief washed over me. Despite the royal mess at the house, Lily was willing to put it behind her. "I think that can be arranged. On one condition," I said, returning her grin.

She looked suspicious.

"You give me a hug."

"How the hell am I supposed to resist you?" She walked right up to me and wrapped her arms around my neck, running her hands through my hair.

My arms wrapped around her waist and we just hugged each other. She was snug against me, her breasts pressed against my chest, her hips in line with my hard-as-nails body part that was constantly awake around her. As my heart raced in my chest, I realized that she fit perfectly against me, and with a tiny adjustment, our lips could touch. I really wanted to taste her.

I slid my hands down to her ass and squeezed gently as I brought her closer and closer. We both moaned. God, I could come just from holding her.

She pressed her hips against me as she tilted her head to the side and nibbled my neck before licking the same area. I couldn't control the shudder that went through me. My hands tightened around her.

"Michael?"

"Shit, that's my dad." I tried to regain control of my body, hoping my t-shirt covered my lower body.

Lily let go of me and took a few steps back. I looked down at her and met her eyes. The heat in them almost brought me to my knees.

"Michael, are you done playing with your little friend?"

Lily giggled.

I turned to face my father, who looked more amused than angry. "For now. Lily, I want you to meet my father, Elias. Dad, this is Lily."

Lily held out her hand. "Nice to meet you, Mr. McKenzie," she said, looking quite flushed.

"You too, Lily, and please call me Elias. Will you take a look at the puppies?"

"Yes."

My father nodded, smoothing the stubble on his chin as he looked at us thoughtfully, "Well, go on in," he looked between us, "I have a few things to take care of." With that, he walked towards the house. I took Lily's hand again. "Come on, let's go see them. Lunch will probably be ready soon."

I took Lily's hand and led her into the coolness of the

barn, which was inviting, and my cock urged me to finish what we'd started outside. Unfortunately, my brain was telling me to behave. I was still hard as a rock and too damn old for a roll in the hay.

We opened the door to the back of the barn and could hear the puppies yelping. They were purebred Golden Retrievers with a four-week-old litter of five. Three of them had to go home eventually, and I was inclined to take the other two, which my mother knew. Until I told her otherwise, I knew she would not give them to anyone else.

"Oh my God, they're adorable." Lily took one look at them, gasped, and ran over to them. She sat right down and let them play on her lap.

I crouched down beside her and petted them. All the while Lily was laughing and cuddling them all. She was really enchanted by them. She kept picking up the smallest one and kissing its nose; this was one of the dogs I was considering keeping. While she was kissing another one, I picked it up in my arms and examined it. Lily looked at me and smiled as she saw me holding the puppy that I had decided to keep.

"Lunch is ready, and don't attack the messenger." Ramon said quickly as he walked towards us.

I stood and looked at him. This was hell and I would never hear the end of it. "Ramon, about earlier..." He wasn't going to make it easy, as the grin on his face showed. I was sure Lily was laughing, but I couldn't really tell because her head was down. "Damn it. I'm sorry, just don't flirt with her again," I growled.

Lily burst out laughing. "I guess you don't apologize that often?"

"Lily, this is the first time" Ramon told her with a grin.

"Shit. This stays between us." I glared at Ramon.

"Like hell it does, brother." Before I could say anything more, he walked away.

I turned back to Lily, who was watching me with laughing eyes. "You enjoyed that, huh?"

I held out my hand, and she slid hers in. "Oh yeah!" I pulled her up and into my arms for a quick hug. I had to keep my distance until she was free of David. It wouldn't bother me to take her away from him, especially considering what he was doing behind her back, but it would bother Lily. A lot.

With our fingers intertwined, I led her back to the house for lunch.

11

Lily

WITH MY HAND CLASPED TIGHT IN MICHAEL'S, WE walked back to the house for lunch and it filled my heart with happiness. It also made me more determined to end things with David.

For a very long time, I'd always feared losing him, but, somewhere along the way, that had changed. Over the past few months my attachment had dwindled. I still cared about him, but my love was gone. I think it disappeared years ago, became something more akin to friendship, but I was only now realizing it.

One thing was for sure, David had never looked at me the way Michael did. I knew it was unfair to compare the two of them, but it was something that couldn't be helped. When Michael looked at me, my panties became wet and I had the urge to squeeze my thighs together to stop the ache. I hadn't experienced that reaction to David, which was sad really.

Being in Michael's arms had soaked my panties and left an ache that only he could alleviate.

"Earth to Lily." He pulled me to a stop on the porch. "Hey, penny for your thoughts?"

I blushed. He noticed and his eyes sparkled. The smile, which had been hovering on his lips, was growing into a huge grin. "Pretty good thoughts, huh?"

Embarrassed, but not enough to keep quiet, I took hold of the door and leaned into him. "I was thinking about how wet you've made my panties and how badly I want you between my legs," seeing the hunger on his face, I continued, "and how badly I want to taste you." I quickly pulled the door open and entered the house before he had a chance to respond.

Teasing the 'tiger' was going to get me into trouble, especially since I worked myself up as well.

"Lily, are you all right? You look rather flushed," Pippa asked as I walked into the kitchen.

"Ah yeah, I'm fine." I looked toward the table just in time to catch Ruben's smirk.

"I'd ask Michael what he's been doing to her." Pippa smacked Ruben across the back of the head. "Hey, what was that for?"

"Stop embarrassing Michael's woman," she told Ruben, just as Michael walked into the kitchen.

The statement was met by silence. Everyone stared at Michael for his reaction. Instead, he grinned and said, "She isn't yet, but she will be." He pulled me into him and kept an arm wrapped around me.

"Oh hell, Lily. If you get fed up with him come find me!" Ruben said grinning, while I felt Michael start to tense. I tightened my hold on him.

Pippa, who obviously sensed the rising tension between her sons, started to place the salad, meats and bread onto the table. "Let's eat." She shoved a bread roll into Ruben's mouth when he opened it to respond.

I took my jacket off, placed it over the back of the chair and took a seat between Michael and Ruben.

"Keep your hands to yourself, brother," Michael growled at a grinning Ruben.

"Does that apply to me as well?" Ramon questioned as he took his seat at the table.

"Shit." Michael put his head into his hands.

"Michael Elias McKenzie, you do not curse at my table, and if you two want to eat," she said pointing to Ruben and Ramon, "I suggest you stop winding your brother up."

"Yes, ma'am," all three replied.

I tried to hide my laugh behind my hand, but no such luck.

Pippa looked at me and pointed the butter knife at me. "And you," she startled me, "whatever you're doing to Michael, carry on. I've never seen him behave with a woman, like he is with you." I smiled and heard Michael groan.

Ruben choked on his drink. "Mom, we don't want to know what she's been doing to Michael."

Oh my God. I felt my blush start at my neck and slowly work its way up into my face.

"That's enough. Lily is a guest here and I don't want you two frightening her away." Elias managed to shut them up. I braved a look at him and he winked my way.

Michael placed some food on my plate and I just sat back and watched him; amused. I couldn't remember anyone ever doing that for me before. With a quick glance around the table, I saw all eyes on us. Michael realized everyone was watching him, and as he glanced at me he looked embarrassed.

"Sorry," he whispered.

I leaned forward slightly and took his hand. "Thank you. I'm glad you know what I like."

I was about to take a bite out of the French bread, when I noticed Ruben about to open his mouth, so I glared at him. He shut his mouth and winked at me. I started to laugh. He was a gorgeous flirt. But it was Michael for me.

Suddenly, Michael pushed his chair away from the table and with his fist clenched; he walked out of the kitchen door and down the porch steps, before anyone could react.

It was so odd. I started to stand to go after him, but

Pippa stopped me. "Lily, leave him for a short time. Finish your lunch and then go to him. He'll have calmed down some by then."

I didn't know what to say or do; so staying quiet I tried to eat, but my stomach was in knots. One minute everything was fine and the next, well, I wasn't actually sure.

Unable to finish eating, I took a drink and sat back in my chair. I couldn't stay there anymore. I pushed away from the table and stood up. "Do you know where he went?"

"Probably the barn," his father replied.

"Thank you, Elias. If you'll all excuse me, I need to go to him." I took my jacket from the back of the chair, walked out of the kitchen and headed for the barn hoping Michael was there.

What the hell happened to make him leave so abruptly? I certainly didn't think I'd done anything to make him react the way he had. I slowed my steps as I neared the barn, feeling nervous. When I pushed the door open, I stepped inside and looked around. Once my eyes adjusted to the dim light, I could just make him out, sitting on a bale of hay to one side.

Slowly, I walked over to him. He was sitting with his elbows resting on his thighs and his face in his hands. Standing in front of him, I decided to crouch down, placing my hands on each of his knees. "Michael?"

His shoulders tensed. He hadn't known I was there. I

went down to my knees and pushed his thighs apart, so I could move closer to him. I smoothed my hands up his arms until I got to his hands and pulled them away from his face.

"Please talk to me? Tell me what happened back there?"

He met my eyes and just stared at me; his eyes filled with heat. He pulled his hands free from mine and cupped my head. Perhaps kneeling in front of him wasn't the brightest thing I'd ever done.

"I saw you laughing with Ruben and I just saw red. I left so I wouldn't hit him." He looked so lost. Desolate.

"Michael, you can't go around wanting to hit everyone I laugh with. Just because I laugh with someone, doesn't mean I want to do something else with them."

He sighed. "Viv, she slept with a lot of guys while we were married."

So that was why he reacted so quickly. "Oh, Michael." I reached up and took his face in my hands. "I'm not like her."

He groaned and started to pull me closer. "Lily, deep down I know that. I've just always been one to react first, think second – unless it has to do with work."

"I've only ever had sex with David and I've never wanted anyone the way I want you."

"Fuck!" He slammed his lips down on mine, pulled me up and astride his lap. I opened my mouth and our tongues fused together. My blood roared through me as I reached up and wrapped my arms around his shoulders, threading my fingers through his hair. He shivered. I moved my hips closer to his and felt the hardness beneath.

With our mouths and tongues still fused together, I started to rub against him. I was wet and close to orgasm. Every time his penis rubbed against my pussy, the pressure would push my panties into my sex – it felt incredible and made me tingle all over.

Michael

Christ. Lily was hot and heavy against me, and her closeness was playing havoc not only with my body, but with my intentions. I never wanted this to happen. Oh, yes, I wanted it to happen, but not while she was unavailable.

She was in my arms and my tongue was still wrapped around hers. All my blood had traveled south, giving me one hell of an erection. If she didn't stop wiggling around, I was going to explode in my jeans.

She kept rubbing her pussy against my cock. I ran my hands down her back and gripped her hips tightly. I pushed her down against me as I arched into her. She began to whimper, indicating that she was close.

I held her tight against me as I slowly rubbed against her as I kissed the life out of her. She pulled her mouth away and looked right into my eyes.

Then it hit. "Oh God, Michael." She collapsed in my arms. Her orgasm seemed to go on and on. I just held on and tried not to join her.

My breath was heavy on her neck, where I had buried my face as she climaxed while I fought to prevent my own. I was exhausted and in desperate need of relief, but holding Lily in my arms was both heaven and hell wrapped together in the finest agony. I took a deep breath as Lily lifted her head from my shoulder to look at me.

"Michael, you need relief."

I shook my head. "No."

With unsteady legs, Lily climbed out of my lap, then knelt down between my legs again, looking at the obvious bulge in my jeans. She looked uncertain, and then she had my jeans unzipped before I could get my confused brain to work. I grabbed her wrist. "Lily, no."

"You gave me the best damn orgasm of my life." She licked her kissed, bruised lips and I almost fell apart. "You're uncomfortable, so let me take care of you." Grinning, she moved back to my crotch. Hell, I was an idiot.

Standing up, Lily's hands fell away. "Lily, I want nothing more than to have your hands and mouth on me, but if that's going to happen, we're going to need a bed and more time than we have." I held out my hand and helped her up from the floor.

I quickly re-fastened my jeans and pulled her back into my arms for a hug. "I really didn't mean for any of this to happen; you caught me at a weak moment. But I'm not sorry that it did. God, I could never be sorry for having you hungry in my arms."

"I'm not sorry either." She kissed my chest and stepped out of my arms. "Do you want to talk about the picnic? It might be safer."

"Um, about that." I met her gaze. "That was an excuse to get you to spend the day with me." I chuckled at the look on her face. "I have to admit, I didn't expect to have such a strong reaction to you with my brothers.

"I enjoyed meeting your family and getting a good look at the barn!" She grinned.

"Is it safe to enter?" Ramon asked.

Lily quickly glanced at my groin and then met my eyes. She grinned.

"It's safe." She called back.

Ramon walked in and stopped some distance away, probably wanting to stay safely out of reach. I didn't blame him, considering how I had acted.

He grinned. "Mom wanted me to come and see if everything was okay. I guess she didn't want to catch you with your jeans around your ankles."

Lily started to giggle, which ended in a full belly laugh. She covered her face to hide it, but it didn't help.

I couldn't help but grin back at her. "We haven't gotten that far yet."

"I really didn't need to know that. Besides, I think George is anxious to get back, something about a date with a lady named Janet."

I looked at him in shock. The sly devil, he never said a word to me. "Come on." I took Lily's hand. "Let's go and embarrass George."

"You'll do no such thing," Lily said as I frowned at her. "I think it's sweet."

I groaned and Ramon laughed behind us. He knew damn well that Lily had me wrapped around her finger.

Pulling her along, I walked over to where George was standing with my parents by the side of the car. I just hoped Lily wasn't having second thoughts about what was about to happen between us. I was her boss, which I knew bothered her, but I had no intention of letting that keep us apart. Hopefully she'll leave David after this afternoon. I couldn't wait much longer. It drove me crazy that she was going home to him instead of with me.

There was nothing I wanted more than to ask her to move in with me, but I didn't want her to regret it. I needed her to come to me on her own, without my influence, even though I should have left her alone this afternoon. Until she was free, I had to keep my hands to myself, no matter how many cold showers I had to take.

"George! What's this I hear about Janet?" I asked him, grinning as he turned red as a beet.

Chuckling, I turned to my parents. "Mom, Dad, thanks for lunch; even though I didn't eat much, it was good to see you both."

"Likewise, son." My dad hugged me and walked over to Lily as my mom took his place.

"She's lovely, Michael. Don't blow it. She's nothing like Viv," Mom whispered as she hugged me tightly, her arms tightening as she said the words. I kissed her on the cheek before stepping back and helping Lily into the car.

As soon as the car doors closed, I pulled Lily back into my arms, unable to keep the promise I had made to myself just seconds before. "Let me hold you. We'll be back in the real world soon." She snuggled further into me, making my heart race. The erection that had remained semi-erect since the barn had returned to full attention, pushing on my zipper.

With Lily against me, I used my other hand to try to move it into a more comfortable position, but of course Lily caught me.

"Would you like some help with that?" She offered. I chuckled.

"You stay away from there." Just to be sure, I took the

hand that was resting on my chest and, after kissing her palm, held it to my chest.

"Michael, are you going to tell me about your past?"

I exhaled. She wanted to know what I had told her about Viv in the barn. "We were married for three years. In those three years, she slept with more men than I can remember. It took me a while to realize that she had the commitment problem, not me. I guess I wasn't enough for her to stay faithful. But I did not love her, Lily. I thought I did, but when things came to a head, I was irritated, but not heartbroken. Although I wanted her out of my life, I did not want her to die. That happened in a car accident on the way to meet the divorce lawyers. Her flavor of the month was driving.

She tightened her grip on me. "I'm sorry, Michael. You didn't deserve any of that."

She kissed my chest. "You're enough for me. I feel burned every time you touch me."

My erection jumped at her words, so I thought it best to change the direction of the conversation before George got a hell of a view. A look only for my eyes.

Three days. That was all it took for her to get under my skin.

I held her close all the way to her apartment building, not wanting to let her go.

She pulled away from me and straightened her ponytail, which had gone crooked during the car ride back to the city. "Michael," she said so softly. She turned her head to look out the window. I watched her swallow and my heart dropped. She turned back to me. "We can't be close again until I'm free." She wiped away a single tear. "It won't be easy for me, but I have to keep my distance from you."

I reached out and pulled her into my arms. "Lily, it's okay. I'll be waiting for you. Always."

She sniffled into my chest. "I promise you have nothing to worry about. We may share a bed, but he won't touch me again. I won't let him."

"Okay," I choked out. I walked away and opened the car door. As I stepped out, Lily followed close behind.

She took a deep breath and met my eyes. "Thank you for today. You have no idea how much I enjoyed being with you and your family. I look forward to doing it again."

I was at a loss for words. I wanted to grab her and take her home with me and not let David near her. She started to walk away from me, caressing my hand as she went.

"Goodbye, Lily," I whispered.

I stood in front of the car, holding on to the door to keep myself from following her. I just watched as she walked up the stairs and then disappeared through the security doors.

12

Lily

IT WAS HARD, VERY HARD, TO TURN MY BACK ON MICHAEL, but I straightened my spine and forced myself to walk away. With the security door closed behind me, I walked through the inner door to the stairs and dropped to the step; my legs refused to hold me up any longer.

My life was a mess. The thought of walking up the stairs to my apartment filled me with dread. I knew David would be there because he'd decided to work from home.

I sighed and got to my feet, then began a slow climb up the two flights of stairs, thoughts of Michael in my head. The look on his face when I'd told him we had to keep our distance had almost crushed me.

Today was amazing and he made me feel so cherished and desired. Then in the barn...wow. That had been hot, and the first time in my life I'd come without someone inside me. Part of me was so disappointed when he refused to let me touch him. I really wanted to see him and give him the same pleasure he'd given me. I wanted to wrap my mouth around him one day. Something I'd only done once or twice before, but never really enjoyed. I certainly never let David come in my mouth, but I wanted to do that with Michael.

I hesitated in the foyer of my apartment, listening to the commotion coming from the kitchen. I put my purse and jacket on the chair by the small table in the hall, then looked at the photograph of my parents sitting on the table in a Victorian frame that my father had made years ago. My grandmother had made the intricate lace cloth on which it sat.

When I was feeling so confused, I missed being able to cry on my mother's shoulder. She always knew what to say and what to do.

With a heavy sigh, I continued down the hall toward the kitchen and stopped dead in the doorway. Oh God, not again.

David was completely naked, his cheeks flushed, and he was wearing an apron tied around his waist. What the hell had gotten into him?

"David?"

He jumped slightly and turned to face me. I couldn't help but look at him. As my eyes fell to his waist and lower, the apron began to twitch, outlining his growing erection. He grabbed his shaft through the apron and moved his hand up and down a few times as he watched me.

"Hey, babe. I didn't expect you home yet. I'm making beef bourguignon and rice as a surprise. How did it go with the boss today?" He continued cooking as if there was nothing out of the ordinary, as if it was perfectly normal to cook naked while fondling your erection.

"I need a drink." I turned and walked out of the kitchen, straight to the cabinet where he kept the whiskey. I knew full well I would regret it, but I poured three fingers' worth into a glass and knocked most of it back in one go. Heat filled my face from the strong liquor, but I ignored it and tried to take a few soothing breaths before I swallowed it all. Hell. It burned as it went down, and frankly it tasted disgusting, but I hoped it would numb me enough to get through the rest of the evening.

When I was absolutely sure that the whiskey would stay down, I went into the bedroom to change into my lounge clothes, which consisted of yoga pants and a long-sleeved t-shirt - my usual attire when I was lounging around at home. Now to face David.

Back in the kitchen, I was just in time to see him putting dinner and a glass of wine on the table for me. He had taken off the apron and still had a pretty solid erection; it was bobbing around like nobody's business as he walked around the kitchen. Enough already!

"David, what the hell has gotten into you? Never in the seven years we've been together have you acted like this. First the other night and now... this," I said, waving my arms in his direction.

He leaned back against one of the cabinets, a calculating look on his face as he watched me. I sat down before I fell over; the whiskey was starting to kick in.

"I want you to watch me," he said.

"I already am." I sat back in the chair and watched him fist his cock. Shocked would be an understatement of how I felt.

"It's a huge turn-on, having you watching me." He picked up his beer and took a drink, as casually as if he were standing in a bar, fully dressed.

"This is different. I mean, you've never done this before. Have you?" I picked up my wine glass and took a rather large drink. I really had to be drunk.

"I watched a movie the night I stayed at Luke's. It was hot, so I thought I would try it...and it really is." Then he smiled at me. "Of course, the woman the actor was beating in front of was actually turned on by what he was doing and ended up stripping for him and bringing herself to orgasm...Christ, look what that image did to my cock." I looked down and, oh boy, his cock had grown, which I didn't think was possible.

Staring at David, I remembered why I'd been

attracted to him in the first place. He was a good-looking guy; well-toned, over six feet tall, and he had muscles that would impress anyone. But a relationship couldn't be about looks, and I didn't like who David had become as a person. Still, I'd be lying if I said I wasn't turned on by the porn show he was doing. Shit, I'd forgotten that alcohol made me amorous as well as giving me a headache.

I didn't want to have sex with him because my heart and my body belonged to Michael now.

"Babe, will you play along?"

He wanted me to watch him so I could do it without losing my clothes.

I met his eyes. "I'll watch, but my clothes stay," I told him. Did I really just slur that? And what the hell was I doing agreeing to watch him when I had promised Michael that there wouldn't be anything sexual between David and me?

When I looked at David, his eyes went hot as he grabbed his shaft and began to run his hand up and down his skin. He spread his legs and slowed the motion with his hand. I looked at his cock, which had begun to leak at the tip in excitement.

I took a big gulp of wine and licked my lips to catch a few drops that didn't quite make it into my mouth.

David moaned. "Fuck... Touch me, Lily. Let me come when you touch me," he begged.

What the hell am I going to do? I stood up and tried

to walk in a straight line to him, but judging by his laughter, I didn't think I had succeeded.

"How much whiskey did you drink?" he asked me as I knelt on the ground.

I frowned now that I was at eye level with his dick. I was really unsure what to do. I didn't want to put my mouth on it.

"Turn around." He had a stunned look on his face and then he did what I asked. "Spread your legs and put one hand on the counter and the other on your cock."

He shivered. "God, babe, it's hot when you tell me what to do."

I really hoped I could survive this.

I quickly grabbed the feather duster from the cabinet to my right and tore off the cover before taking a deep breath for courage. I reached out and slowly moved it up his calves to his thighs and then further north. His breathing became ragged as I stroked the feathers over his back and between his legs.

"Close," he croaked.

Tilting the duster slightly, I tickled his balls; he called out a name, but it wasn't mine, and came all the way down the door in front of him.

I stood on wobbly legs and went into the bathroom. I locked the door, undressed and climbed into the shower. I needed to sober up and wondered who the hell Lucy was. Did he know he'd called out someone else's name?

Michael gave me the only orgasm I had had in months in the barn, and I would have gone down on him if he had let me. The thought of having his penis in my hand, my tongue licking along its length and lapping up his creamy white cum, was a hell of a turn-on. Shit, I shouldn't be having these thoughts.

Out of the shower, I dried off and put my clothes back on, then took a deep breath before opening the door and walking into the bedroom.

David was sitting on the bed, having obviously showered in the guest bathroom.

"Are you okay, Lily?" he asked.

How did I answer that? "I've been better."

He patted the bed next to him, so I went over and sat down.

David took my hand and just held it. "I'm sorry, Lily. I really am. We've been drifting apart for a while now and I don't know what to do to stop it. I really don't want to lose you. Please promise me you won't leave me."

I'd started to get a headache as I sat and listened to David. The truth was, I didn't know if I should believe him or not, and did I mention Lucy? I should be angry, but I wasn't. I probably would have been if I hadn't met Michael.

I turned my head to look at him. "Who's Lucy?" He froze, his eyes almost popping out of his head. So he knew a Lucy. "Who is she? And don't even think about lying to me." My voice came out hard.

He looked at me and let go of my hand. "How..."

"You called her name when you came."

"Fucking hell." He put his face in his hands. "God, babe, I'm sorry. I didn't know." He sighed and seemed to hesitate, "She's the woman from the video."

I was stunned to say the least. "Are you serious?" He looked embarrassed, so I decided to let it go. My need to sleep off the whiskey took precedence over the conversation. I'd had enough. "I need to sleep."

He sagged in relief.

As I climbed into bed, the last thing I remembered was David telling me he loved me. I had no answer to that. I couldn't lie and tell him that I loved him, too.

Michael

It had been twelve days and eleven hours since I'd dropped Lily off at her apartment building after the day we'd spent together at my parents' ranch house. Twelve days since I'd touched her. Twelve days since I'd brought her to orgasm. Twelve days of cold showers several times a day.

The first day back at the office had felt strange. Lily

basically went out of her way to avoid any contact with me, which only made me want to try harder. My attempts were short-lived when Lily ended up in tears. I felt like the world's biggest bastard.

I could not bear the sight of my Lily in tears, so I jumped out of my chair and pulled her into my arms, half afraid she would refuse contact. But she came willingly. I just held her as she wrapped her arms around me and cried. I whispered apologies to her over and over until we both felt better.

When she calmed down, she admitted to me that she'd kept her distance because it was safer that way. She really wanted to be with me, but she had some things to work out with David first, and she thought it best to keep her distance, but I was making it difficult.

I was angry, not at Lily, but at the bastard she called her boyfriend. He was still cheating on her behind her back, and yet he still had some kind of hold over her.

It had felt good, too good, to hold Lily in my arms that day. Even though it was short, I loved every minute of it. I just wish there had been no tears involved.

I'd planted a soft kiss on her lips and promised to keep my distance until she said otherwise. I also admitted that it was going to kill me and cause a lot of cold showers.

Lily really got under my skin, and the thought of her having sex with anyone but me made me want to hurt someone. Badly. As far as I was concerned, she was mine and I had no intention of letting her go.

The woman who was warming my frozen heart was living with someone else, which was extremely frustrating. The number of times I'd almost asked her to move in with me in the past twelve days was in the triple digits. Keeping my mouth shut was proving to be very difficult for me, but for Lily, I would try.

With only two days until the McKenzie picnic at my parents' estate, I had no meetings scheduled. We had some last-minute preparations to make, and I was looking forward to spending the day with Lily uninterrupted. It was crazy to seek something as simple as being in the same room with her. I knew that being so close to her would bring my body to life, but I'd made it through the last twelve days; one more wouldn't kill me. I hoped.

I got up from the kitchen table, where I'd just eaten a bagel and drunk my third cup of coffee of the day before rinsing the cup in the sink and leaving it to dry.

George would be waiting for me outside for the first time in three days. He'd been sick. I had to call the doctor to his cabin because the stubborn son of a bitch refused to go to the doctor's office. He was never sick and insisted he was fine, but he was coughing like he'd been smoking for years. He never smoked. It turned out he had a pretty bad chest infection, and I threatened to make Ruben stay with him if he refused to rest.

So, after three days of rest, he was on the phone at five in the morning begging me to let him work today. He told me he was fine and would go crazy if he had to spend another day in the cabin. He sounded much better, so I agreed. As I walked out the front door, I saw him resting on the hood of the car, looking a hell of a lot better than he had.

"Good morning, George. I hope you're really feeling better today," I said, stopping in front of him. On closer inspection he still looked a bit pale.

"I'm almost back to normal, Mr. McKenzie. I really need to work. A man can only sit around for so long before he goes crazy with boredom."

"How on earth can you be bored with all the DVDs and books you have stashed away in that cabin?"

"I've already watched them all and read all the books, but I was more restless than anything else, especially after I started feeling better."

"Okay, George, but if you start feeling sick again, tell me this time. Don't suffer in silence. Do you understand me?"

"Yes. Are you going to get in the car or are you going to stand here all day giving me instructions, because I'm sure there's a little lady who's going to be mighty disappointed if you don't get downtown?" He grinned.

I let out a groan and got into the car, my thoughts going straight to Lily. They didn't last long when George pulled out of the driveway with a little jolt. It smoothed out after a few minutes and soon he was whistling a tune from the front seat.

"Someone's in a good mood today," I commented.

He cleared his throat. "Janet's working today."

"Ah, that must be love," I replied, grinning as I saw George blush through the mirror.

"Not yet, but she's growing on me. What about Lily?"

I shifted uncomfortably in my seat. "What about Lily?"

"Why isn't she with you?" In all the years George had worked for me, it was the first time he'd asked me anything personal. It surprised me.

"It's complicated," I replied, frowning and turning my attention to the window, effectively ending his inquisition.

I closed my eyes, thinking of Lily and how easily she could disarm me with a single look. Once or twice I'd caught her lost in space, staring at me. I would grin at her until she came back to reality, and she would blush with embarrassment. It was cute.

When I heard a car horn outside the car, I looked up in my seat just in time to see an SUV slam into the side of our vehicle. My heart pounded as metal collided with metal. I heard glass shattering as I was slammed into the car door and my head hit the window. As a ringing sound filled the air, my vision went black.

Lily

Sitting in my office, I took a sip of coffee and wondered what today would bring. I had missed being close to Michael these past few weeks. It had to be done for my own peace of mind, as much as I hated it. I could see he was waiting for a signal from me to move forward, and the minute I gave that signal, he'd be on me like a starving tiger without hesitation.

My life really revolved around work. I would have a very brief conversation with David over a bowl of cereal in the morning and spend the day at the office, making sure I worked late every night. Then I would go home and eat alone. I would spend a few hours alone, then crawl into bed and cry myself to sleep. David would go to bed around midnight. The routine was set, and we did the same thing every day.

Why was I still with David? Well, besides the fact that I had nowhere else to go, I would feel bad about ending our relationship. He told me he loved me every night as he crawled into bed, thinking I was asleep, but the sound of doors opening and closing always woke me up. It was hard, and I didn't have the courage yet, no matter how much I wanted to be with Michael.

I didn't believe David anymore. Some nights he came in smelling of perfume that wasn't mine.

I'd finally found an apartment to look at in a nice neighborhood, and the lady I'd talked to said she'd allow me to pay the rent as soon as I got paid. All I had to do was come up with the deposit if I wanted the place. I was relieved when she said that and made an appointment to see the apartment on Sunday, the day after the picnic.

I couldn't wait until Monday to tell Michael that I had an apartment. A small part of me hoped he would offer to help me move. I looked at my watch again and wondered where he was. It was just after eight, and Michael was usually at his desk. It was strange; he usually arrived at seven.

As eight-thirty came and went, the growing sense of worry began to gnaw at me. I couldn't help but glance at the big clock above the door every few seconds. When it was ten minutes to nine and he still hadn't arrived, I began to really worry. I was about to grab my purse, determined to hunt him down, when the melody of my cell phone began to play. I grabbed it and looked at the screen - Michael. The sight of his name made my body sag with relief.

"Michael, I was really worried. Are you okay?" I asked hastily.

"Lily."

My heart sank. Something was wrong. I could hear it in his voice. "Michael, what's wrong? Where are you?"

"I'm okay," he paused. "An SUV crashed into the car on the way to the office."

"Oh God, Michael!" My voice trembled and tears began to fall down my face. I felt sick to my stomach.

"Shit, Lily, please don't cry. I'm really okay. Apart from a few stitches on my forehead, I'm fine, but George had a heart attack," he sighed. "It was only mild, so he's going to be okay, thank God."

Where are you? I need to see you."

After Michael gave me the name of the hospital, we ended the call and I burst into a flood of tears. The thought that Michael might have been seriously injured scared the hell out of me.

"Lily, what is going on?" Dale asked, coming around my desk and putting his arm around me. I hadn't heard him come into the office.

I swallowed some air into my lungs and managed to calm down. Dale handed me some tissues and I wiped my tear-stained face. "Michael was in a car accident. I don't really know what happened, but he said an SUV hit them and George apparently had a heart attack. I don't know if that was the cause of the accident or if it was the shock of the accident that caused it. I have to get to Michael. I jumped out of my seat and quickly grabbed my jacket and purse. "He said he was okay and that he had a few stitches in his forehead, but I have to go anyway."

Dale looked at me for a moment. "He's more than a boss to you, isn't he, Lily?"

I met his gaze and looked him straight in the eye. "Yes," I whispered, nodding my head in agreement.

"Come on. I'll get Jacky to cover the phones in here," he said, a huge grin spreading across his lips. "Jacky's going to be pissed that she has to do some work for a change instead of gossiping all day."

Dale led me out of the office and accompanied me in the elevator to the ground floor. He managed to get someone from security to drive me to the hospital. I think I surprised Dale when I reached up and kissed him on the cheek and whispered a 'thank you'. He was an incredibly sweet and caring man.

On the way to the hospital, scenarios raced through my mind, bringing new worries about what had happened to Michael. A chill ran down my spine at the thought of arriving at the hospital to find Michael unconscious in a bed with wires sticking out of him. I felt another lump of hysteria clawing at my throat as the car sped toward the hospital.

I was an idiot. I knew Michael was fine, except for a few stitches on his forehead, but I hadn't seen him yet and my imagination was running a little wild. I was stressed out, to say the least.

As soon as the security guard pulled up in front of the hospital, I was out of the car, running to the entrance and through the doors to the receptionist. "Excuse me, can you help me?" I asked a nurse who looked like she'd swallowed a whole lemon.

"I suppose so," she said in a tone as sour as her appearance.

"Can you tell me where I might find Michael McKenzie?"

"Are you a relative?" she asked me with a sneer.

The words to explain my relationship were on my lips when a heavy hand landed on my shoulder. I looked back and smiled in relief at Ruben. "She's his fiancée and I'm his brother, so can you please tell me where I can find him? Or do I have to call Simon Summer, your administrator? He's a good friend of mine."

Flustered, she pressed a few keys on her keyboard and pointed us in the right direction.

"Lily, I talked to Michael. He said he was okay except for a few stitches. You look really upset," Ruben said worriedly.

"Ruben, I just need to see him, okay?"

He put his arm around me and pulled me in the direction the receptionist had indicated.

"He made the right choice this time. I like you, Lily. I hope one day you'll be a McKenzie, too. But you have to promise me that you won't tell Michael what I just said, unless you want him to beat me up."

I smiled at him. "I won't. Thanks for saving me back there. She was actually about to see my temper."

"So I guess I actually saved her from you?"

We turned a corner and found Michael sitting on a chair in the hallway with his head in his hands. I started to walk towards him with more speed. "Michael."

His head shot up. He blinked and then got up and walked toward me. "Lily," he said as I threw myself into his arms and began to sob my heart out, overwhelmed with relief that he was okay.

"Um, I think you might want to come in here," Ruben said, leading us into an empty room.

I wasn't really aware of anything other than being wrapped tightly in Michael's arms. I heard a door close and a lock click into place.

"Lily," Michael said in a cracked voice. "I'm really okay, love. Look at me."

He pushed me slightly away from him. I raised my hand and caressed his cheek. "I needed to see you for myself." I looked at him. All his desire for me was there for me to see, and dared I hope that love was mixed in? "Kiss me, Michael."

He moaned. He reached for me at the same time I reached for him. My purse fell to the floor and he pushed my jacket down my arms.

Our mouths locked, our tongues fused, and I never wanted to come up for air. I was wrapped so tightly in Michael's arms as he devoured my mouth. My sex pulsed between my legs. I moved even closer to him and felt his excitement, hard and firm against my stomach. I rubbed against him. He moaned and moved his hands from my waist to my ass, then pressed me against him. It was my turn to moan.

"God, Lily, make me stop." He began to kiss down my neck to my collarbone.

I grabbed his head and met his eyes. "No."

He lifted my skirt over my hips and I pressed my lips to his, sucking his tongue into my mouth. He moved his hands to my ass and lifted me up. I wrapped my legs around his waist and began to rub my sex along the length of him.

He turned around and my back hit the wall as he continued to ravage my mouth. My nipples were pebbled under my bra, my stomach quivered with need, and my thong was soaked. Nothing had ever felt so good.

Our breathing was erratic and my orgasm was just out of reach. The lips of my pussy opened as I continued to rub against his hard erection, and he pulsed in just the right place.

I'd waited two weeks to be in his arms again, but we had too many clothes on.

Michael

Damn, Lily felt hot and amazing in my arms, the place I never wanted her to leave. I had my tongue fused with hers, my hands on her delicious ass, and my cock rubbing between her legs. What more could I want?

I pulled my mouth away from hers and swallowed some air into my lungs. "Lily, I want you, but don't--" Lily cut me off as she locked her mouth on mine again.

"Take me, quickly," she begged in a whisper.

Fuck.

All reason vanished completely. I moved my lips down to her collarbone again and looked up to see her passion for me flooding her eyes. I moved one hand to cradle her breast while keeping the other on her bottom. Her nipple was hard as I rubbed it between my thumb and finger. She moaned and arched her body against me. Fuck this.

In one frenzied motion, I pulled my cock out, ripped her thong, and then thrust into her sex - we both froze. God, she surrounded me with her warmth. She was so fucking tight. I thought I was going to lose it before I even moved.

She ran her hands through my hair. "Michael, please make love to me."

"Oh God."

I had both hands on her butt. I lifted her up and then impaled her back on my cock. My legs almost buckled with pleasure.

"Oh my God! Don't stop Michael. I'm so close."

Stop? No fucking way.

I continued to hold her in my arms, pressing her hard against the wall with my chest as I began to pump in and out of her.

She was so wet and had me so excited that I was probably going to end up on the floor in a heap the minute I came.

Our lips sealed again. I mimicked what my cock was doing with my tongue. She then broke the kiss and began to pant as her sex began to contract around me. I thrust into her two more times as all the blood rushed to the tip of my cock, my balls pulled up and I came in long bursts of pleasure.

Christ! My orgasm went on and on as my cum covered her walls, and it suddenly hit me - I hadn't used a condom. Shit.

She was limp as she held on to me. I staggered backwards, and when my ass came in contact with what felt like a table, I turned and laid her on it.

Breathing heavily, I gently pulled away from her, my cock soaked in our shared juices. I looked around and found some paper towels, which I rinsed under the tap before cleaning up and zipping up my pants. When I looked back at Lily, her expression almost broke my heart. Her eyes were downcast and she seemed hesitant. Soaking more paper towels, I crossed the room and gently cupped her chin in my palm. Brushing my thumb across her cheek, I lifted her head and kissed her lips softly before bending down and parting her thighs.

I groaned. This was not a good idea. My cock was on the rise again as I breathed in her scent and placed my hand on her pussy to clean it.

I took a deep breath. "Lily, we didn't use a condom. I didn't. I'm sorry. I've never done this before. It wasn't until I was inside of you that I realized what I'd forgotten." I sighed. "I'm clean, though. I haven't had sex in over two years." Hell, I wasn't going to blush.

"When I used to have sex with David, he wore a condom and I was on the pill, but I'm not anymore."

"Don't worry, I have no intention of letting you go. We're in this together."

She smiled at me and my heart started pounding again. What the hell was going on with this woman?

I helped Lily up from the table and bent down to get her purse. I turned to look at her and ended up dropping it on the floor. She was standing with her skirt around her waist, exposing her bare ass, and then she grabbed the torn thong and shoved it down her thighs.

She saw me watching her. "It annoyed me."

I was speechless. My cock was throbbing and my head was throbbing. While I was ravishing Lily, I'd forgotten all about the accident and the fact that I had stitches. The doctor tried to tell me I had a concussion and recommended I spend the night in the hospital. Like hell.

Lily was impeccably dressed, though I knew she had nothing on under her skirt. She would have to go home and change or stop at a store before returning to the office. There was no way I could keep my hands off her knowing she was panty-less under her clothes.

Ever since I'd met Lily, I couldn't stop fantasizing about having her in my office. She wouldn't be wearing any panties and I would push her face first across my desk, lift up her skirt and fuck her from behind. Nice fantasy, but one that shot instant desire through me.

She walked over to me and brought us chest to chest. She looked up at me smiling and wrapped one of her arms around my waist to hold me tight. She sighed as her other hand rested on my chest. I wrapped my arms around her and rested my chin on her head.

"I'm looking at an apartment on Sunday."

I pushed her away and held her shoulders. "You are? That's the best news I've heard in a long time."

She looked hesitant.

"What's wrong?" I asked.

"Um, I was wondering if... I mean, if you're not doing anything..."

I couldn't stop myself from grinning. "Are you going to ask me to come see the apartment with you?"

"Yeah."

I kissed her lips. "I'd love to."

She lifted her hands to my face in a caress, running them gently around my stitches. "It really scared me, Michael, when you called and said you were in an accident." Her eyes filled with tears again.

"Lily, I think I just proved to you that I'm fine." She blushed. "But I think you need to change something before we get back to the office; otherwise I won't be able to stop myself from lifting up your skirt and impaling you on my cock again."

She moaned. "That was cruel; now I'm wet again."

Someone knocked on the door, ending our moment.

"Michael, you need to get out of here fast. Mom and Dad are here."

Hell. I was hard as hell, and my mother would take one look at Lily and know exactly what we just did.

Oh, what the hell? She's my girl, so it didn't matter. I grabbed Lily's hand, unlocked the door, and pulled her through just in time to see my parents coming around the corner.

As soon as my mother saw me, she started to cry and hugged me. "Oh, Michael. I was so worried when Ruben called. Are you really okay?" She asked as she began to pat me down.

"Mom, I was fine as soon as Lily got here." I pulled Lily back into my arms as she nestled against my chest. For once, it felt amazing to finally have someone who cared about me and not my money.

I looked at my parents who were watching us. My mom still had tears in her eyes, but she was grinning.

"If you're done with all this mushy stuff, do you think we can get a move on?" Ruben said, rolling his eyes.

"Let me just check on George and make sure they have my contact information."

"I already have. He'll be fine, but some things will probably have to change. No one can see him for twenty-four hours. They have your information and mine, so let's go."

I took Lily's hand as we walked out of the hospital to Ruben's SUV. I opened the door and put my hands on her ass before shoving her inside, remembering she needed panties - and damn fast. "Ruben, can we stop by Lily's place on the way back to the office?" I asked, not daring to look at Lily.

"Do I want to know why?"

"No."

I sat back in the seat and pulled Lily close to me. All I had to do was convince Lily that she didn't need an apartment. She could move in with me.

14

Lily

SITTING CUDDLED UP WITH MICHAEL IN THE BACK OF HIS brother's car was wonderful. I'd been desperate to get to the hospital earlier, but as soon as I turned the corner and had his arms wrapped around me, I was fine, even though I was crying all over him in relief.

Never in my life had I done to anyone what I did to Michael in the hospital. Sex in a room where anyone could have walked in. The door was locked, but they could have had a key.

It was the hottest sex I've ever had. I sat with Michael so close to me with my bare bottom and all I wanted was for him to be inside me again. He'd felt huge and filled me to the brim. As soon as he'd entered me, the walls of my sex had closed in on him. Oh God.

I started to wriggle in my seat, squeezing my thighs tighter together, trying to get rid of the pain between them.

"Are you okay?" Michael whispered in my ear.

I turned to face him. "No. I need you under my skirt," I whispered back.

His eyes glowed. I kept eye contact with him. "Ruben, just take us back to my place," he said to his brother.

Ruben grinned and it was obvious that he knew his brother well.

"Are you sure, Lily?" he whispered in my ear.

"Yes."

"What about..." Michael couldn't finish.

"I'm going to tell him that I'm moving out and that we're done. I have never been unfaithful to him in the past, and to be honest, I would not even consider being with you unfaithful. The only relationship I have with David right now is that of roommate. He's also seeing someone else; he smells of her perfume when he comes home. The fact that he's seeing someone else relieves me. If I loved him like I should, I wouldn't feel relieved, so that says a lot about our current relationship."

"Lily, in case I haven't made myself clear, I want you, but not just for one night. Do you understand what I'm saying?" He asked me with a growl.

I smiled and turned my head to look at him. "I want

you just as much," I whispered and caught Ruben grinning like an idiot in the rear view mirror.

I started to laugh and really giggled when Ruben winked at me, which made Michael frown. "Keep your eyes on the road. One accident is more than enough," he growled at Ruben.

"Sit tight, brother. I'll get you and Lily back to your place in one piece. And I was thinking of staying for dinner."

"Like hell."

He roared with laughter. "You're too easy to tease. But I'll call you in a couple of hours to take Lily home."

"Enough!"

"Michael, I need to go home tonight and talk to David. The sooner the better." I put my hand on his chest and looked into his eyes.

"I don't like the idea," he whispered to me.

"Neither do I, but I have to do this and get it over with once and for all."

Michael leaned forward and put his forehead on mine. "I can't believe I'm about to say this, but I think Ruben should drop you off at your apartment." I opened my mouth to argue, but Michael put his hand over my lips. "If you come home with me, I can't let you go back to him."

I snuggled against him again. "I'm not sure I would have been able to leave you, so take me home."

He ran his hands through my hair, which I wore

loose. "All right. Take the rest of the day and tomorrow off and I'll see you at the picnic. No fighting. Starting Sunday, you're mine."

I smiled against his chest. "That's fine with me."

"If you need me before, or a ride to the picnic, call me. You have my cell number."

"Okay, I will."

"Call me anytime, because I'm going to miss you."

"I'm going to puke," Ruben blurted out. He met my eyes in the mirror.

"I'm going to have so much fun telling everyone about this car ride. Aren't I glad I got chauffeur duty?"

"If you know what's good for you, you'll keep your mouth shut, Ruben," Michael threatened as the car came to a stop in front of my building.

"Don't get out with me." I put my hand on his arm to keep him from getting out of the car. "You have to stay here and just drive away as soon as I'm on the sidewalk. Otherwise, I'll probably drag you in with me." I was on the verge of tears, so I quickly kissed Michael on the lips, said goodbye to Ruben, and got out of the car.

Michael

I really hated leaving Lily. I'd done what she wanted by staying in the car, and Ruben had driven off as soon as he saw her enter her apartment building. But I didn't like it.

Lily was mine, and hopefully after Sunday, my home would become our home. That was what I wanted more than anything - to have her by my side. I couldn't help but wonder what she liked for breakfast and which side of the bed she preferred to sleep on. Not that the latter mattered. I planned to have her fall asleep in my arms every damn night and wake up in them every morning.

On the weekends we could ride my Harley north to the lakes, maybe stay in one of the hotels. Mmm, we could stay up there for a week and give George a vacation too.

George, my boyfriend and chauffeur. I knew there was no way he was going to rest if he knew I wasn't going to let him drive me again. I had to think of something, and quickly, because he was awake. The hospital let me talk to him briefly, and in the two minutes they allowed, he insisted that I didn't need to find anyone else, that he was still capable of driving me around. Like hell.

He needed to take it easy, and driving downtown in rush hour traffic wasn't what I'd call taking it easy.

He was a pretty decent cook, and I hated cooking but

valued my privacy, so who could be better than George, who lived ten minutes away? But could I stand having him underfoot, especially if Lily moved in? I guess there was only one way to find out, because he sure as hell wasn't driving again.

With any luck, he'd lose his license because George had caused the accident earlier. It wasn't exactly his fault; he'd been in the middle of a heart attack and swerved at the first sharp pain. I don't remember anything after that because the blow to the head knocked me out.

Had I lived to be a hundred, I don't think I would have ever forgotten the look on Lily's face when she saw me in the hospital. She'd thrown herself into my arms and then sobbed her heart out. But hell, I had never intended to drag her into a room and ravish her. She'd felt damn good in my arms, though. I'd waited almost two weeks to get her back in them, so it was impossible to let her go when I needed her the most.

I'd slipped into her warmth so easily, considering how wet she was. When she used her inner muscles to squeeze my shaft so hard, I thought I would lose her right then and there without even moving. At least I could hold out for a few more strokes. But when I crouched down in front of her to clean her pussy, it took all my control not to throw the towel aside and eat her alive. She smelled so good with our combined juices on her thighs.

Thinking about Lily in my arms, all excited and wet, was not a good idea while I was lying in bed. I'd decided on an early night, not only because of the pain in my head, which had started to ease up a bit, but also because I figured if I was in bed, I'd be less likely to drag my bike out and go see Lily.

With the covers kicked off, I turned on my side to grab my phone. I wasn't going to visit Lily, but I could text her.

I found her number on my phone and typed my first text to her.

How are you?

Two seconds later she replied.

I miss you. How are you feeling?

I thought about my response for a few minutes. In general, I felt better than I expected, although I would have felt much better if Lily had been with me. Instead of telling her that, I answered.

Headache almost gone. Where are you?

In bed, naked ;-)

She better not be naked in bed waiting for him. I

couldn't see straight as the anger started to roll through me when my phone beeped again.

I'm fully dressed and waiting for D to come home so I can talk to him.

Relief washed over me. Tonight would be it. She would be mine before the weekend was over.

Sorry, I don't share. When's he getting home?

In a few hours.

My smile deepened as an idea popped into my head.

You want to get naked and lie on your bed?

Are we going to have text sex? Wouldn't a phone be better?

I'll text you instructions, and then I'll leave you alone.

Okay. Will text when clothes are off.

Fuck, was I really going to tell her what I wanted her to do to give herself an orgasm? My dick jerked in agreement.

I'm naked on my bed. I've also locked the bedroom door.

I moaned in response to her text. I could imagine her lying on the bed, her long legs spread, her sex exposed to the world. My cock stiffened even more - if that was possible.

Good girl.

I wish I was with you so you could do these things to me.

I dropped my phone on my chest with that last one. I'd never been so aroused on my own. Hell, I'd probably jerked off in the shower too many times to count, but just reading Lily's words made me hard as a spike. I couldn't hold back anymore, and I ran my hand down my aching cock to my balls, imagining that it was Lily's hand. I shuddered and leaked from the tip.

The phone buzzed against my chest, indicating a new message.

Are you still there?

I chuckled. Such an impatient girl.

Yeah - you got my dick so damn hard, I'm leaking.

If I was there, I would lick it up!

I arched off the bed and my breathing had become uneven. Shit, I was supposed to be working Lily up, but she was the one working me up.

My cock and balls were throbbing with the image of Lily's hot mouth locked around the tip. I pulled my hand away. I had to get Lily excited.

I want you to massage your breasts and play with your nipples until they're pebbled and imagine it's my hands on you.

Already pebbled.

I longed to see those nipples. In my mind, they were a dusty pink, the perfect complement to your flawless complexion.

Put the phone down and do as I say.

Okay.

I did the same, running my hands over my own nipples, over my ribs and stomach until I reached my shaft. Once there, I wrapped my hand around it and started running my fingers up and down. I wasn't sure how long I could go on before I came; it felt good, too good.

You have to touch my pussy. I'm so wet and aching for you.

God, her words alone were enough to bring me to orgasm. The next few texts had to be enough to send her over the edge, because I really was seconds away.

Keep one hand on your chest and move the other hand between your legs.

I ran my hand up and down my length, desperate for relief.

Dip your finger into your sex and then rub your clit for a few seconds, then put your fingers to your mouth and taste yourself.

My breathing became erratic and my hand on my cock moved faster and faster, up and down. I had to send her another text because I wanted us to get together. I could imagine her on her bedspread, my fingers dipping into her pussy as she rocked her hips to the words I was typing.

Put two fingers in your sex and play with your clit. Come for me.

I imagined Lily lying on her own bed, one hand massaging her breast and nipple, the other between her legs, pleasuring herself.

My climax erupted from somewhere deep inside me. I ejaculated all over my stomach and some of it landed on the pillow next to my head.

I reached for my phone and typed another message to Lily with a shaky hand.

> Are you okay?

> Oh yeah! That was hot. You?

> I'm still shaking. It was that good.

> I don't want to leave, but I need a shower.

I grinned. I didn't want her to go either, but I needed a shower too.

> Me too. Good night, Lily. See you on Saturday.

> Night, Michael. I can't wait. xx

She added two kisses at the end of her text. I smiled all the way to the bathroom and through the shower, and I was pretty sure I fell asleep still grinning.

15

Lily

LAST NIGHT MICHAEL GAVE ME AN ORGASM BY TEXT. IT was amazing. It was also the first time I'd ever done something like that. My only wish was that I could have heard his voice. He had a rich, dark chocolate voice that made me hot and bothered the minute he said anything to me.

I showered and dressed, then sat and waited for David. He didn't come, at least not while I was still awake. Instead, I fell asleep in my clothes, only to find him in the shower in the morning. He avoided me when I waited for him in the kitchen. In fact, with a shouted excuse that he had to get to work, he got dressed and left the apartment before I could catch him. He thought

I was an idiot. He didn't speak to me at all, and that really pissed me off.

After I finished cleaning the kitchen, I went to the bedroom and took out three of the biggest suitcases I could find and put them on the bed.

I started with everything that was in the tallboy and put all my lingerie in the elastic pockets. I left the sexiest piece out to wear for Michael. Sometime during the picnic I'd let Michael know what I was wearing under my dress.

Exhausted from cleaning and packing, I threw myself on the sofa and stared at the ceiling. I felt restless and didn't really want to be in the apartment. The sun was shining outside, so I managed to drag myself up and quickly changed out of my lounge clothes into stonewashed jeans and a t-shirt. I slipped my feet into my lilac ballerina pumps, grabbed my purse, and opened the apartment door to face Michael.

"What are you doing here?"

I hadn't expected to see him until the picnic. He seemed speechless, so I took matters into my own hands. I stepped out the door, took his face in my hands, and brought it down to plant a soft kiss on his lips before moving to kiss his forehead over the gauze covering his stitches.

"I had to see you. I couldn't wait until the picnic."

He stroked my face down to my neck, but before he could go any further, I grabbed his hand and held it in mine. "How are you feeling?" I asked. I'd been worried about him ever since the accident.

"My head hurt when I woke up this morning, but after a couple of Advil, the pain eased up." He smiled at me. "Of course, I feel much better after seeing you."

"Aww, you're sweet."

"I'm not sweet... I'm a guy."

I burst out laughing. "You're also an idiot." I reached up and quickly kissed his cheek. "I was going for a walk in the park. Want to come with me?"

He took my hand and began to pull me toward the stairs. "I'd love to. It's been a while since I had a hot dog from that stand over there." He grinned, looking like a big kid.

I rolled my eyes at his enthusiasm.

"Lily, where is your sense of adventure?" He held the door open for me.

I walked by and couldn't resist rubbing up against him. I turned my head and met his eyes, then winked. "My sense of adventure happened last night. Text adventure!"

Michael pulled me to a stop and into his arms.

"Oh." He was long and hard against my stomach. "I didn't expect such a quick reaction to my comment."

"All I have to do is think about you and voila... rock hard," he growled.

I licked my lips.

"Oh no. You're not doing this to me. We're going to

the park, buy some hot dogs, find a spot on the grass, and we're going to sit there cuddling while we watch the world go by. Now come on, move your ass." He pulled me behind him to get me moving.

"That sounds great." My throat was dry after his speech. He had me all choked up. I wanted to do everything he said.

In the seven years I'd been with David, we'd never once gone to the park to chill. David's idea of chilling was watching hockey, which didn't bother me because I was a fan too, but we were with a few thousand people. The park would be crowded, but we wouldn't have any trouble finding a secluded spot - at least I hoped not.

"Lily, do you want everything on that?"

"Yes, please," I replied, watching the guy working the stand assemble our hot dogs.

Michael put his arm around my shoulders and pulled me close. I wrapped my arm around his waist, under his t-shirt. When my hand started to go down the back of his jeans, he growled at me. He actually growled at me! The guy with the hot dogs looked at us and apparently decided he was hearing things, so he finished preparing our food.

"You. Must. Behave."

"I can't believe you growled at me."

"Thanks," Michael said as he took the hot dogs and sodas from the guy.

He pointed me toward the lake and the trees that

hung low, providing a semblance of privacy. "I was having a hard enough time keeping all that blood above my belt. You shoving your hands into my jeans sent it south fast."

I chuckled. "You need to learn to control your libido before it gets you into trouble."

"I wouldn't have to control it if you weren't so damn sexy."

"Ha." I stuck my tongue out at him as we sat down under one of the trees that offered more seclusion than the others.

Michael

Lily really tested my patience. I'd done nothing but dream about holding her in my arms again. She was the sexiest woman I'd ever met, and I knew she was all mine, or soon would be. After spending most of the morning tidying up, I finally gave in to my need to see her and grabbed my car keys.

When I'd shown up at her apartment, I'd been nervous as hell. I had no idea if David would be there or not. I was surprised when she opened the door and walked in and planted a kiss on my lips for all to see. It had taken everything in me to stop myself from grabbing her and pushing her against the wall. All I'd wanted was to feel her curves pressed against mine again.

The low hanging branches of the tree we were relaxing under partially hid us. I rested against the trunk with Lily between my legs, resting against my chest. I ate my hot dog with one hand while rubbing her belly with the other. I waited for her to finish eating before I touched her skin. We couldn't do what I wanted to do under here, but we could play - a little.

With a quick gulp of our sodas, we wiped our hands on napkins and put everything in the bag, which I set aside to throw in the trash when we left.

Lily lay down between my legs with the back of her head against my groin - not a good idea!

"Um, Lily?"

"Yeah." She grinned up at me. "You want me to move?"

"That would be good," I croaked.

She laughed and turned around and sat down again - this time with her face in my groin.

My head hit the tree behind me. She really was going to kill me. Lily's hand crawled up my thigh and landed right on my twitching dick. My breathing began to quicken as she traced the outline of my growing shaft with her finger. Without warning, she leaned forward slightly and used her mouth to gently bite me through my jeans. I almost shot off the floor.

"Fuck!" She looked up at me. "You have to stop.

Seeing you with your head in my lap is such a turn-on, I'm not sure I can stop."

Lily began to climb on top of me, straddling my thighs. She wiggled on top of me until I stopped her hips with my hands. "What makes you think I want you to stop?" she teased.

I didn't get a chance to answer because her mouth came down hard on mine. She wrapped her arms around my neck and sucked my tongue into her mouth. My hands tightened on her hips as I arched into her.

She whimpered into my mouth. I released my grip on her hips and grabbed her head to intensify the kiss. She began to rub against my fully engorged cock. If she didn't stop, I would come with her.

Gradually I managed to pull away from her kissing mouth and looked into her eyes. "I want you," I laughed as I took her face in my hands, "as if you couldn't tell, but today I want to spend it lying here in the park, relaxing and talking. Yes, I'm going to be uncomfortable, but I can handle that as long as I'm with you and I know you're here with me."

Lily, with tears in her eyes, stroked my face before leaning in to give me a light kiss. "Just hold me, Michael. Hold me really tight."

With those words, Lily lay back down, pulling me with her before cuddling up to me as I wrapped her tightly in my arms.

My body was still aroused as Lily slid her leg

between mine and her hand into the back pocket of my jeans, but my intentions for the afternoon were going to be as I told her. No matter how much it would kill me, I planned to stay zipped up.

With Lily flush against me, I distracted myself with the goings-on around us. For a weekend, the park wasn't as busy as one would expect. There were families with children; one or two had even brought their dogs, who seemed more than happy to join in the family Frisbee game. It made me sad to realize that I'd never have that, but maybe I could have a piece of it with Lily.

"Hey, why do you look sad?" Lily asked, rubbing the frown from my forehead with her fingers.

"I'm not sad. I have you in my arms; how could I be sad?" I leaned over and planted a kiss on hers. "Lily, do you need a ride to the picnic tomorrow? I can pick you up if you need me to."

"Don't worry about me, Michael. I'll be there."

I didn't like her answer, but it would have to do.

16

Lily

ALL I COULD THINK ABOUT WAS THE TIME I'D SPENT IN the park with Michael. After the hot interlude, we'd settled down on the grass and he'd held me close while I slept. Yes, I'd dozed off on him, but who could blame me? I'd been worried about him the night before, so I hadn't slept much.

Michael had let me sleep for a few hours and then woke me up with sweet kisses all over my face.

I smiled at the memory - so sweet.

"What put that smile on your face, or should I ask who?"

David! I turned to see him watching me from the bedroom doorway. I suddenly felt vulnerable lying on the bed as I was.

"So, you decided to come back."

He walked further into the room and stopped dead when he saw my pile of shoeboxes and suitcases.

"What's going on, Lily? Are you moving out?"

I sat up on the bed and he came over to sit next to me. "Yes. Our relationship has been over for a while, and I know you have someone else."

He looked startled. "Lily, I don't know what to say. I tried to keep my friendship with her just that, but along the way it turned into something else. I'm sorry. You don't deserve that from me. You don't seem too upset though?"

"I'm sad that it's come to this after all the years we've been together. But to be honest, I'm relieved. I'm sorry if you don't like it, but I can't help the way I feel."

"Where are you going? I assume you're not kicking me out?" he asked, taking my hand.

"I'm looking at an apartment tomorrow, so hopefully I'll be moving out tomorrow night." I sighed in relief.

It was getting late, so I got up to get my cowboy boots, which matched my above-the-knee sundress. I'd left my hair down and added more curls. I planned to leave Michael speechless.

"Lily, would you mind if I came to the picnic as your guest?" I looked at him and frowned. "Our company was sent invitations, but there are two other people the boss wanted to attend. You were my girlfriend at the time, so

I told him he could use my invitation since I was going with you anyway."

"Okay, but don't introduce me as such," I said. David looked startled at my answer, but grabbed his clothes and went to the bathroom.

While David took a quick shower, I made my way to the living room and collapsed on the sofa. That went much better than I thought it would. Maybe David felt the same relief I did. He wasn't usually so calm about things he wanted. Part of me was sad to realize that he didn't want me anymore. I shook my head, trying to rid myself of the emotions I was feeling. The last thing I needed was to feel sorry for myself; it was ridiculous since I had Michael.

The bathroom door opened, so I dragged myself out of the daydream I was in and walked over to the dresser to get my purse.

I could hardly wait to see Michael again. I had missed him last night; it was going to be hard not to be with him at the picnic. I just hoped we would get a chance to dance together.

"Are you ready to go, Lily?" David asked me as he came out of the bedroom.

"Yeah, as ready as I'll ever be." I followed David out of the apartment, down the stairs, and out of the building to his car, which he managed to park right outside.

He opened the door and waited for me to get in

before closing it, then ran around to get in the driver's seat. He didn't put the key in the ignition. He sat for a few seconds before turning to look at me. "Lily, are you going to be, okay?"

I remained silent, trying to organize my thoughts before I screwed things up. "If this had all happened at once, I would probably say no, but it didn't. So, yeah, I'm fine. I'm enjoying my new job, and I've met some great people and made some new friends. Part of me is sad that our relationship is ending, but I will always have fond memories of our time together. You've been there for the good and the bad in my life, and I'll never forget that, but it's time for both of us to move on."

We sat there for a minute or two before David finally put the key in the ignition and drove off.

Michael

I stood in the shade of my parents' ranch and watched everyone arrive with their partners and children, and it made me feel lonely as hell. I wanted Lily to be with me, standing next to me. Since her soon-to-be ex had no idea about us or the fact that Lily was moving out, she'd asked me to be patient for one more day. It wasn't what I wanted to do, but I'd agreed. Another day couldn't hurt, right?

"Brother, why are you hiding here?" Sebastian's voice interrupted my thoughts. He gave me a questioning look, one eyebrow raised as he walked towards me.

"I'm not hiding. It's hot," I replied, draining the beer in my hand.

He laughed.

"You two pussies having your own party?" Lucien asked as he came around the corner with Ramon and Ruben.

"No, Michael was hiding out here," Sebastian announced, sliding out of range.

"I was not hiding. I was having a quiet drink before I had to be social." I took the bottle of beer Ramon offered and downed about half of it.

"Are there going to be any hot chicks here today?" Sebastian asked.

"They're all married," I replied, causing Ruben to choke on his beer.

"Not all of them are married. Wait till you meet his assistant."

I wanted to kill Ruben.

Sebastian stopped in the middle of his drink and looked at me. "Well, Michael, you've been keeping a secret." He looked at Ruben. "How hot?"

Ruben's smile deepened and he looked back at

Sebastian. "Curves, lots of them. Long, dark, curly hair and breasts to fill them."

"You better stop right there," I told Ruben. My fists ached to be used and I knew I had to get Ruben to stop before I resorted to violence.

"Looks like the hot assistant is already taken," Lucien commented.

"If you'd seen her in the car after Michael's accident, you'd have no doubt," he grinned. "In fact, I'd ask him what they were doing locked up in the hospital room."

Lucien choked on his beer while Ramon and Sebastian just stood there looking at me.

"What?" I asked. There was no way I was going to get into a discussion with my brothers about Lily.

"You've been on your own for six years. You finally met someone, and you don't want to tell us. Is that true?" Lucien asked.

I put my beer to my mouth and froze. Lily walked in my direction, and she looked sexy as hell. The sun was behind her, making her dress see through. She took my breath away.

"Who the fuck is that?"

Sebastian's comment brought me back to my senses and I realized that all four of my brothers were standing with me, staring at her. Lily looked up and stopped when she saw all of us just standing there, probably with our tongues hanging down to our knees.

"Michael, don't just stand there; go get your girl." My mother's words brought me back to my senses.

"She is mine. You four can keep your hands to yourselves," I growled.

As I started to walk towards Lily, her whole face lit up. I could hear my mother sighing behind me and a few snickers, not to mention Sebastian making a comment under his breath.

Before I wrapped Lily in my arms, I quickly looked around for David and saw him disappearing around the barn with his boss's daughter.

Standing in front of her, I cupped her face in my hands. "You're gorgeous. Hell, I think I'm going to have to beat up my brothers for looking at you and drooling!" I leaned down and kissed her softly on the lips. "I've missed you."

She placed her hands on my hips and threaded her fingers through the belt loops of my jeans, then pulled me close before sealing her lips to mine.

As soon as our mouths touched, I slid my tongue in and fused it with hers. Our bodies began to melt together as I heard more than one throat being cleared behind me. Reluctantly, I pulled my mouth away from Lily's and met her eyes. She licked her lips, drawing a groan from me.

"You're going to kill me today, you know that?" I breathed heavily, dreading having to introduce her to my brothers.

A quick glance over my shoulder confirmed what I already knew. They were standing where I'd left them, but in a line to meet my wife.

Lily followed my gaze and started to laugh. "Come on, introduce me to your other two brothers."

"Do I have to?" God, could I sound any more pathetic? CEO here, not idiot!

Lily slipped her hand into mine and gave me a gentle tug to get me moving. "I told David I'm moving out and about the apartment I want to look at tomorrow. He seemed okay, I guess. Which was a relief."

"About the apartment."

"Hey, come over here and share," Sebastian called.

Lily laughed and walked over to my mother, who held her arms out to her. "Lily, it's so good to see you again."

"It's good to see you too, Pippa." My mother pulled away and slipped her arm through Lily's to introduce her to my brothers. Why she needed to be introduced to those idiots was beyond me.

"Lily, you already know Ruben and Ramon, and this is Sebastian; you might want to stay away from him."

As Ruben roared with laughter, he got a dirty look from our mother. Then she moved on to Lucien

Because of his accident, Lucien was badly scarred from the tips of his fingers, up the back of his right arm, along the back of his shoulder, and down part of his side and back. I was nervous for her to meet him because he was going to test her, and if she failed, he'd be cold, which would probably upset her, and then I'd have to hit him.

"Lily, this is my oldest son, Lucien." Lily held out her hand to him, and of course he held out his right hand to her. She looked down and then back up at his face before taking his hand, wrapping her fingers around his as they shook hands. Lucien was surprised.

"I'm not afraid of you, Lucien," Lily told him.

"I like you. The next time I'm in town, we can have coffee together and I'll tell you all about Michael."

No way was that going to happen. She didn't want to have coffee with anyone but me.

"I'd like that. Don't forget."

Did she just agree to meet Lucien?

I frowned.

"Don't get your panties in a bunch. I'm not poaching." With that, Lucien left.

My mother still had her arm through Lily's, as if they had been friends for years.

When I looked closer, Mom had tears in her eyes. She turned to Lily and kissed her on both cheeks. "Thank you for being nice to him."

Lily looked shocked. "I wouldn't be anything else."

"It's just that since his accident, he's shut himself away in that shack he calls home, and I worry about him. He needs a friend, and I think he's chosen you."

Was what my mother told Lily the truth? Was he

lonely and in need of a friend who could accept him for who he was? I hope that was all it was. I really had to stop being possessive or she wouldn't take it for long. We also had to have the 'will you move in with me' conversation.

17

Lily

SEBASTIAN AND LUCIEN WERE BOTH ATTRACTIVE MEN, and if Michael hadn't made it clear that I was with him, I was pretty sure that one of them would have made a move on me. My guess was that it would have been Sebastian, although there was something about Lucien that appealed to me. He was wounded, and his mother thought he needed a friend. Well, I could do that, provided Michael behaved himself.

"Lily, I've been looking all over for you," David said as he came up behind me and put his arm around my shoulders.

I shook him off. "David."

He started to speak before I could finish. "Lily,

Robert is over there, and he wants to talk to you." The cheek of him!

"I have nothing to say to him." Robert was my former boss and I owed him nothing.

"Lily, stop being awkward and come talk to him."

"Who are you?" Sebastian asked with a look on his face that I couldn't decipher.

"I'm Lily's boyfriend, David. And who are you?" David replied.

"Okay, that's enough," I said. "David, you're not my boyfriend anymore, so you don't get to tell me what to do and who to see."

"Lily, we agreed to come here together," David argued.

"We agreed to come here together, but not as a couple. Robert is looking for you; tell him I'm busy."

"Lily?" He finally realized that I had no intention of playing nice, which was just as well, because I could feel the anger rolling off Michael.

He turned and stalked off, and before I could even turn back to Michael, David was being dragged into one of the tents with my ex-boss's daughter.

"What's he doing with Lucy?" Ruben asked.

Lucy, the name he had yelled when he came into the kitchen. He was an idiot. Her father would go crazy if he found out, which he probably would if they continued like this. I had met her when we spent the weekend at her father's house, although I didn't remember her being called Lucy. In fact, I remembered that she'd been introduced to me as Jennifer. Wait a minute, was she the reason I lost my job? Okay, I wasn't going to freak out, because if I hadn't lost my job, I wouldn't have met Michael, but I was still annoyed.

"He's been having an affair for a while, I'm not sure how long, but I just found out it was with his boss's daughter," I said.

"Shit, Lily. That sucks."

"Thanks, Ruben, but it really doesn't. I'm okay with it. I shouldn't be, but I am."

"Michael, come over here and help me a minute," Elias called.

Michael put his hand on my back and leaned down to whisper in my ear. "Are you going to be, okay?" I shivered and turned my body against him to hide my pebbled nipples.

"We'll go see what Dad wants; you stay with Lily." One of his brothers said, which one? I couldn't tell because Michael had me so turned on, I couldn't think straight.

"Lily, you're going to kill me," he whispered again.

"Then stop whispering in my ear. It turns me on to have you so close, and when you whisper in my ear, I get goose bumps. Not only that, but my nipples have also become pebbly."

"Fuck, you're really playing with my libido. The next time I take you, it will be in a bed, not in the barn or against a wall in a hospital, but in a bed where I can spend hours touching your skin, tasting your body, especially your pussy."

I moved closer to Michael and wrapped my arms around his waist. "That was cruel. I need..."

"What do you need, Lily?"

I clenched my fists into his shirt. "I need you, Michael. Just you."

I could feel his heart rate increase at my words.

He pulled away, took my hand, and dragged me into a small office at the back of the garage.

As soon as the door closed, he sealed his mouth over mine, sending all my senses into overdrive. God, he knew how to kiss and the taste of him was intoxicating. I ran my hands through his hair and his whole body shivered against mine. His penis felt long and hard against my stomach. I reached down with one hand and stroked it through his clothes, but I really wanted to see it, to touch it without any clothes between us.

"Lily, you have to stop." He moved my hand away and knelt on the floor. "I want to taste you. I want to go back out there with the taste of you on my tongue."

My legs almost buckled.

He grabbed my hips and backed me up against the wall for support, then grabbed the hem of my dress and lifted it. He moved closer, spreading my legs further apart so he could place his tongue on my thighs before dropping my dress over his head as I practically melted into a puddle.

My stomach quivered, my breathing was ragged, and my thighs trembled with need as Michael kissed my pubic bone and then used his fingers to move my thong aside. I was so aroused I could come just from his touch. My sex began to clench, and he wasn't even inside me.

"Michael, I really need you.

"I know, baby. I'm trying not to lose control. This is about you, not me."

He rubbed around my clit, moving his fingers to rub the entrance to my sex; I couldn't hold back the moan. It felt too good. "Don't stop."

"Fuck, your pussy is soaked."

He slid two fingers inside me. I clenched and started to come as he put his tongue on my clit and sucked it into his mouth. My orgasm went on and on as I writhed on his mouth and fingers as he brought me back down to earth.

"Hell," Michael said. He sounded rather muffled.

He removed his fingers from me and then stuck his tongue in me as I erupted again and came on his mouth. Well, he said he wanted my taste on his tongue.

Michael slowly let go of my hips and put my thong back on, then moved out from under my dress. I looked down at him and his mouth looked wet - he was licking his lips. My eyes darkened.

"Now you."

"Later," he croaked, getting to his feet.

Observing the bulge in his jeans, I exclaimed, "Oh my." "Michael, you've brought me to orgasm four times now, and you've seen my pussy twice. I haven't seen your cock once, not even in the hospital. I've felt you, boy, but I haven't seen you," I pouted.

His eyes burned into my body, and I ached to have his skin branded against mine

I told him what I wanted: "I want to touch you naked. I want to stroke your length, get to know your girth. I want to lick up all the milky cream from the head of your penis, and then I want you to come in my mouth like I just did with you."

"Fucking hell, you keep talking like that and I'm going to come in my jeans."

I licked my lips.

"Michael, get your ass out here!" Sebastian shouted at the same time as he banged on the door, making us both jump.

We looked down at the big bulge in Michael's pants. He grinned and opened the door.

Sebastian took one look at both of us, obviously seeing his brother's condition, then burst out laughing.

"Sorry to interrupt," he said with a big grin.

I started to laugh, and Michael frowned at me. I laughed harder, and of course I set Sebastian off again. Michael seemed to have his libido under control for now and took my hand to lead me out into the daylight.

Michael

Standing in front of the garage with Lily's hand in mine, I faced Sebastian, who had interrupted a very heated moment. Two seconds later and I would have given in to Lily's demand to touch me. Hell, her words about my cock almost made me rip my jeans open so I wouldn't come in them. She was a hot little thing with a sassy mouth, something I hadn't expected.

I straightened up and looked at Sebastian who was still laughing with Lily.

"Okay, fun's over. Sebastian, what was the emergency?"

"Sorry, it wasn't that urgent. I didn't really think you'd get up to anything out here," he said, chuckling. "You know, I think this was the best day I've had in a while, and you, brother," he pointed at me, "will never live this down. Making out in the office with the hottest chick here is not right. That's usually my job."

"You stay away from her."

"You'd have to be a complete idiot to think she has eyes for anyone but you." Besides, I don't want a black eye. It would ruin this perfection," he said, moving his face from side to side.

"I think I really like your brothers, Michael." Lily

looked up at me, leaned in and gave me a quick kiss. "I'm going to go say hello to Sylvia and save Ramon. Are you sure she's old enough to work? She looks like jailbait."

Sebastian chuckled when he heard Lily's comment.

"I had Dale personally check her records before we offered her the job. She likes to talk, but she's damn good at her job." I turned to Sebastian. "You keep your pants zipped around her."

He choked on a swig of beer. Served him right.

Lily walked away laughing.

I watched her shake her sexy ass as she left; the rest of her was just as hot. I still had the taste of her on my tongue and my jeans were starting to feel uncomfortable again.

"Lily is a hot babe." Until Sebastian opened his mouth, I'd forgotten that he was standing next to me.

I scowled at him. "Okay, it wasn't an emergency, but you obviously wanted something."

"Yes, I did. Jacky, the office shark is looking for you. I don't think she had anything to say."

"Hell, this is your fault for thinking with your dick when you hired her," I told him.

I'd been annoyed as hell when I'd come back from a meeting to find I had a new employee who only wanted to get into my pants. She hadn't been successful and turned out to be a nuisance. "You had the hots for her; go and entertain her."

"Like hell. She probably eats dicks for breakfast."

I roared with laughter. I could always count on Sebastian to be blunt and to the point with few words. Unless he was trying to get into someone's pants, then he was all charm and the perfect gentleman.

"Michael, there you are." The tone was bubbly and flirtatious. I jumped at the sound.

I turned to find Jacky standing six feet away in the shortest dress and highest heels I'd ever seen. I heard Sebastian laughing in the background as he walked away, leaving me alone.

"Jacky, you shouldn't be back here. Let's go and join everyone," I suggested, trying to get Jacky to join the rest of the guests. Unfortunately, she had other ideas.

"Oh, don't be silly. I don't want to share you with the others. Why can't we go in there?" She muttered, trying to drag me back into the garage.

No way. Jacky had always been forward at our company events for employees, but never this much.

"Jacky, that's not going to happen. I'm your boss and you're my employee. That is all we are going to be. Hopefully, when you sober up a bit, you will realize that." I ran my hands through my hair as I looked around, hoping to find someone else to blame. "Look, I have to go say hello to everyone. Let me walk you back."

"You're a good man, Michael McKenzie. Let's go." She walked up to me and slipped her arm through mine, then snuggled close. God, I hope Lily didn't see this and misunderstand.

"Why don't you like me?" Jacky asked and I really wished she hadn't.

"Jacky, you seem like a nice woman, but I'm not looking for anyone else." I tried to be diplomatic, but I had to tell her. And technically I was with Lily, so I hadn't lied about not looking for anyone else.

"What about your brothers?" she asked.

I laughed. There was really nothing else. "Jacky, there are a lot of boys out there; please find one."

"You're sweet. I'll see you later." She walked off towards the alcohol tent, and as I watched her go, I caught sight of Lily in deep conversation with Lucien on the back steps. My first instinct was to go and find out what they were talking about, but I had to learn to trust Lily. I took a deep breath and walked in the opposite direction to the barn, which had been cleared out for the dance.

As soon as I walked in, the first person I saw was David. He was standing in a corner with his hands up Lucy's skirt and in her panties. I really hoped Lily didn't catch a glimpse of him like that. She already knew he was having an affair with her, but she didn't need it thrown in her face.

It killed me to know that Lily was out there, sitting, talking to Lucien. I just wanted to be there with her and know what he was saying.

The truth was, Lucien needed a friend, someone to talk to, because God knew he wasn't going to talk to me or our other brothers. I knew deep down that I could trust Lily, but after what Viv had done, it was hard to trust people completely, and I felt sad that sometimes that included my brothers, who I knew would never betray me.

18

Lily

I HAD STAYED AWAY FROM MICHAEL MOST OF THE DAY because I didn't trust myself not to touch him. We'd been acting like teenagers in the office, and it had felt good. I really wanted to see Michael and touch him, but he didn't let me. In the end, it was a good thing, because his brother would've interrupted at a crucial moment.

He spent most of the afternoon with Lucien. He was a nice, handsome guy who had been through a lot and still needed time to recover. We'd become friends over the last few hours. Michael had come over to talk to us a few times, probably to check on us and make sure Lucien wasn't poaching. He wasn't subtle about it either, because each time he reminded Lucien that I was his wife. Lucien just laughed and told Michael that he'd adopted me as his sister.

We had also attracted the attention of other staff members, which wasn't good. Although I wasn't sure how it would look if they found out I was dating Michael.

As the evening dance began, I looked around for my man. I really wanted to dance with him.

The music was loud, but no one seemed to mind, and we still had a good time. The McKenzie family certainly knew how to thank their employees. Looking to my right, I leaned against the wall and saw David with his tongue down Lucy's throat. I was shocked that he would do it so openly, but I was surprised that it didn't bother me to see him with someone else.

"Hey, are you okay?" Michael asked, standing so close to me that his chest was pressed against my back. He nibbled on my ear as he ran his hand down my arm, intertwining our fingers. I held on tight.

"I'm fine. Would you mind if everyone knew about us?" I asked.

"I don't want to hide you, but if that's what you want, I'll go along with it. Hell, I'll go along with pretty much anything you want if it means you're mine."

I turned and looked up at him. The heat emanating from him was searing.

"Dance with me, Lily?"

"Okay," I whispered.

He took my hand and led me to the dance floor, causing a bit of a stir in the room. He pulled me into his arms and put one hand on my hip; the other hand he intertwined with my fingers. My arm went to his shoulder, and I moved my hand to the hair at the back of his neck. He shivered.

Pressed together, without an inch between us, we began to slow dance. Within minutes, Michael let go of my hand and wrapped me in his arms as he stroked my back. I was turned on to the hilt and really needed him. From the feel of it, he needed me just as much.

I slipped my hand under his t-shirt and met his skin. He jerked against my stomach and tightened his grip on me.

"Be careful, Lily. I really want you," he growled into my ear.

I responded by rubbing against him. My nipples were rock hard, which I was sure he could feel. His hands slid down my back and rested on my ass. He danced us into a dark corner that was less crowded. I pushed both my hands into the back of his t-shirt, digging my nails into his skin.

He moaned and pushed into me as his hands pulled me even closer. All I wanted to do was unzip him so I could climb on for a wild ride. He had soaked my thong, and I was seconds away from orgasm.

"Michael, I need you inside me...now!"

He breathed heavily into my ear. "I don't think I can

move yet." He let me go slightly, but I kept my hands in his t-shirt, landing on his hard, muscular stomach. Watching his abs quiver, I moved further up his chest to his chiseled abs. I was shocked to see the tip of his penis peeking out of the waistband of his jeans.

I licked my lips.

"Jesus, Lily," he croaked as I watched him leak. Before he could stop me, I took a finger and rubbed the creamy liquid over the head of his cock.

"Fuck."

He grabbed my hand and pulled me through a door in the back that I hadn't noticed before.

"Let me taste you?" I begged.

"I want you in a bed. You deserve a lot of loving, but not out here."

"Michael, I want you too much to care where we are." I stepped inside him again and pushed my hand down the front of his jeans before wrapping it around him. His shaft was silky to the touch and so large that I could barely wrap my hand around it. His eyes were practically rolling back in his head.

He reached out and locked the door as I unzipped his zipper and freed his cock.

I knelt and pushed his jeans over his hips. His cock jerked in front of my face. I leaned in and put my tongue to the tip, licking it along the slit, never breaking eye contact.

With my hand, I gently stroked down to his balls and

back up to the tip, then down again. Keeping my hand around the base, I used my tongue to lick him up and down, then swirled it around the head. His breathing was erratic, and his eyes were heavy. I took him in my mouth and heard his head hit the wall.

I'd never liked doing this before, but finally having Michael's cock in my hands and mouth was a huge turn-on. His reaction told me I was doing it right. I took as much as I could in my mouth and used my hands to caress his thighs. With one hand, I gently stroked his balls as I sucked on his shaft.

"Lily...soon," he panted, then moaned loudly.

I moved my other hand up to his root and took a firm grip, sliding my hand up and down in sync with my mouth. I released his balls and rubbed my fingers between his legs. He shivered. He put his hands on my head as I took him further into my mouth. I pressed lightly where I thought his perineum would be, and as he roared in release, I sucked him dry.

He moved my head away. "I can't take any more." He slid down the wall and unzipped his jeans, then pulled me onto his lap. I laid my head on his chest and listened to his uneven breathing. "Come home with me tonight, Lily...please?"

"Yes," I whispered. Now that I'd found him, I had no intention of letting him go. Not ever.

"I can't move. Turnover on my lap and let me put my fingers inside you."

"No. I desperately want you inside me, but we need a bed. We'll have that when we get to your place."

He chuckled. "When we have a bed, I have no intention of ever letting you out of it."

"Ha. If you want an assistant at work, you won't have a choice."

"Spoilsport. It's a good thing I have an amazing imagination."

"Yeah, well, that imagination better stay subdued for now, because you have to get back out there. Oh, my God. Everyone's going to know what we did."

"No, they won't. Come on, let's get up." I climbed off him and helped pull him up off the ground. "There's a door to the outside, right there," he said, pointing to a door I hadn't seen.

Michael zipped up his jeans and led me to the door, which he unlocked and opened for me. I stepped outside and stopped dead in my tracks.

David was about four feet away with his jeans around his knees, fucking Lucy from behind.

"Oh my God," I said, stunned. David whipped his head around and saw me, then started to climax. To say I was embarrassed was an understatement. I wasn't jealous; how could I be after doing for Michael what I never would have done for David? But I certainly never expected to see them doing it.

Michael wrapped his arms around me as they reunited. David turned back to us and looked shocked.

"So that's why you're not bothered that I'm having an affair, because you are too."

"I've only been with Michael for two days. Can you say the same about Lucy?"

He looked embarrassed. "Are you coming home tonight?"

"She won't be back until sometime tomorrow to get her things," Michael said as he continued to hold me.

David nodded and pulled Lucy away with him.

Michael

"Lily?"

"I'm fine. Please don't worry about me. Sure, it was a surprise to see my ex in this state. I can't complain, though, considering what I've been up to with you." She licked her lips. "You tasted so delicious and hot."

I moaned. "If you're sure you're okay, let's go up to the house and see my parents before we go back to my place.

"I'd like that." I took her hand in mine, and after a chaste kiss, we walked up to the back porch of my parents' ranch house.

I opened the door for her, then led her into the living room where my four brothers were lounging. Lily was about to sit down when she spotted a pile of photographs on the piano by the window. My mother loved to look at our photos almost every day.

"You don't want to miss these, Lily," Sebastian advised as I tried to pull her into a chair.

I groaned. "Yeah, she really does."

"Okay, now I'm really curious." She winked and walked over to look at them.

The photos were of my brothers and me from childhood to adulthood. My brothers giggled in the background until they saw Mom standing in the doorway watching Lily. She had a strange look on her face.

"Do you like my photo gallery?" she asked Lily.

"Yes, I do, although when they were younger it was hard to decide which one was Michael."

"Don't worry, Lily. I had that problem when they were running around. In fact, sometimes I'd put them in different colored shirts. Anyway, Michael said you would like some coffee, so make yourself comfortable and Michael can get your coffee for you."

"Oh, that's fine. I'll get it myself." She followed my mother out of the lounge, and I collapsed into the chair across from Lucien.

Sebastian, Ruben, and Ramon got up and started to leave the room. "Just remember, Lily is mine.

"Yeah, we know," Sebastian grumbled.

I looked back at Lucien. "Was a departure planned?"

"What do you mean brother?"

"Go on then, because I assume they've gone to distract Lily in the kitchen while we have this conversation."

"Did you tell Lily?" Lucien asked me.

I could play dumb and pretend I had no idea what he was talking about, but if I did, I'd end up having to give him the same answer. "No," I whispered. "You don't tell her, it's up to me."

"She has to know, Michael. I'm not blind. I see the way she looks at you, and I've seen the way you look at her. Whatever is between the two of you is more than just a passing fancy. It's not fair to keep something this important from her.

I clenched my fist as my temper began to rise. The last thing I needed was a lecture from my big brother. "This has nothing to do with you, Lucien."

"I know that, but I like her."

I started to rise.

"That's all, Michael. She's more like a sister. I can talk to her, and she listens. All I want from her is friendship, and just so you don't get the wrong idea, I'll tell you, the next time I'm in town, I plan on taking her out for coffee during lunch. I figured you would go crazy if I suggested after work."

I trusted my brother, and realistically, I'd begun to trust Lily. She was nothing like Viv, so I could handle Lily being friends with my brothers. But there was no way I was going to have the conversation with Lily that

Lucien wanted.

"I'll tell her when I'm ready, not before, and certainly not when you tell me to."

"Is it safe to come in here? Sebastian told me you two were having a discussion."

I was still angry at Lucien and couldn't quite wipe the scowl off my face.

"Lily, ignore Michael; he's a bit out of it. Come and sit here." Lucien patted the seat next to him.

She walked over to the sofa where Lucien was sitting and hesitated slightly before sitting down. I realized that I should have sat where she could join me.

Not liking the look on Lucien's face, I got up, walked over, and sat next to her, pulling her to my chest just before my other three brothers came back into the room, followed by my mother.

"Where's Dad?" I asked.

"He's outside, insisting on supervising the guards."

That was my dad; he always had to be in control. Probably where my brothers and I got our control issues.

My mother sat in the window seat, and every now and then I would catch her looking over at me and Lily. I knew what she was doing. She wanted me to admit that Lily was more than just my assistant. She'd seen how I'd reacted when I'd brought Lily here a few weeks before. I couldn't claim her as my woman then.

I kissed Lily on the back of her head and then turned to face my mother. "Lily is with me now."

My mother burst into tears. I hadn't expected that. Lily started to get up to go to her, but my mom waved her back down.

"I'm sorry. I don't know where that came from. After all these years of worrying about him, he finally has a nice girl."

"Mom, Lily's a little bigger than a girl," Sebastian pointed out, only to have Lucien kick him. He was sitting closest.

"Sebastian Elias McKenzie, you will not embarrass Lily. She is a guest in this house and Michael's girlfriend. I don't want her to be frightened away by you."

"Yes, ma'am." My brothers laughed until Mom glared at them.

"Well, with that in mind, I think Lily and I will take off. The security people know what to do, so tell Dad to leave them alone. That's what they get paid for.

Lucien stood and held out his hand to Lily. She put her hand in his as he pulled her up from the sofa. I joined them and pulled her back to me.

She grinned up at me. "Stop acting so jealous," she whispered.

"I'm not acting. I am!" She rolled her eyes.

"Now that we've established that Lily is your woman, do you think we could give her a goodbye hug without you throwing punches?"

"Just get it over with." I just wanted Lily all to myself.

She hugged my brothers, but when she got to Lucien, they hugged, and Lucien gave her a card with his phone number on it.

"If you ever have a problem or just want to talk, my cell number is on there," he told her.

"Thank you. I'll see you for coffee soon," Lily replied.

"You sure will."

At that point, I just grabbed Lily's hand and practically dragged her out of the house to my car.

19

Lily

Sitting in Michael's car, I rested my head on the seat and looked out the window. Seeing nothing, my mind drifted back to the picnic. It had been an amazing day and being with Michael made it even more special.

I hadn't expected the orgasm he had given me in the garage. I thought I would end up a puddle on the floor. The pleasure shooting through me was indescribable.

His brothers were great, and Sebastian was obviously the flirt of the family, but it was Lucien who had quickly become my favorite of his brothers. He had scars, and although I could only see the ones on his hand, he had talked to me about them and about the accident he had been in.

Afterwards, he was shocked that he'd opened up so much, but I had told him that he could talk to me anytime without it getting back to anyone, including Michael.

When Lucien asked if I'd meet him for coffee, I told him I would, but as a friend. He'd told me that since the accident, that was all he had to offer. I wasn't sure what he meant by that because he only mentioned that his upper body was scarred, not his lower body. Then again, I guess it wasn't something you'd talk about with a woman.

He'd been teasing me a bit about his brother until Ramon interrupted. Of all Michael's brothers, I would say Ramon was the most reserved. The others liked to flirt, not as much as Sebastian, but the flirting was there, except for Ramon. He seemed to have a lot on his mind.

We'd walked over and had some delicious food. I ate a lot more than I normally would have during the day, but when I stood in front of bowls and plates of my favorite foods, I couldn't resist.

Oh, I was aware that Michael was watching me, and he was never too far away. A few times he'd started to walk over to me and ended up being stopped by Jacky, Dale, or someone else. He seemed to be popular with the staff. I also noticed that all the single women were looking at him, and I was proud to say that he never once looked in their direction.

Being in his arms on the dance floor for all to see

had been amazing. He'd claimed me and our relation-ship in front of everyone we worked with. I knew it was the beginning of our relationship, but it had felt right to be in his arms and not have to hide anymore.

I had been aroused in his arms and wouldn't have cared if he had picked me up and impaled me on his dick in the middle of the dance floor. When he'd dragged me into the dark corner and I'd seen the head of his penis peeking out of the waistband of his jeans, I'd been hit with a wave of lust so strong that he was lucky I hadn't fallen to my knees right then and there.

I coughed and squirmed in my seat, trying to find a more comfortable position, because I'd managed to arouse myself again. The pain throbbing between my legs was almost unbearable.

"Are you okay?" Michael asked.

"Sore and wet!" I replied without hesitation.

He cursed and shifted slightly.

"I think you need to focus on where we're going." I chuckled.

"I think you need to think before you speak."

I laughed. "I was... I was thinking about the time we danced in the barn and the feeling of heat that accompa-nied the sight of the head of your penis sticking out of the top of your jeans, all wet and glistening. I licked my lips.

"Fuck, please stop." He adjusted his jeans. I looked down and saw he was fully aroused again.

"How far away are we?"

"It doesn't matter because we won't be intimate again until we have a bed."

"Michael," I whined.

"Ten minutes. Just wait ten minutes. Think of something else for now."

Think about something else. How did he expect me to think of anything else when I was sitting so close to him?

I grinned. "I like your brothers. They're nice and handsome. Don't tell the others, but I have to admit that Lucien is my favorite."

"Lily," he growled.

"Michael," I said in a sarcastic voice. "I said I like your brothers. They're your family. Don't you want me to like them?"

He cursed. "Lily, you are testing the patience of a saint. Yes, I want you to like my brothers. I'm trying to accept you developing a friendship with Lucien. But it's not easy because of what Viv was like. I know you're not like her, but she really messed me up. This is the first time since then that I've taken a chance on someone. Please, just be patient with me and kick me back in line if you must. Okay?"

I wiped away the tears that escaped my eyes as I listened to him. "Okay."

Michael turned onto a narrow, tree-lined road. The way the trees had grown, they'd formed a tunnel of kissing trees, and it looked pretty. I could barely make them out in the early evening light that was quickly fading into night.

We came to a stop at the foot of a large rustic cabin that looked amazing.

"Home," Michael announced. "Now I just have to figure out how to get out of this car without embarrassing myself."

"I don't have a problem." I grinned and climbed out. I went around to open Michael's door. "Are you coming?" I asked.

"I'm just about to."

I could barely contain my laughter as he led me to his cabin. I decided it was best to change the subject. "This is a beautiful cabin. Did you build it?"

He raised an eyebrow. "Yes, I did. I drew up the plans and then hired the McKenzie brothers."

"Well, they did a wonderful job," I said as I walked inside. "A really wonderful job."

He laughed. "Although a McKenzie was in charge of the inside, my brothers and I can't take the credit. It goes to Ma McKenzie."

"Ah, she has good taste."

Still holding my hand, Michael walked to a set of large double doors. He pushed one open, and wow. He made this room; it was his.

"This is the only room in the house that I decorated and furnished," he said.

"Oh, Michael! It's wonderful. Look at all these books...and somebody likes Apple technology." I laughed. Not only did he have a desktop computer, but he also had a laptop, an iPad, and, if I wasn't mistaken, an iPod docking station.

"I like it best." He wrapped his arms around me from behind and nuzzled my neck. "You smell good."

I moaned and sank into him. He felt so good behind me. I could feel practically every inch of him, including his fully engorged cock. "I think we need a bed."

He took me in his arms. "Then let me show you where it is."

Michael

I had Lily exactly where I wanted her: in my home, and very soon in my bed. But right now, she was in my arms, and I had no intention of letting her go.

I'd been hot for her most of the day, and when we danced, I couldn't hold back anymore. I was going to let her feel exactly what she'd done to me. I certainly never expected her to see the tip of my dick. And when she touched me, I'd almost blown my load.

"Michael, what are you thinking about?"
"You."

She grinned at me. "Good answer."

"I was thinking about dancing with you and what you saw that led to you having my cock in your mouth."

She moaned and I almost stumbled.

"Where the hell is this bedroom?"

"Don't be so impatient. Good things are usually worth the wait."

I kicked open my bedroom door, marched over to my bed, and dropped her on it. She giggled.

"One minute." I ran back downstairs to the kitchen to get a bottle of wine and a couple of bottles of water.

I quickly ran back upstairs and into my room, dropping the water and barely holding on to the wine.

Holy fuck.

I had to be dreaming. The kind of vision that was on my bed had to be a dream.

"Do you like it?" She was sitting in the middle of my bed in all her naked glory.

"You're not a dream?"

She started to laugh, making her breasts shake. "You have too many clothes on. Take them off."

"Yes, ma'am," I replied as I began to take them off. In five seconds, I was standing in front of the bed, just as naked.

Her eyes widened. "You're huge!"

"I'm a McKenzie, what did you expect? All McKenzie men are hung like horses."

"Oh. My. God! I can't believe you just said that! Did I

really have to know about your brothers?" She wiggled her ass to get closer to me, then spread her legs on either side of mine.

I placed my hands on her shoulders and stroked along her collarbone to her gorgeous breasts. I gently ran my hands over her nipples. She got goose bumps.

Then it was my time to get goosebumps as she touched my hips and around to my ass, kissing along my shaft to the already wet tip. I just had to think of Lily, and I was in that state, but seeing her naked in my room with her hands on me drove me crazy.

"Mmm, that feels damn good." She was sucking and licking me like a Popsicle, and my hands were tangled in her hair.

She pulled her mouth away and put her hands on my balls. "I love touching you. Putting my mouth on you. I've never let anyone come in my mouth until today."

I froze. "Lily, you mean you've never sucked cock before?" She burst out laughing. "Sorry, I guess Sebastian rubs off on me. He has a foul mouth."

She was really giggling.

I stood in front of her with my hands on my hips and just stared. I probably looked like an idiot standing there naked and aroused.

"Okay, I think I'm okay now. Sorry, you're just so proper at the office; hearing you blurt something like that really tickled me. I guess you'll have to pay the price," she said, sliding back onto the bed and pointing her finger at me to follow.

"Lie down on your back." She kissed me. "I'm going to love you like you've never been loved before." She grinned and I did exactly as she asked.

She started at my feet, caressing them, and rubbing between my toes - it felt good. She slowly moved up my shins and tickled the underside of my knees before moving to my thighs. I wasn't sure how long I could hold out, but I knew I wanted to come inside her.

I lifted my head to look at her. "Lily, I need to touch you."

"You can do it later. It's my turn. I've wanted to see you naked and touch you since the first time I saw you in the elevator."

I dropped my head back onto the pillow and let her have her way. My turn would come soon enough.

She licked my hipbone, then moved to lick the other, avoiding my throbbing shaft. I felt her dip her tongue into my navel and move slightly up my body to rub my cock between her ample breasts.

"Fuck." I arched off the bed and into her. "That's so hot! If you keep doing that, I'm going to come all over us," I panted. She rose slightly above me, and the view was amazing. She was slender and curvy with large breasts and pink nipples. She was every man's fantasy, and she was mine.

"Behave." She swirled her tongue around my nipples

and then bit down, sending a rush of blood to the tip of my cock.

As she sat on top of me, the lips of her pussy parted, enveloping me in her warmth and wetness. And then she moved.

She shivered as I began to massage her breasts and got goosebumps as I rolled her nipples between my finger and thumb.

"That feels good."

"I want to be inside you right now."

She made a slight movement and wrapped her fingers around my cock before positioning me at her sex. As she slowly slid down my rigid dick, my eyes rolled back in my head.

My jaw clenched as I grabbed her hips. "Don't move," I hissed.

I breathed heavily as I tried to regain some semblance of control but lost it again when Lily leaned in and brought us chest to chest. She sucked my lower lip into her mouth, nibbling playfully.

Groaning, I pulled her in for more of a kiss and sealed our lips together as I held her hips against me with my hands.

When I pulled out, I started fucking her with just the head of my dick before losing control and going deep. Her wet, hot, and tight channel closed around me seconds before I felt her sex as it rippled down the length of my cock. With a loud moan, the fire in my sac exploded, shooting thick ribbons of cum into her.

No one had come inside her before me, and as far as I was concerned, no one ever would.

She was wrapped around me with my arms on her ass while I was still buried deep inside her. I never wanted to move.

20

Lily

OUR BREATHING BEGAN TO SLOW, AND FOR THE FIRST
time I could remember, I felt completely happy.

"Are you okay, Lily?"

I smiled into his chest, tears of happiness prickling
the back of my eyes. "Oh yeah."

He moved us both onto our sides, slipping out of me
before reaching for the blanket and pulling it over us,
and then I was in his arms, both of us satiated.

"You're amazing. You've been driving me crazy these
past few weeks."

The tears that had been threatening to fall slid down
my cheeks. "No one has ever turned me on like you or
given me so much pleasure."

"Move in with me," he blurted out.

I was stunned. "What?"

"I didn't mean to just blurt it out. I guess I'm nervous. I want you here with me, so I know you're safe and because I just want you here. I want to spend all my free time with you, and it's pointless to pay rent for an apartment if you're going to spend your nights here with me." He grinned and looked too adorable.

That was fast. Okay, we'd wanted each other for a few weeks now and I knew all his quirks, likes and dislikes. He was also right about the rent and where I'd sleep. But was moving in with him the right decision? My relationship with David had really been over for a while, and I was tired of being lonely. It would be nice to spend time with someone who wanted me as much as I wanted him, so I took the plunge. "Yes. I'd like to move in with you."

I didn't think his smile could get any bigger. I knew I'd made the right choice.

"Thank you." He kissed me deeply, almost curling my toes. "Let's get some sleep."

"Really?"

He chuckled. "Don't you want to sleep?" he asked me as he caressed my face.

Our legs were intertwined, my head resting on his arm and my hand stroking down his side. I was in heaven.

"I'm tired, but I just want to talk to you."

He moved his hand from my face and rested it on my hip before pulling me closer.

"What do you want to talk about?" He kissed me and pulled away so I could answer.

"Tell me one of your fantasies." I couldn't help but grin at his reaction as his eyes almost popped out of his head. "I'm serious. If you tell me one of your unfulfilled fantasies, I'll tell you one of mine."

"Why can't you go first?"

"Are you serious?" I rolled my eyes. "I asked the question."

He groaned. "Okay, but just remember that you asked when I tell you. Because you won't be able to get it out of your head."

"Okay, maybe we should talk about something else."

"Not a chance. Okay, the fantasy I've been having for the last few weeks takes place in my office."

It must be a hell of a fantasy because his erection started to twitch against my stomach.

"You're in a dress and a pair of those stilettos you wear. Those shoes are driving me crazy."

I laughed. "After that first day, I wore them to torture you. I caught you looking at my legs a couple of times."

"Damn right. Anyway, you come into my office and stand close. Close enough that I can feel your nipples through our clothes. You lean in and whisper that you don't have any panties on."

I moaned as Michael started to play with my nipples.

"You walked back to the office door. Giving me a dirty look over your shoulder, you close the door and lock it. You turn back to me, and with agonizing slowness, you walk back to the conference table, slowly sliding your dress down your arms. When it hits the floor, you step out of it and then bend over the conference table, spreading your legs. Then you ask me to fuck you."

He slammed his lips down on mine and ravaged me. There was no other word for what he was doing. I moved my leg and wrapped it around his hip. He arched his hips back and thrust into me. Heaven.

Once inside me, he began to slide in and out of my sex so slowly that he drove me wild. It felt so good, and as he rolled me onto my back, I moved my legs so that they were intertwined with his as we moved in sync.

"Keep it slow, Lily. I want to enjoy you."

He planted soft kisses all over my face as the pleasure began to build. I was so close to coming when I dug my fingers into Michael's ass.

"Lily?"

"Yes." We moaned as my sex squeezed the life out of Michael's penis. My orgasm went on and on, kicked up a notch when I felt Michael come inside me.

I was glad I was already on my back because that's where I would have ended up. Michael got up from where he'd collapsed on my chest and tried to pull himself out of me. "No, I want you to stay."

"I'm too heavy."

I pulled him back down onto me.

He grunted, then settled down.

"That was...fuckin' amazing," he murmured into my neck.

"Mmm."

After lying on top of me for a few minutes, he rolled over and lay down on his back. He found my hand and intertwined our fingers.

"You didn't tell me your fantasy."

"I'm too tired."

He laughed. "Oh no, you're not. I told you mine."

"I'm not sure I'd survive mine."

"After that comment, you're not going to sleep until you tell me."

I huffed with indignation and gave him a wicked smile. "I have this fantasy involving you and a motorcycle. A Harley, to be exact."

"I have a Harley."

"You do? I didn't know that."

"I'm going to take you out on it sometime soon."

I laughed. "Mmm, you are really going to take me on when you hear this."

"Oh, Lord."

"We're out on your bike and you pull over to a secluded spot. We get off the bike feeling horny, and you can't keep your hands off me. I step out of your arms and undress while you watch. I walk back over to you and start taking off your jacket and t-shirt and then your jeans. I make you sit astride your bike and then climb on your lap and impale myself on your cock. In this position you go so deep and feel so good that it only takes a few strokes before we both come hard. When we finally get off, we're both a quivering mess."

God, if I wasn't so tired, I would jump on top of him after my little fantasy. And he had a Harley.

"Michael, are you still with me?"

"Oh God, maybe I should have waited for that."

I rolled onto my side and reached for him with my free hand. He was hard as steel.

"Sleep." His voice rumbled in the darkened room.

"But..."

"I know. I'll survive. Go to sleep, Lily."

"Good night, Michael."

"Good night, Lily." He planted a sweet kiss on my lips and moved us so that he was spooning me from behind.

Michael

Lily slept in my arms, exhausted from the events of the day. She was an amazing woman and had turned me inside out. Sleep eluded me; my brain refused to shut down and settle, as did my body.

I shifted my body slightly away from Lily so that I could look at her. I reached behind me and turned on the lamp so I could see her more clearly.

My breath caught in my throat. She was beautiful, which I already knew, but watching her sleep made my heart flutter. I didn't want to wake her, but I couldn't control my impulse to touch her. I reached out and gently ran my hand down her arms to her delicate hands and back up again.

Without waking her, I turned her on the bed so that she was lying on her back.

Her breasts hadn't been felt yet. I'd touched them, but I still wanted to taste them - that would have to wait until she was awake.

I knelt beside her and just took my fill. She excited me like no one else, and unfortunately it always happened at the most inappropriate times.

My hands slid over her ribs and down to her pubic bone. I continued down her thighs to her ankles. I kissed her feet and moved back up her body, stopping when I reached the junction of her thighs. She was completely naked, her sweet pussy and clit peeking out.

My dick swelled with excitement and my breathing began to increase as I looked at her more. I desperately needed to be inside her, but I wanted her to sleep so she would be rested when morning came.

I took a deep breath and after planting a kiss on her

peeping clit, I forced myself to move up to her navel. I licked up from her navel to the underside of her breasts.

She had perfect breasts, not too large and not too small. They were firm with pink tips. Just a touch, that's all I would do.

I leaned over her and kissed one nipple, then moved to the other. I sat back up and both nipples were rock hard.

Hell.

"Michael?"

I looked up at her face. Her eyes were open, and she looked at me like I was the only man she'd ever seen.

"I didn't want to wake you. I couldn't sleep and I had to look at you."

She held her hand out to me and stroked my thigh, then rubbed the bead of moisture on the head of my cock.

"Make love to me." She began to manipulate my shaft, wrapping her hand around it and moving it up and down. On the upward motion, she rubbed her thumb over the head, which made me shiver. It felt so damn good.

Her hand fell away as I moved my hips out of reach and stretched out next to her.

"I need to taste your breasts. I've touched them, but I haven't tasted them. I can't believe I've been neglecting these beauties." I reached out and caressed them with my hand, leaning forward to put my mouth on the next one.

"Michael," she moaned, arching off the bed as my mouth and tongue made contact with her flesh. I reached up with my hand and used it to massage her other breast. Her nipple was rock hard as I rubbed it between my fingers.

She was panting and moaning, her legs spread open, so I rolled on top of her and wedged my cock between her thighs. I began to rub between her legs as I switched breasts with my mouth.

"Michael, please."

She was close and I wanted to make her come while I sucked her breasts without any stimulation inside her.

Her hips began to move beneath me as she ground her pussy against my balls.

With my cock hard as hell, pre-cum leaked out onto her belly, and I knew it wouldn't take much for me to shoot my release all over her.

"Michael," she screamed as she started to come. I released her breast from my mouth and thrust into her, slamming my mouth down on hers. As our tongues fused, I came and came and came in the longest orgasm I'd ever had. I could still feel the aftershocks inside of Lily. The little spasms milked me and drained me of every drop.

I rolled us both onto our sides and stayed connected to the aroused woman in my arms.

As she snuggled against me, I watched her sleep.

I couldn't sleep and buried my face in Lily's hair, excited that she had agreed to move in with me. I couldn't wait for her to move out of her apartment and into my house. I couldn't wait to make my house our home.

Our home. As soon as I had that thought, it dawned on me that we might need to redecorate. My home was decorated for a single man, and at the time I had no intention of letting a woman move in, but of course that all changed.

Lily would be treated so well that she'd never want to leave me, no matter what. One day I would have to tell her about my past unless Lucien took it upon himself to tell her. I trusted him not to, but he had grown fond of Lily.

21

Lily

I REALLY DIDN'T WANT TO WAKE UP. I HAD THE MOST wonderful dream of being naked in Michael's arms while he was doing some naughty things to me. I turned over and came into contact with a hard body. My eyes opened.

"Good morning," Michael whispered. He leaned over and kissed me. He tasted of coffee and oh God, I had morning breath.

"Don't kiss me until I've brushed my teeth," I yelped as I pushed him away.

"You taste delicious." He grinned at my embarrassment. "I brought you breakfast in bed."

"You did?"

He sat up in bed and pulled me forward, then fluffed my pillows. He helped me sit up, handed me one of his t-shirts, and tucked the sheets around my legs before reaching for the tray and placing it between us on the bed.

"This is a feast." He'd made me a toasted bagel, a bowl of fresh strawberries, cantaloupe, and grapes, a small plate of cheese and crackers, a glass of fresh orange juice, and coffee.

He just grinned and took a bite of his bagel. I reached for the coffee first because I needed a caffeine fix so badly. It was delicious.

I choked back tears. He was so thoughtful. "No one has ever done this for me before. Thank you, Michael. It means everything to me."

Michael looked at me and looked angry. "You better get used to it, because this is going to be a regular weekend occurrence. Now eat up. We have a busy day."

"We do?" God, I sounded like an idiot this morning.

"We're going to visit George in the hospital, then move you out of the apartment and into this place. Sometime during the day I'll give you a tour of the house so you know where everything is."

The fruit went down pretty well as I sat back and listened to Michael. I could listen to him all day long with his husky, deep "come to bed" voice. I took in his bedroom, painted a deep green with dark mahogany furniture and a green and gold sofa in the window with a coffee table. I couldn't help but wonder who he had entertained in his bedroom.

He started to laugh. "You're broadcasting pretty loud," he said.

I glared at him and shoved a piece of melon into my mouth.

"The only woman who has ever been in this house is my mother. The decorator was male, but he was gay, and my mother hasn't set foot in my bedroom, nor has anyone else but you. Ever."

I couldn't help the smile on my face. It felt good to know that I was the only one. My heart fluttered when I finally realized that he wanted me for more than a few weeks. He was in it for the long haul. Thank God.

When I finished my breakfast, I stretched and looked over at Michael. His eyes were fixed a little lower than my face.

He licked his lips and met my eyes. "Okay, we won't have sex until tonight. I want you to move in here this morning," he said, then jumped out of bed. He moved the tray and pointed to the bathroom. "You shower in there; I found some old sweats of Ruben's that shouldn't fit too bad, and one of my clean t-shirts. They're on the shelf next to the towels. I'll take a shower in the next room."

I couldn't believe my ears. "You're not going to shower with me?"

"Lily, if I get in the shower with you, we're not going

anywhere. Lucien and Ramon will be here in about twenty minutes to help us. So get to it."

"Yes, sir," I said with a salute.

"Cheeky...now, Lily."

"Okay." I threw off the covers and heard Michael groan as he caught a glimpse of my bare bottom as I climbed out of bed.

"I'm going." He turned and walked out of the room, closing the door behind him.

I laughed and walked into the spacious bathroom. It had a large glass shower off to one side, with the biggest bathtub I'd ever seen. It was more like a Jacuzzi you would find in a gym.

With the shower turned on and the t-shirt I was wearing tossed into what appeared to be a hamper, I stepped into the shower and pressed the button to start the water. The hot water felt so good.

After about ten minutes of letting the jets hit my body, I turned off the shower and stepped out. I wrapped a fluffy towel around me and searched for the clothes Michael said he'd left for me.

Once I found them, I placed them on the towel rack while I dried myself and then quickly pulled them on. The sweatpants were a bit big, but I rolled them in at the waist a few times. Michael's t-shirt was too big, which was not unexpected considering his broad shoulders. The only problem was that I'd left my bra in the bedroom. My breasts were on the large side, so there was no way I could go without a bra unless I was wearing a dress with a fitted bodice.

I opened the bathroom door and stepped out to find Michael lounging on the bed.

"What took you so long?" he asked, watching me walk over to him. "You need to put something on under there."

I climbed astride him, then leaned in to kiss him. "I know, I left my bra in here."

"Good, because I don't want Lucien to see you without it," he grumbled.

I sealed our mouths before he could say anything else. I moaned and wiggled on top of him. He felt and tasted delicious.

He broke the kiss. "Lucien and Ramon are downstairs," he said, his voice hoarse.

"Why are they here again?"

"To help move you in. I think Lucien just wanted to see you again."

He looked worried. "Michael, you know I'm nothing like Viv, right? It will only piss me off if you keep comparing me to her." I pulled away and stood up. He followed me.

Holding my face in his hands, he looked straight into my eyes. "I know you're nothing like Viv; you wouldn't be here if you were. She screwed me up big time, and to be honest, I've never seen Lucien so possessive. He acts like your big brother and not mine."

I laughed at him. "Then that's good, right? If he thinks of me more as a sister than a lover. Why aren't you happy about that?"

"I am, I guess."

I kissed his lips again. "Come on. Let's get this morning over with so we can have the rest of the day to ourselves."

Michael

We pulled up in front of Lily's apartment and waited for Lucien and Ramon to arrive. They should only be about five minutes late because of the traffic light we hit after leaving the hospital. George was feeling better and did nothing but complain. He wanted us to get him out of there, but Lily soothed his ruffled feathers. He had calmed down, and Lily had made him promise to behave, or she wouldn't sneak in some chocolate when she visited again.

Lily was happy, which made me happy. In fact, I couldn't remember the last time I'd been this happy. After breakfast in bed and a shower away from her that nearly killed me, I held her hand and walked her downstairs to meet my brothers.

She kissed my hand and then let go to hug them. I

noticed that the hug she gave Lucien lasted longer than the one she gave Ramon. Lily and Lucien caught my frown. Lucien laughed before Lily walked back over to me and pulled my head down for a kiss. When she lifted, she'd almost lost her sweatpants, which made Ramon's eyes bulge out of his head.

"Hey, what are you smiling about?" Lily asked me.

"I was thinking about you almost losing your sweat-pants and Ramon's reaction."

"Oh my God! I was just glad your t-shirt covered my butt."

"I think I would have hit my brothers for looking at your butt."

She started giggling and had trouble stopping until Lucien opened her door and let her fall out. Luckily, he caught her.

I shot out of the car and ran over to her. "Are you okay?" I grabbed her and pulled her into my arms.

"Of course I'm okay. Lucien caught me so I didn't end up on the sidewalk. But I think I hurt your brother."

"He'll be fine. Come on, let's get this over with."

"Michael." She slapped my arm, not hard, but enough to get my attention. "I can't believe you're leaving without bothering to make sure your brother is okay."

I looked over at Lucien and he looked in pain. He was white around the mouth and looked like he was protecting his side. "Lucien, is Lily, okay? Did she hurt you when she fell on you?"

"I'm fine," he replied in a tight voice.

"Okay, Lucien. You're not fine. Come with me." She left Ramon and me on the sidewalk as she grabbed Lucien's arm and pulled him toward the entrance of the apartments.

"I think they've adopted each other," Ramon said. "I meant as brother and sister. He won't try to steal her from you. If he tried, she wouldn't go anyway. So, you have nothing to worry about, brother."

"Thanks, Ramon. Are you okay? You've been acting kind of strange lately."

"I'm fine," he said and followed our brother and my wife into the building, leaving me behind.

I knew he was right. I'd just never been possessive of a woman before, or anything for that matter. The depths of my feelings for Lily were truly intense. I didn't want to suffocate her, but I needed her with me and no one else.

I shook my head and tried to get rid of my possessive tendency, then went into the apartment, which wasn't what I expected. Considering how messy Lily's desk always was, her apartment was a nice, tidy surprise.

"Michael, would you mind grabbing the two pictures on the table next to you?" Lily asked as she walked from another room to my brother on the sofa.

The pictures were obviously of her parents, and it looked like maybe her grandparents as well. Holding them, I walked further into the living room so I could hear what was going on.

"Lily, please stop fussing. Michael, will you tell your wife that I'm fine and that I don't like being pampered?" Lucien grumbled.

"Oh, Lucien, be quiet. You're in pain. You are going to take those pain pills. Just sit there and let them work, then you can move."

Both Ramon and I tried not to laugh at the image of Lily standing in front of Lucien with her hands on her hips while Lucien decided whether she was serious.

"Lucien, you're in pain because I landed on you. Please take the painkillers and sit down for a while, otherwise I'll be stressed out all day worrying about you. Please."

"Fuck," he said under his breath. "Give me the painkillers and go bother someone else."

She watched him take the pills like a prison guard, then patted his head. "Good boy." She walked quickly into what looked like the bedroom while Lucien glared at her from behind.

"Don't say a word to anyone," he warned.

Of course, we just laughed.

"Michael, Ramon, can you come and carry these into the front room?" she called.

"Have fun, brothers." Lucien put his feet up on the coffee table and settled into the chair.

I went into the bedroom she'd shared with David

and tried not to picture them in bed. At least I didn't have to see David. Lily had called and told him we were on our way over. He'd told Lily he was taking Lucy to breakfast so their paths wouldn't cross.

To be honest, Lily didn't seem too bothered that David was with someone else, which made me feel relieved. I was a little worried that she'd buried her feelings to keep them from me, since he'd been seeing Lucy for a lot longer than Lily initially thought.

"Michael, move." Ramon shoved me from behind and I bent down to pick up a stack of shoeboxes. I walked into the lounge and placed them on the sideboard just as I felt someone pinch my butt. I jumped and turned to find Lily in my arms. She had her arms around my waist.

"Thank you for this, Michael," she murmured into my chest.

I ran my fingers through her hair and cupped the back of her head. "I'd do anything for you." Our mouths met in a soft caress of lips and tongue. I tasted her.

"Get a room," Ramon grumbled from not too far away.

"I've got plenty of rooms I'd like to get back to soon, so let's load this lot up."

I reluctantly set Lily aside and watched her walk over to sit next to Lucien.

"I'll help you in a minute. I just want to check on your brother." She gave me a big grin and winked.

Ramon grabbed two of the suitcases and I grabbed the same pile of shoeboxes as before. I trudged down the stairs behind my brother, leaving my wife upstairs to bother Lucien.

Ramon turned to me and did a double take. "Why are you looking at me with that grin on your face?"

"I'm thinking about Lucien and how Lily is fussing over him."

"And you're laughing about that?"

We loaded the back of the car with some of Lily's things. "Yes, I am. Come on, Ramon, you know how he hates people fussing over him. Lily will drive him crazy."

"Yeah, he usually puts up with Mom for five minutes before he tells her to get out."

"Exactly, except something tells me that Lily won't be so easy to get rid of, especially since she feels responsible for his pain right now."

I opened the door for Ramon on our way back in, only to be greeted by Lily on her way down with a suitcase and a rather large rolling pin.

"Give me that," I said, jokingly taking the rolling pin from her. I laughed at the look on her face.

"Okay, if you insist."

I grabbed the case while she and Ramon burst out laughing.

"Why do you have a rolling pin?" I asked.

"I thought I'd take it out now so I wouldn't be tempted to use it on your brother."

"He can be stubborn. You'll be lucky if he doesn't try to escape while you're down here."

"He wouldn't dare," she looked from me to Ramon, "would he?"

"You better go check."

She turned and ran back up the stairs with us behind her.

We stopped on the landing because she was standing in front of Lucien with her hands on her hips.

"You're a pain in the ass, you know?" she said to him.

"Everybody tells me that. Lily, I'm okay. I promise. I really appreciate your concern, but I have to go."

She let out a puff of air. "Oh, all right. But don't you dare forget coffee next week."

"I won't." He leaned forward and kissed her cheek as he hugged her. "Thank you, Lily."

He walked over to Ramon and me. "See you later. I'm going to walk a little and take a cab back."

22

Lily

BACK AT MICHAEL'S HOUSE, WE WERE LYING ON THE SOFA in the living room after lunch. All my clothes and things were packed away in the room I shared with Michael, and the photographs of my parents and grandparents were on display in the foyer of his house. Michael kept reminding me that this was 'our' home, but it would take some getting used to.

Ramon had left after lunch and went back to the cabin he'd built on his parents' land. His brothers were great guys, stubborn, but great guys. At my insistence, Michael had called Lucien until he answered to make sure he was okay. The chicken didn't talk to his brother and immediately handed the phone to me. Lucien swore and then apologized when he realized it wasn't his brother. I could curse with the best of them now.

Michael had wanted to rest in his room as soon as Ramon left, but I'd told him I really needed to rest. I was tired and full after eating the huge sandwich Michael had bought me at Subway on the way back to the house.

Michael was more than ready for the next round of lovemaking, as the hardness pressed into me could attest. I pressed closer and heard him moan.

"If you want to rest here, I suggest you stop struggling," Michael whispered. He might be trying to be noble, but his body had other ideas - his cock twitched behind his zipper.

"I think we've rested enough. Take me upstairs, Michael. I want you to make love to me...now."

He shot up from the sofa with me in his arms. After a quick kiss on my lips, he rushed to our room.

Once inside, he just held me.

"Put me down. I want to strip for you."

"Oh God."

He released me and let me slide down his body until my feet hit the floor.

I moved out of his arms and headed for the bed. As I looked back, evil thoughts of him naked filled my mind. "I want you naked, sitting in that chair," I said, pointing to the chair about four feet from the bed.

He clenched his fists. "Lily, I don't know if I can take this. You already got me all worked up."

"I promise not to touch you yet."

"Fuck."

He kicked off his shoes but wasn't wearing socks. He pulled his t-shirt over his head and stood in just his jeans. I looked at him and licked my lips. He had the body of a god, tight and muscular. I moved my eyes to his zipper where his hand was. He unzipped the zipper very slowly, revealing his cock, which was hard, the head wet with excitement. He took a deep breath and pushed the jeans down his legs until they were off.

Michael stepped back and put his butt in the chair as I'd asked. He was magnificent. He had strong thighs with only a light coat of hair covering his groin. His penis protruded toward his belly, long and thick. I licked my lips and gave him a secret smile as he arched out of the chair.

"Lily, you're going to get more of a show if you don't stop staring at me. You look like you want to put your mouth on me."

I smiled. "I do."

"Lily," he growled.

I kicked off my boots and pushed the sweat down my legs. I grabbed the hem of the t-shirt and slowly pulled it up and over my head, then tossed it to the pile of Michael's clothes.

Standing in just my bra, I reached around the back and unhooked it, slowly pulling it down my arms until it joined the rest of the clothes. I was naked and it was Michael's turn to lick his lips.

I stood in front of him and started circling my nipples with my fingers, something I'd never done in front of anyone before. "Mmm, that feels good." I began to twist and pinch them between my finger and thumb.

My arousal would be obvious if he touched me between my legs, and the throbbing inside my sex would soon have me squirming to ease the pain of frustration.

Michael's cock twitched, and a bead of fluid ran from the head down to the root.

I licked my lips.

He cursed.

"Stroke yourself," I begged.

His eyes moved from my breasts to meet mine in shocked pleasure.

He wrapped his hand around the head of his dick and stroked down. A moan escaped between his lips.

Michael continued to jerk off and watched through half-closed eyes as I slid my fingers through my wet folds.

He growled.

My fingers were soaked with cum and when I pulled my hand away, I presented my fingers to Michael. "Taste me."

"Fuck, Lily. I don't know how much more of this I can take. You've got me on a tightrope."

I straddled his legs and leaned against him as he took my fingers in his mouth. He sucked and flicked them with his tongue.

His hand was still clenching his cock as I used my finger to rub the moisture he was leaking into the head.

"I need you now, unless you want me to come all over us."

I moved his hand away. "Next time." I impaled myself on his erection.

He held my hips and stayed still while he caught his breath. Putting my hands on his shoulders for balance, I arched against him and nearly came apart when his mouth wrapped around one of my beaded nipples. He brought his free hand up and rolled my other as I rocked against him.

I shattered into a million pieces, repeatedly. My sex was so tightly wrapped around Michael's cock, it was a wonder it didn't shatter. Before I had a chance to come back to earth, Michael came inside me and filled me with his cum. The thought of his hot cream filling me sent waves of pleasure through me and I came again.

Michael held my hips tightly and cursed with his head thrown back.

I collapsed against his chest and wrapped my arms around his neck. He pushed me away slightly and took my lower lip between his teeth. He nibbled along my lips before sealing our mouths and tongues together in a kiss of hunger and possession.

He brushed the hair from my face. "Don't ever leave me, Lily; I couldn't survive without you."

He brought tears to my eyes. "I won't. You mean the world to me."

Michael

I was sitting on the chair in my bedroom holding a naked Lily in my arms after the most extraordinary sexual experience I had ever had. She had completely knocked me out. At first she seemed shy and maybe a little hesitant, but God, there was nothing hesitant about what we had just done.

For her to stand there naked in front of me and touch herself, wow, that was hot. And sexy.

"Michael, how can you be ready to go again after that?" She asked into my neck. I shivered and my cock swelled even more inside her.

"You standing in front of me with your hands on your breasts was so fuckin' hot," I said and arched into her, fully aroused.

Lily lifted her head and ran her hands through my hair as she looked into my eyes. "You're amazing. I thought fisting your dick was hot; you made me wet."

She lifted herself up and then slammed back down on me. My eyes rolled.

I don't know where the hell she got the energy to ride me, but she did, and it felt good. I grabbed her hips and pulled her down onto me and held her there. She tried to wriggle around, but I wouldn't let her.

"Michael, oh God. I'm so close...please."

My wife begging me was a huge turn-on. Before she could think, I had her off my cock and turned her around to face outward and then back down on me.

I reached in front of her and placed my hands on her breasts. I massaged the soft mounds, pinching her rock hard nipples. She leaned forward and put her hands on my knees. Then she began to slide up and down my shaft as I continued to play with her flesh.

"Oh God," she moaned.

"I know." I looked down and watched my cock disappear into her sex and then emerge again, covered in her arousal.

I moved a hand from her breast down to her clit. The moment I touched it, she shattered around me. I swelled even more and came as she continued to spasm around me, milking every drop of cum out of me.

She collapsed back onto me. My arms were wrapped around her and my ass was probably stuck to the wooden chair.

"If I can move, I'll carry you to the shower."

She started to shake.

"Lily?" Was she crying?

I found the strength from somewhere and lifted her off of me. The action made us both catch our breath because it felt good. I sat her on my lap and noticed that her face was full of tears.

"Oh God, Lily. Please tell me what's wrong. Did I hurt you?"

She shook her head. "No, you didn't hurt me. I've never done anything like this before. I didn't know anything, wow... You really are amazing... Thank you for making me feel..."

I did the only thing I could after her little speech and kissed her, gently. "You're the amazing one. Come on, let's take a shower and sit on the deck. I'll put some steaks and potatoes on the back grill for dinner."

"I'd like that."

I picked her up and carried her to the bathroom. I placed her on the edge of the Jacuzzi so I could turn on the shower.

"You're hot," she said out of the blue.

I turned to see her eyes on my ass. "Lily, I want to wash you. Please behave so we can get through this shower without me being inside you." I cupped her face in my hands. "I want to spend the rest of the afternoon with you, sitting around our house," I grinned, "with you in my arms, just talking."

"Let's take a shower, and I promise to behave myself the whole time we're in there," she said, then walked past me and stroked my cock.

"Minx," I hissed.

She laughed. "Coming?"

"Almost!"

I stepped into the shower with her, wondering if I was going to survive this. She began to rub her body with shower gel. I groaned. She was slick with water. Her nipples were rock hard and peeking through the soap. She was every man's fantasy and I told her we were going to behave. It was official - I was crazy.

I took a deep breath and grabbed the shower gel. I began to coat my chest, down to my cock, which was ready to play. My breath came out as she came up behind me and wrapped her arms around my waist. Her wet breasts pressed against my back. "Lily?"

"I've never had sex in the shower before. I want you to make love to me in here," she purred in my ear.

"Fuck!"

She moved her hands down my stomach, stroking my dick from tip to base before dropping to her knees in front of me. Grabbing my ass, she pulled me forward and right into her mouth. Heaven.

Her tongue swirled around the tip before she sucked; my legs almost gave way. She licked down to my balls and sucked one into her mouth. She sucked gently before doing the same with the other. My toes curled.

She moved back to the head and swirled her tongue around the leaking head. After a few more swipes with her tongue, she stood up, turned around and bent over to rest her hands on the built-in ledge.

With her legs spread and her ass in the air, I could see the wetness around her pussy and her swollen clit. My mouth watered and I hoped she was as ready as she looked. I couldn't wait another minute.

I put one hand on her hip and the other on my cock as I slowly entered her. God, she was so tight, and after her mouth was on me, I was ready to explode. Inside her to the hilt, I held both her hips and pulled out almost all the way before slamming back into her. The eroticism of watching myself slide in and out of her almost brought me to my knees.

"I'm close," she said, followed by a moan.

"So am I." I couldn't take my eyes off my cock as it disappeared into her sex - it was such a turn-on. I felt a tingle at the base of my spine and clenched my teeth to hold out a little longer.

I fought for breath. I was going to come.

"Think what this would be like on your conference table," she said.

Fuck. I began to come at the same time Lily began to contract around me, moaning. I was sure the tip of my dick had flown off. I came so damn hard.

God, Lily was going to kill me.

As my breathing began to even out, I pulled away

slightly so I could slip out of her warmth. "Come here, baby," I whispered as I helped her up and wrapped her in my arms.

"I can't move. You're deadly."

"It's you, Michael. Just you."

23

Lily

THE BACK DECK OF THE HOUSE HAD THE MOST AMAZING views. There was a large, manicured garden, which Michael told me was big enough for him and his brothers to play rugby in. Beyond it were some magnificent views of the mountains.

Michael had gone inside to sort out the meat and potatoes for the outdoor barbecue. He'd told me to stay put because we needed to eat a substantial meal before bedtime. I just laughed at him. He quickly returned with a glass of wine and told me to relax, which I did.

I was still a little stunned at how outrageous I'd been that afternoon. Not once had I behaved with David the way I had with Michael. I wasn't sure why, but with Michael I felt totally comfortable being who I was, and I didn't feel embarrassed. The fact that he had the hottest body I'd ever seen might have had something to do with it.

He really was like a sculptured god. I just had to look at him and I melted.

The biggest problem I had was getting to work tomorrow. I was Michael's assistant, and I was worried that people would think I got the job because I slept with him. Not true, but people loved to gossip, and especially about Michael because he had never dated before. At least Dale would be in my corner and dispel any gossip with the truth.

"Hey gorgeous! Have you had enough of my brother yet?" Sebastian asked, coming out of the house.

He made me jump, lost in thought as I was.

He sat down in front of me.

"No, I haven't," I replied and took a big gulp of my wine. "When did you get here?"

He grinned. "Trying to get rid of me?"

"Sorry, that didn't sound very polite. I enjoy watching Michael and you interact. I'm an only child, so I never had that. It's fun to watch."

He sat back in his chair and just stared at me. "I can see why Lucien took you as his sister. I like you and you're good for Michael. I don't remember him ever being this happy," he hesitated. "Don't tell him I said that."

"I won't."

"Won't what?" Michael asked, coming out of the door, followed by Ruben.

Michael sat down next to me and put his arm around my shoulders.

I grinned at Sebastian before turning back to Michael. "That Lucien adopted me as his sister."

"As long as that's all, we're good."

"Michael, please don't start that again." I looked at him, trying to gauge how much it bothered him that I'd started to be friends with his brother.

"I'm really okay with you being friends with them," he said, turning to Sebastian and Ruben. "What are you two even doing here? No hot dates?"

"Nope. We decided to come and flirt with your wife and maybe get some food out of you. That was only if we didn't catch you in bed."

I started to giggle as they both sat across from us with grins on their faces.

"Okay, that's enough. Stop embarrassing Lily."

"I'm not embarrassed."

"I should have known."

"So, Seb and Rue, why don't you both have girl-friends?" They both looked at me in shock.

"They don't like their names shortened," Michael told me, trying not to laugh.

I looked at them both and Sebastian winked at me. "You can call me whatever you want, honey."

"Dick comes to mind," Michael muttered.

I slapped him on the arm. "Be nice, they're your brothers and I like them." I reached up and kissed him on the mouth.

"Do you two mind? Two single guys over here," Sebastian said, trying not to laugh.

"I think we need to find you both a nice woman, so I have some female company when you visit." I laughed. The look on their faces was priceless. Michael roared with laughter next to me.

"Um, Lily, we can find our own women if you don't mind," Sebastian looked worried.

I'd decided to make them sweat. I pushed Michael slightly out of sight and looked at them both.

"No, no, you don't have to do that. I'll find you both a hot woman for a date. Just one date and you can take it from there. Just think how happy it would make your mom to see all her boys happy with one woman."

"Lily...we don't mind sharing you!" Ruben said. He'd been quiet since they arrived, as if something was bothering him.

Michael tensed.

"You know he's just kidding. I thought you were making steak and potatoes."

He looked at me. "You want me to put them on now?"

"I'm getting hungry, and this wine you keep plying me with is going down pretty well." I grinned at him.

"Is that your way of saying you're getting drunk?"

"Yep!"

"Oh, brother. I would get her sobered up if you, um, have things planned for later," Sebastian said.

I couldn't help but laugh - and blush.

"You two are going to get kicked out of here without food if you keep this up," Michael warned with a grin.

"Hey, I've been behaving. I think I should get Sebastian's share," Ruben said.

"What about 'we don't mind sharing you'?"

"Okay, we'll both shut up. In fact, I'll cook so you can stay with your wife."

Ruben got up and went into the house to get the meat and potatoes. I was really looking forward to this. The wine had really started to make me tipsy, so some food would be good.

It was nice to sit outside with Michael and two of his brothers. They made me feel like I was part of their family, which made me feel all warm and fuzzy inside.

Michael held me tight as his fingers tangled in my hair. I cuddled up to him and put my face on his chest, then kissed him. I decided to close my eyes for a few minutes. I was so comfortable.

Michael

I couldn't concentrate on my work. The object of my desire was sitting outside my office while she sorted some spreadsheets for me.

Yesterday had been amazing. Lily was living with me, and I had no intention of letting her go. A little over two weeks ago, I'd been okay, not happy, but okay. I had every intention of staying single, because from experience it was easier to be alone, even if I was lonely.

After two weeks of pining for her, she was finally sharing my home.

We'd woken up together two mornings in a row. Twice I'd brought her breakfast in bed. I'd awakened abruptly in the morning when I came down her throat. I had no idea what she was doing and thought I was dreaming until I came and felt her sucking me off.

I reached under my desk to rearrange my shaft, which had hardened thanks to the image in my head. She had a wicked mouth on her.

As soon as I walked into my office, I'd taken one look at the conference table and stiffened. I'd remembered her words about what it would be like on the conference table. Yesterday, her words made me instantly shoot my load. And if my wife had anything to do with it, this fantasy would come true when I least expected it.

I was really looking forward to this surprise. I'd never fantasized about having a woman in my office until I met Lily, and now I couldn't get it out of my mind.

She had charmed all my brothers, especially Lucien. When I saw her with Sebastian and Ruben yesterday, I realized that I had nothing to worry about. She treated them like her own brothers, and if I was honest, it thrilled me that she felt so comfortable with them. It felt like she'd been a part of it for much longer than a day.

I pushed away from my desk and stalked to the door. Just one look and then I would get some work done.

The door opened silently, and as I was about to step out, I heard Jacky say, "He won't want you for long, that's the way he is. He'll always go to bed with you at your place. He'll never take you to his house; he never does." I stepped out at this point, anger flared from my nostrils as I searched for the object of my anger.

"Jacky," I barked.

They both jumped.

I walked over and pulled Lily up from her seat. I cradled her against my chest and watched as Jacky's eyes widened at my show of affection. "If I ever hear you talk to Lily like that again, you'll be looking for another job. Are we clear on that?"

"Yes, Mr. McKenzie."

"Good. On your way back to your office, please let the staff know that Lily's address is now the same as mine. Have them add me as her emergency contact as well. You got that?"

"Yes," she said and practically ran out of the office. She was angry, but she should have been terrified - no one talks to Lily like that.

"Are you okay?" I cupped the back of her head and lowered mine to plant a kiss on her luscious lips.

"I'm fine. In fact, she was about to be told to mind her own business and exactly where I live when my knight in shining armor showed up." She grinned at me.

"Well, that should take care of everything. Within thirty minutes, the whole company will know we're living together." I kissed her right eye. "You're addictive." I kissed her left eye. "I can't concentrate on anything because you're out here instead of in there with me." I kissed her on the lips.

She pushed me away. "If I sat in there with you, we both know we wouldn't get anything done.

"Yes, we would." I grinned. "At least I'd be able to see you without having to get up from my desk. So, you see, I'll get a lot more done because I won't be spending my time running to the door just to look at you.

Her arms were wrapped around my waist as she stroked my back. It felt good and right to have her in my arms. "If I was in there with you, we both know you still wouldn't get anything done; you'd spend all your time staring at me!

"Exactly," I said, laughing at her.

We both turned at the sound of a cleared throat. "If

you're both done, do you have a minute, Michael?" Dale asked, amusement in his eyes.

Lily chuckled and turned away.

"Yeah, let's go to my office so Lily can get back to work. She gets distracted easily.

"Like someone else," Lily said under her breath.

24

Lily

AFTER THE RUN-IN WITH JACKY, A FEW PEOPLE GAVE ME strange looks every time I passed, but most of the staff were pleasant, if not a little curious. I kept my relationship with Michael private because it was nobody else's business but ours.

Michael made me feel loved and appreciated. It was a wonderful feeling.

To celebrate our week together, Michael had insisted on taking me away for the weekend to a beautiful hotel on the river. The hotel was a small, family-run, two-story colonial ranch house with ten rooms available to the public.

I stood on the balcony, taking in the beautiful view of the river and the mountains beyond, while Michael finished getting dressed. He'd asked me to pack a cocktail dress because he wanted to take me out to dinner. The dress I'd packed was red, with one bust covered in red sequins and the other in silk, the same as the rest of the dress. It fit me like a glove, and if that didn't drive Michael crazy, my shoes would. They were high, and I mean sky-high. I just hoped he wouldn't be so distracted by my legs that he walked into something.

"How am I supposed to eat dinner with you looking so hot?" Michael asked, sliding his hands around my waist from behind.

"You're going to have to behave. This dress is not made for making out...mmm..." He started to kiss my neck. "Michael...stop."

Michael took a deep breath and stepped back, turning me around to face him. He left me speechless. It was the first time I'd seen him in black, and he looked gorgeous.

"I don't know what to say, but wow. You always look hot, but in that black suit and shirt with the red tie, you leave me speechless."

He grinned at me, took my hand, and pulled me outside. "We have to go before I forget about dinner and go straight to dessert."

"I agree! I love being naked with you, but I didn't go to all this trouble to avoid being seen. Besides, I was planning on torturing you the whole meal."

He groaned, handed me my purse from the bed and

opened the door. "You're going to drive me crazy in that dress."

"Think how hot it's going to be when we get back to the hotel - all that pent-up energy."

"Fuck. Don't say another word until we're in the car and on our way to the restaurant."

I snickered. He was funny and in for a treat. I had told him the truth when I said I wanted to torture him, but I didn't think he realized how far I was willing to go.

"Why are you grinning like the cat that got the cream?" he asked as he waited for me to get in the car.

"No reason." I patted him on the cheek and got in.

Michael ran around to the driver's side, got in, and started the engine.

We sat in silence as he drove the car down the mountain road into town.

I was looking forward to eating at the restaurant because it would be the first time we'd done something like that. Our first date. I started to giggle and saw Michael frowning at me.

"I was just thinking about tonight being our first date. I think we've been doing the whole thing backwards."

"That's why I wanted to fix it this weekend. I don't want you to miss anything." He blushed.

"You really are the sweetest guy." I had to quickly reach into my purse for a handkerchief; he'd brought tears to my eyes with his declaration.

"Hell, I never meant to make you cry."

"I'm fine. Just take us to the restaurant. I'm kind of hungry now, but I want your arms around me before we go in."

"You got it."

Michael

Lily crushed me. It made me angry to realize that she'd never been treated like she was special. She was special to me, and I spent every day making sure she knew it.

I was sitting in a meeting on Friday when it suddenly hit me that I hadn't taken Lily out on a date. My concentration went to hell for the rest of the meeting. As soon as they left my office, I was on the Internet looking up phone numbers to arrange for the hotel and restaurant.

The hotel was amazing and had everything we needed. There were even strawberry and chocolate flavored condoms in the bathroom. When Lily discovered them, she giggled hysterically.

I pulled up to the restaurant, turned off the engine, got out of the car, and ran around to open Lily's door. I took her hand and pulled her straight into my arms, holding her tight.

"You feel amazing against me. You always do."

"Thank you, Michael. For this weekend, for this dinner, and for changing my life."

I was at a loss for words after her "thank you," so I took her hand and led her into the restaurant, where the maître d' led us to a cozy table in the back of the room.

After we ordered, we sat close together on the high-backed sofa. I held Lily's hand on her stomach, our fingers intertwined. Her free hand rested on my thigh.

"You're playing with fire." I leaned over and kissed the side of her neck.

"Mmm, I want to see how much you can take," she said. Her hand continued to creep up my thigh toward the family jewels.

I grabbed her wandering hand and placed it on the table just before it reached my groin. "You need to stay away from there."

The last thing I needed was for Lily to feel my erection. I was having a hard enough time controlling it. One touch from her and it would want to come out and play. This was not going to happen in the restaurant.

We needed to talk about something other than us, but what? George!

"I got a call from the hospital while you were in the shower. George is getting out in the next few weeks, so I need to find a nurse for him. No matter what he thinks, he will not be left alone. If he is, he'll end up back in the hospital or worse."

"Don't worry, Michael. I'll tell him. He'll probably be

less likely to refuse if it comes from me, but if you suggest it, he'll probably curse the idea to high heaven."

Why did Lily's smile look so... sweet? Too sweet. Then her hand landed right on my semi-erect cock. I growled. She laughed.

I inhaled, trying to control my body's reaction to her, to no avail. "Lily..."

"Our food is here."

She sat back and removed her hand from my crotch. She picked up her napkin and spread it across her lap, then reached for mine and did the same, applying pressure where I really didn't need any.

The waiter left as Lily grinned and turned to start her meal. I reached for my glass of burgundy and took a sip, almost choking when Lily's hand landed on my cock again.

She gave me a wicked slap and then my zipper went down. That was so not supposed to happen here.

I reached under the table and grabbed her hand.

"No, I'll play, but no one else will know what I'm doing. And by the way, I took off my panties, just for you."

"I..." My brain had completely shut down.

"Eat."

Eat. How did she expect me to eat with her hand under the table caressing my cock while she was naked under her dress? I met her eyes as they moved to my plate and back again.

She continued to eat while I tried to swallow the lump of beef stuck in my throat.

"I'm not going to make you come, but I'm going to get you so hot that you'll park and take me in the car. Although I think I should have worn something a little easier to take off," she whispered.

"Then you better move your hand because I'm too excited to hold on."

She cupped my shaft in her fist and stroked her fingers up and down over my balls.

I was shaking with need and seconds away from coming. The thought of being in a public place where everyone could see us, combined with her touch, had me beyond excited.

Before I could explode, I removed Lily's hand and quickly strapped myself in. I rested my elbows on the table and put my head in my hands... and breathed.

I glanced at Lily, who was sitting next to me, eating as if she hadn't nearly brought me to orgasm in a crowded restaurant a few seconds ago.

"Michael, you should really try this. It's amazing and melts in your mouth. Here, have a taste of mine."

She cut a piece of meat from her own plate and forked it to me with a wicked gleam in her eye.

The rest of the meal would be hell.

25

Lily

IT HAD BEEN FIFTEEN DAYS SINCE I'D MOVED IN WITH Michael, and I'd never known what true happiness was until I did. He was the most amazing, sexiest man I'd ever met, and he filled my heart to bursting.

Every morning I'd wake up cuddled up in his arms. He'd make slow love to me, then climb out of bed to go downstairs and make us both a cup of coffee. After the coffee, we'd shower together, and most of the time we'd make love again in the shower. Then we'd get dressed and go to the office.

In the evening, we'd leave work, go home, and cook dinner together. We both preferred quiet evenings at home, just the two of us, talking or watching a movie from the huge collection of Blu-rays that Michael had hidden in the closet in the "boy's room.

At the restaurant he'd taken me to during our hotel stay, we'd barely finished our meal when he'd dragged me outside, into the car, and within two minutes he'd pulled up behind some trees, off the main road. He had my dress undone and off, his cock inside me within seconds. It was hot and gave us both a hell of a memory.

On Saturday we stayed in town and went grocery shopping and then basically did what normal people do on weekends - housework.

Sunday, we went to his parents' ranch for dinner. It was a beautiful afternoon. I'd helped his mom in the kitchen while Michael, his dad, and his brothers tinkered outside until dinner was ready.

While visiting his parents, Michael received a phone call from a distraught George. Apparently, one of the nurses had taken a liking to him and refused to leave him alone. He begged Michael to get him out of the hospital. Michael laughed and told him to enjoy it while he could. He hoped to get out of the hospital in a few days, but Michael had told him that he could only go home if he promised to rest. George was unaware that Michael had hired a nurse to take care of him during the day. That would not go over well when he found out.

Michael was in a meeting in his office that was about to end, and I was bored. I'd finished the database Michael wanted me to put together. I'd typed up the report from this morning's meeting and was twiddling my thumbs in boredom.

There were no more meetings for the rest of the day, and Michael didn't know that I had a surprise planned for after the meeting. I had a fantasy to deliver.

I got up from my desk and went to the ladies' room. Locked in a stall, I carefully removed my matching panties and bra. I wore a dress to work today with seduction in mind. The bodice was tailored to support my large breasts, while the dress fanned out to just above my knees. It was made of a thin, flyaway material, so I wore a light cardigan over it to hide my nipples. Because of my braless predicament, they would be visible, and considering how aroused I was thinking about Michael and my state of undress, they'd be more than noticeable.

I ran my hands down my hips and then over my breasts. They ached and were hard as stone. My sex pulsed. God, I had to calm down or I would jump on him the minute everyone left instead of seducing him.

I took a deep breath and walked back to my desk to stash my purse in my bottom drawer, which I kept locked. I quickly looked down and made sure my nipples were hidden behind the cardigan, then knocked on Michael's door and entered.

Someone else was talking as I walked in, and Michael's eyes went straight to me. I winked at him and walked over to the conference table to clear away the empty cups.

I started at the opposite end from where Michael sat. He never looked away from me, no doubt wondering what I was up to. He would find out soon enough. I moved over to Michael and made sure he felt my breasts as I leaned over for his cup. He did feel them if his sudden stiffness was any indication. I smiled to myself as I wheeled the cart out of the room, leaving the dirty cups in the small kitchen. I walked back to his office, pretending to have a message for him.

I opened the office door and walked back in.

"Sorry to interrupt, but I just need to deliver a message."

"Okay, Lily."

Michael remained in his chair as I walked over to him. I leaned in front of him and heard him swallow. He looked down my dress and I leaned over to his ear. "I'm not wearing any panties. I need you inside me," I whispered, feeling bad. I pretended to stumble and put my hand in Michael's groin, feeling the evidence of what I'd done to him. He was trembling with longing.

How the hell I got out of his office, I don't know, but I heard him tell everyone that the meeting was over; he had something important to do. I chuckled.

I hadn't been back at my desk for more than two minutes when they walked out. When the last one left, I got up, locked the outer office door, turned off the lights, and returned to Michael's office. I locked his door and stood staring at him, still sitting at the conference table.

"There was no way I could move after your little show."

I smiled. "Stand up." He did.

Oh my God, he gave new meaning to tent pants. I licked my lips.

"Lily."

I walked toward him, and as soon as I was out of sight of the windows, I stopped and took off my cardigan, which I tossed on a chair. I reached behind me and unzipped the back of my dress. I let it fall from my shoulders to my arms. I stepped out of the puddle that had formed at my feet.

Michael was extremely excited and frozen to the spot. I walked over to him in my stilettos, stood in front of him and pressed myself against him. He inhaled as I massaged his face. "This is your fantasy," I said.

I turned and walked to the back of the conference room, where the table was free of papers, then threw a cheeky grin over my shoulder and bent over it. The cool table felt good against my hot breasts. I spread my legs to show him how wet my pussy was before looking over my shoulder at him.

"Fuck me," I said, my voice hoarse with desire.

He tossed his shirt somewhere and his pants, shoes

and socks followed. He was naked, all muscle, his dick hard as steel, dripping with pre-cum.

He stalked up to me and stopped with his hands on my ass. He made me so hot and wet.

On his knees behind me, he grabbed my ass and kissed each cheek. I could barely hold myself still as I fought not to push back against him. He chuckled at my impatience and placed an intimate kiss between my legs, right on my genitals. I almost collapsed right there as a deep moan escaped my lips.

"You're so fucking sexy. All wet and swollen for me."

"Yes," I croaked, and boy, was I wet with wanting him.

He stayed on his knees and plunged his tongue into my sex. I almost jumped off the table; it was intense.

"Hold still, I want you to come for me like this."

He put his mouth on my clit and sucked. Then he pulled away and put two fingers inside me and started cutting them in and out as he rubbed my clit.

I cried out, "Oh, Michael," as I came. He took his fingers out and put his mouth on me. He continued to fuck me with his tongue, prolonging my climax. When I finally began to return to earth, he took one last swipe of his tongue and stood up.

"I can't wait," he said and thrust into my tight sheath.

His invasion almost made me come again.

He thrust forward before pulling back and sliding his

dick along my ass. He grabbed my hips and thrust back into me, filling me to the brim.

He grabbed my hips and slowly rocked back and forth inside me, bringing me to the brink of another orgasm. As he massaged my bottom, he slipped a hand into the crevice and gently pushed the tip of his finger into my ass.

I started to come around his cock, banging my head from side to side. "It won't stop," I screamed.

He roared in release as my orgasm still milked the life out of him. "Fuck, Lily." He quivered.

My sex rippled with small aftershocks, and when he removed his finger from my ass, I couldn't help the trembling pleasure that ran through me. It caused Michael to curse and begin to harden again.

He slid out of me and pulled me back with him to sit in his lap on the chair he had collapsed into.

I kicked off my shoes and snuggled into him. "That was out of this world," I whispered into his chest.

"You're destroying me, Lily. Do you know that? I've never done this before. I've never done it in my office or touched anyone where I touched you."

I looked up at him and did the only thing left to do - kiss him. I held his face in my hands and kissed him, never taking my eyes off his.

I loved this man. My heart was his. I realized I'd never given it to David, not really, but I had given it to Michael.

Michael

Sitting naked at my conference table with an equally naked Lily in my arms, I had just had the best sexual experience of my life. Before Lily came into my life, I had not had sex in a long time, but I had never touched a woman as much as I did with Lily. I enjoy sex. She had fallen apart in my arms the moment I'd pushed my finger into her ass. It had been hot.

She started wiggling in my lap. "We can't do it again, at least not here."

I just grinned.

"We have to act out your fantasy now."

Her eyes widened.

"I've changed my mind. The fantasy I've had since we've been living together is one where I have you tied to your bed while I do nasty things to your body."

I couldn't keep the stunned look off my face.

"Oh yes, I want you naked, spread out on your bed, and then I'm going to put my mouth on every inch of you," she said, stroking my cock, which wanted to play again.

She jumped up and ran to the bathroom. I followed and stopped in the doorway when I saw her using one of the towels to clean between her legs. She rinsed it out a few times, then walked over, stood in front of me, and put the cloth on my cock, wiping her juice off and around my groin. She got a towel and dried us both.

"I better get dressed before we get caught like this."

I watched her go back into the conference room while I washed my hands and splashed some cold water on my face.

I went back out to join her and quickly got dressed, watching Lily the whole time.

When we were both fully dressed, she walked over and kissed me, planting a kiss on my lips. "We'll continue this when we get home tonight," she said and strolled out, her sexy butt swaying.

I walked behind my desk and sat down heavily. I was in love with her. When the hell that happened, I had no idea, but I loved her. It was as clear as day. But what the hell was I going to do about it? There was no way in the world I'd ever be able to let her go; that was out of the question. But did she feel the same way about me?

She always looked at me like I was the only one in the room, and once or twice after we'd been intimate, I'd felt like she was about to say something, but she'd held back. Part of me was afraid to push it with her in case I was wrong, and she crushed me instead. I'm so screwed.

"No need to ask what you're thinking about," Lucien said, taking a seat across from my desk. I hadn't even noticed him come in.

"What are you doing here?" I grumbled.

"Well, I figured since Lily looked pretty flushed, you were in a good mood. Guess I was wrong."

"Leave Lily out of this. What are you doing here?"

"I came to take your assistant out for coffee."

"I don't think..." He didn't let me finish.

"I know she's your wife, Michael. I'm your brother. If you can't trust your own brother, who can you trust? I promise you, the only thing I want from Lily is friendship. I can talk to her, and I know it will stay with her. She's becoming a friend, and I guess you could say a sister."

He was right. He was my brother and had never given me a reason to doubt him. "Sorry, Lucien. She has me tied up in knots."

He laughed. "I can see that. I can also see how much you love her." I met his eyes. "You're my brother, and I've never seen you act like that with anyone else... That's why you have to tell her."

"No." I got up and walked to the window, resting my forehead against it.

"I can't lose her, Lucien. She's my life."

"What if she finds out later and leaves you because you didn't tell her?"

"That won't happen."

"Michael."

"This conversation is over."

"I think Ramon is gay," Lucien said.

I just stared at him. "What?"

"You heard me. Sit down."

"I think I need to for this conversation."

"Why do you think our brother is," I waved my arms around, "you know."

"You can say it, Michael...gay."

"Do you know or are you just guessing?" I asked him.

"He's never been seen with a woman, ever. I mean, have you ever seen him with a woman?"

I shook my head.

"Exactly. Besides, Ruben saw him in town the other night at his club. He said he was about to go over and let him know he was around when another guy walked up and put his arm around him."

"That doesn't mean he's gay. He could have just been a friend."

"I don't think so, but I'm not going to ask him. I don't want him to confirm it. There's nothing wrong with it, but it would be weird, him being our brother, you know," Lucien said and looked like he was squirming.

"Okay, I can't talk about this anymore. Go and take Lily for that coffee and look after her."

"With my life," Lucien said, and I believed him.

26

Lily

I'M BACK AT MY DESK AFTER RUNNING TO THE RESTROOM TO put my panties and bra back on. I felt rather flushed after what I'd just instigated in Michael's office. I had no idea where my inner vixen had come from, but she sure as hell turned me on—not to mention what she did to Michael.

I was mortified when I walked out of his office and saw Lucien seated on the sofa in the guest area. He said he had just arrived, but I had my doubts. He smirked as he moved into Michael's office.

"Hi, Lily," Sylvia said. "Can I come in?"

"Of course you can," I replied, wondering why she was asking. She never had before. "Sylvia, is everything all right?"

She sat on the corner of my desk. "Yes. Are you all right, Lily?"

I raised an eyebrow. It was an odd question for Sylvia to ask. "Yes, I'm fine. Why wouldn't I be?"

"No, no, it's okay. I just thought I'd ask." She jumped up from my desk and headed for the door.

"Sylvia, wait up." I walked toward her. "Please, tell me what's going on."

She looked pale. "Jacky said she heard you and Michael arguing, and that you'd be moving out soon."

I was annoyed. Jacky needed to mind her own business. "We haven't argued, so I don't know where she got that idea. And as for me moving out? There is no chance of that. Everything between Michael and me is fine. I've never been happier."

She seemed to sigh in relief. "Thank God. I should have known better than to believe anything she said. But I needed to hear it from her, you know."

"Yeah, don't worry about it. Next time, don't believe anything she says about us. I think she's jealous."

"I won't. I better get back to work," she said, walking out of the office.

"Shit."

"Nice vocabulary for a hot young woman," Lucien said. I turned around, and there he was, sitting at my desk.

"Comfortable?"

"Actually, no. This chair is rock hard. How the hell do you relax on it?"

I laughed. "That's the point. I wouldn't get any work done if I relaxed on it," I smirked. "Besides, that's what Michael's for."

"I really didn't need to know that. Grab your purse. The big boss gave me permission to take you out for coffee."

"You asked his permission?" I asked as I retrieved my purse from the bottom desk drawer.

"Not really. I did tell him, though. I don't want a black eye for kidnapping you for a little while. I have an appointment in an hour, so I can spare thirty minutes. I can't wait to find out what you were doing in there when I arrived because I had to use my own key to get in."

I blushed. There was no way I was telling anyone what we'd done in there.

He laughed. "Mmm, that's good, huh?"

"Shut up, Lucien."

He took my hand, pulled me out of the office, and led me straight to the elevator. Before I could get my thoughts together, he took me to Starbucks.

As we sat down by the window with our drinks, I noticed Jacky sitting across from us with a couple of other women who worked on a different floor of the company.

Lucien followed my gaze, then turned back to me.

"Ignore them, Lily. Jacky might be acting jealous because you live with Michael, but she'd go with anyone who has money. And before you ask, no, none of us have taken her up on the offer. She works for us. Until you came along, employees were strictly off-limits. But you're the exception." He smiled. "You have Michael so tied in knots, it's funny. I've never seen my brother like that before, so you need to let us tease him."

I rolled my eyes. "Boys will be boys." I took a few sips of my drink, aware that Jacky and her friends were glaring at me. They were probably wondering why I was living with one McKenzie and drinking coffee with another.

"Lily."

"Sorry, they're annoying me now..." I shot one last glance at them before my face brightened with a grin. "So, Lucien, I think you need..."

He didn't let me finish. "I don't need anything or anyone," he said, emphasizing the "anyone."

"You know, one of these days, I hope you meet a woman who really drops you on your ass. When that happens, I will laugh my socks off!"

"Wishing that on me is just cruel." He sulked.

I really did like Lucien. He was serious most of the time, but he was playful with me. There was no sexual tension; he just needed a friend, and I wanted to be that friend. Michael had started to settle down around his brothers when I was around, and he had started to trust our relationship.

Realizing in his office earlier that I loved him came as a shock. I never loved David the way I love Michael. Michael was my whole world. Without him, I'd crash and burn.

"Earth to Lily! Where did you go? Never mind. I know where you went." He roared with laughter.

"I'm telling you, one of these days, a woman will drop you on your ass, and I really can't wait to see it."

You are asking for trouble," he said, pointing his finger at me. I must leave, or I'll be late for my appointment. I'll take you back upstairs, so Michael doesn't yell at me."

"Really, I'm quite capable of walking into an elevator and then walking back to the office on my own."

"Humor me. Besides, your friends just climbed aboard. Come on." He practically dragged me to the elevators. "Play along," he whispered. Then he wrapped his arm around my waist and pulled me into him.

He started to pretend to nuzzle my neck. I moved slightly, drawing my body closer to his. He met my eyes and winked. "Oh, Lily, you taste like heaven," he whispered.

I could feel a giggle working its way up inside me. When the doors opened two floors before ours, Lucien pulled me out, ushering me away through the emergency exit and down the stairs.

We both burst out laughing. "God, that was so funny! Did you see her face?" Lucien asked me.

"Yes." I couldn't stop laughing.

I took a deep breath as Lucien led me up the two flights of stairs back to Michael's office.

"Okay, I'll leave you here. Thanks for having coffee with me, and for the fun in the elevator." I laughed.

"You're welcome. Take care." I hugged him, quickly kissed him on the cheek, and walked back into my office.

Michael

I closed my office door and leaned back against it. I had just seen Lily embrace Lucien, then lean in to kiss him. She kissed him on the cheek, and they laughed. What the hell was going on?

Control. That's what I needed. Deep down, I knew nothing was going on between them, yet I couldn't stop the jealousy that flared up and took me by surprise.

I loved Lily and was terrified of losing her.

She knocked on my door and tried to open it. I stepped aside as she walked in.

"Michael, what's wrong?" She asked, standing in front of me with her hands on my hips.

"You kissed him," I blurted out.

She was speechless at first. Then, she took hold of my face and kissed me. "He's your brother. He took me out for coffee. He walked me up the last couple of floors. I hugged him and kissed his cheek, saying, 'Thank you, and take care.'"

"Why did you walk the last few floors?"

She grinned. "Jacky was in the elevator with a couple friends, so Lucien pretended to be all over me." She kept her eyes locked with mine. "He snuggled into my neck and pretended to nibble it, but he wasn't actually doing anything. He was just trying his best not to laugh." She looked up at me. "Michael, I promise you that's all it was."

She looked close to tears as she pulled away from me. She walked over and sat on the sofa. "I can't keep doing this." She wiped a tear away. "I can't keep explaining myself to you every time you get the wrong idea. I'm your girlfriend and he's your brother. You need to trust us. Lucien needs a friend, and I want to be that friend, but I can't handle your constant questioning whenever I see him. You need to trust me like I trust you."

She had me panicked after what she'd just said. I didn't want to drive her away. Plus, she was right; I had to stop questioning her every move.

I sat next to her on the sofa and pulled her close. "I'm sorry, Lily. So very sorry. I trust you. I know deep down that you wouldn't cheat on me. It's just a matter of getting my mouth to catch up to my brain." She chuckled. "Here, let me." I pushed her away and used tissues to wipe her tears.

"You're so beautiful. You take my breath away."

She climbed astride me, which I didn't think was such a good idea considering her dress was practically around her hips.

"Lily, the door isn't locked."

"I know."

Then she kissed me. As she nibbled my bottom lip, she positioned herself right over my straining erection. When she licked along my lips, I opened my mouth and our tongues met. I took her head in my hands and held her there as we continued to kiss.

"Lily," I moaned into her mouth. "We really need to stop." I gripped her hips, holding her tight against me. I was unable to let her go, but I knew I didn't want to take her in my office again.

Finally, Lily moved her mouth away from mine and looked into my eyes. "I always want you, Michael. I've never acted like this before. Like a nymphomaniac or something."

I burst out laughing. Nymphomaniac?

Lily tried to look serious, even placing her hands on her hips, but her expression didn't last long before she joined in the laughter.

"Nymphomaniac. I like the sound of that. A lot!" I couldn't help but tease her.

"You would," Lily said, swatting me on the shoulder as she climbed off me.

I watched her walk toward the door, swaying her hips seductively. I nearly ran after her and pinned her against the door. Instead, I sat on the sofa and rearranged my cock into a more comfortable position.

She grinned back. "Tonight, I'm tying you to your bed. I hope you're ready." She walked out of my office, leaving me stunned and aroused.

Groaning, I stood up, moved back behind my desk, took my seat, and looked out the window at the city of Lexington below. I wasn't really taking anything in.

I really needed to connect my mouth to my brain before I put my foot in it again. I would take her out to dinner in a few days when we could spend the following morning in bed. I knew I had a difficult time trusting people, but I couldn't keep acting like that every time she went somewhere without me. I did trust her. It's simply that sometimes I occasionally forgot and acted possessively toward her.

I decided to tell Lily my idea. I stood up from my desk and walked to the door. Just as I was about to open it, I heard her say, "David." Was he on the phone?

Instead of going back to my desk, I leaned against the wall and listened.

"David, I'm not interested in going back to you."

There was silence while he obviously talked.

"I'll tell you this one last time: I'm not going back to you. I'm happier now than I've ever been, so I would appreciate it if you would leave me alone. Have a good life because I intend to—with Michael."

She hung up the phone.

I couldn't believe what I'd overheard. I was thrilled to know that she planned to spend the rest of her life with me, despite my caveman tendencies.

"You heard."

I jumped. She caught me. "Yeah."

"He wants me back. I don't think things are working out with Lucy. I feel bad for him, but I'm happier with you than I ever was with him."

"Good." I cleared my throat. "I was just about to ask you out to dinner in a couple of days."

"You were?"

"Yeah. I thought we could go out on a night when neither of us had to get up for work the next day."

"You have a one-track mind. Since you're the boss, do you think we could play hooky for the rest of the day?"

"That can be arranged. What's the hurry?"

"I can't concentrate on work. I'm too busy thinking about you naked on your bed at my mercy."

"Christ, let me get my briefcase."

I walked over to my desk, shoved everything off it into the briefcase, grabbed Lily's hand, and dragged her out of the offices and into my car before she could catch her breath.

Lily

I WAS EXCITED ABOUT WHAT I WAS GOING TO DO TO Michael. The thought of him naked with his hands tied to the bedpost was incredibly arousing. The image of his erect penis pointing toward his navel while I did naughty things to him made me wet.

While Michael was in the shower, I wandered around our room naked, trying to find the scarves I had. Yes, I found them buried under my bras.

With a wicked thought in my head, I smiled and walked to the bed, sprawling on top of it. I put the smaller scarf on the nightstand and draped the larger one between my legs, covering my mound. Then, I used another scarf to cover my breasts. Anticipation and excitement pulsed through me as I imagined Michael's reaction when he walked in. I couldn't wait to see desire in his eyes as he took in the sight before him.

The silk against my skin felt delicious, and I was having difficulty staying still because of it.

"Fuck, you look hot."

I caught Michael's gaze. He prowled toward the bed like a predator. His eyes glittered with hope. My heart beat faster. His dick was already standing at attention, its head gleaming. When I saw him, the pulse between my legs throbbed.

I inhaled deeply, trying to stay calm so he would beg. All I wanted was for his thick cock to be inside me, with my sex clamped around it while I writhed beneath him. I sighed and arched off the bed.

"Fucking hell, you're the hottest thing I've ever seen. Is your pussy wet for me?" He knelt on the bed.

"Soaked."

"Then let me take care of you." He went to touch me between my thighs.

"No, don't touch me there. I'll go off like a rocket." I quickly moved away. "Lie down."

He looked at me and stretched out. I took hold of the two scarves and straddled him.

His eyes darkened as my pussy lips rubbed against his chest. I drew in a breath. "Lily, I can feel you. Christ." He arched his hips up from the bed, panting hard.

I leaned over him and secured one of his wrists to the metal headboard. I grabbed his other wrist and did the same. Only then did he pull my breast between his lips. I shuddered. He smiled and released me. I reached for the blindfold, covering his eyes, and heightening his other senses. As I began to explore his body with my hands, he moaned softly, completely under my control. The power dynamic between us shifted, igniting a passion neither of us could resist.

"Hold tight," I told him with a smirk.

I took the smaller scarf and let it drift along the length of his shaft. His penis jerked as he panted and tightened his grip on the headboard.

My fingers trailed along his thigh while I held the scarf in my other hand, moving it between his legs and balls and back up his shaft. It twitched and glistened at the tip.

I placed the scarf over his erection and left it there until I looked up and noticed that he was looking at me beneath the blindfold.

"Don't move." I pushed his legs further apart, put my tongue to his ass, and licked along to his balls. I applied pressure to his perineum before sucking one ball into my mouth, then the other.

He cursed and panted. His penis kept jerking. I didn't want him to climax yet because I hadn't played with him or the scarf yet.

I moved away from between his legs and took the scarf off his shaft. His stomach was wet with creamy precum. Smiling into his eyes, I pulled the scarf through my fingers while he watched me.

"What are you going to do with that?" He gulped.

"Watch."

I licked along his length. His whole body quivered.

I kissed him there, took the scarf, wrapped it around his balls, and tied it. Not too tight and not too loose. He was beside himself.

"Don't come yet."

"Fuck."

I sat back and admired my handiwork. His balls were all tussled up, and his cock was going crazy. He was desperate to come, but not yet.

"You look...wow." I didn't know what to say. There were no words to describe how he looked. There he was, the naked love of my life, lying on the bed with not an inch of fat on his body, his balls tied together, and his large cock desperate for release.

I was so turned on. I leaned over, licking him from base to tip and sucking the mushroom head into my mouth. I lapped up all his moisture while he writhed on the bed and pulled at his restraints.

Then, I did something I wasn't sure would work.

I sucked my finger into my mouth for lubrication while watching his face. His eyes widened. At the same time, I sucked his cock deep into my mouth and released the scarf, putting my finger in his ass.

He nearly threw me off the bed with his prolonged

roar of relief. He came so forcefully that I couldn't bear it. I closed my mouth and continued enjoying myself with my hand. He cursed and tossed his head back, still experiencing the climax.

Oh my God, that was so hot!

Michael finally stilled on the bed. I crawled around him, removed the bindings from his wrists, and the blindfold, and ran to the bathroom to grab a cloth and a towel.

I wiped his stomach and cock, threw the cloth and towel to one side, and settled back on the bed beside him.

He pulled me into his arms as we lay there. Other than when he was released, he hadn't spoken.

"Michael?"

"I think I'm dead. That was fucking awesome!"

"Awesome?" I repeated.

He turned his head and grinned at me. "Yeah, awesome. Just one question, though: Where the hell did you learn that?"

I smiled and kissed his chest. "I read it in a book once. I thought it was hot, and since meeting you, I've wanted to try it. I was too embarrassed at first, but not anymore. Seeing you like that was hot."

"When I get my breath back, I'm going to take care of you."

I looked down and saw that he was aroused again.

Michael

Lily blew my mind with what she did to me. I had never even fantasized about having that done to me. Wow! I'd never come so hard or for so long in my life. Good God. I felt too weak to move, afraid I'd embarrass myself by falling on my ass.

My cock was engorged and eager for Lily's sex. I rolled on top of her, spread her legs, and slipped into her hot, wet folds. I groaned. Lily moaned.

She was tight and wet. I leaned my elbows on either side of her head and kissed her repeatedly. I loved this woman with all my heart, but I was afraid to tell her. I had never said those three words to anyone before, but I knew they were important. One day, I would have the confidence to tell Lily how much she meant to me. Until then, I could show her.

Our bodies moved together in perfect rhythm, each thrust bringing us closer to the edge. The intensity of our connection was unlike anything I had ever experienced. Lily's nails dug into my back as she arched against me. In that moment, I knew I never wanted it to end. Her sex gently quivered as she prepared to climax. Yet, I wanted to prolong her pleasure for as long as possible.

We never looked away from each other when we made love. When she contracted around me, the pressure and her expression sent me spinning, and I came with her.

"Oh, Michael," she whispered.

"I know, babe."

As we lay there catching our breath, I rolled us onto our sides, remaining connected to her as I drew her into my arms and held her. She fell asleep just a few minutes later. I slipped out of her, but continued to hold her as I wondered what the future might bring.

All I knew was that Lily was my future. There was no way I could ever let her go. If she left me, it would kill me.

I stroked the hair down her back, holding her close for what felt like an hour, though it was probably only five minutes.

I heard movement downstairs, so I reluctantly got out of bed, grabbed a pair of jeans and a long-sleeved T-shirt, threw them on quickly, and took one quick glance at Lily before heading downstairs. I found George sitting in the living room with a beer.

I walked straight over to him, removed the beer, and sat down before he noticed I was in the room.

"Not you too," he grumbled.

"Doctor's orders, as you well know."

I sat down across from him and drank his beer, which caused him to scowl.

I grinned.

"That nurse is driving me crazy. I can't have a burger and fries. I can't have a beer. If I smoked, she'd probably tell me I couldn't have a cigarette, too. She also told me I couldn't have sex."

I just looked at him. "Have you asked her if you can have sex?" I hooted with laughter when I saw the startled look on his face. He wouldn't meet my gaze. I lowered my beer. "Please tell me you didn't hit on your nurse." I sat up and rested my elbows on my knees. "George?"

"Maybe a little bit." He squirmed.

"How much is a little bit?"

"Okay, I asked her if I could have sex, and she threw my salad at me. It was a perfectly good lunch, I tell you. Why would she do that? It wasn't as if I asked her to sleep with me. I just wanted to rattle her cage a little. It worked a bit too well."

"I would say so." I decided against taking another drink. With how this conversation was shaping up, I'd probably spit it all over the place.

I couldn't imagine not being allowed to have sex with Lily. My love for her wouldn't change, but it would be hell.

"How would you feel if you couldn't have sex with Lily?"

I snickered. "I was just thinking about that."

"Thinking about what?" Lily asked, walking into the

room in yoga pants and a T-shirt, her wet hair in a ponytail clipped to the top of her head.

She kissed George on the cheek, walked over to me, and climbed onto my lap.

"I missed you," she whispered, kissing me before looking back at George. "So, what were you talking about when I walked in?"

"Sex," George replied, trying to hide his grin behind a cough.

"Excuse me?"

"Babe, George is causing trouble with his nurse."

She gasped and brought her hand to her mouth. "Oh my God! You haven't propositioned your nurse, have you?"

I couldn't hold my laughter in any longer and laughed at him.

"You didn't?" Lily still couldn't believe that he had.

"Now, Lily, you have Michael to satisfy your urges." I slammed the bottle down, and Lily chuckled.

"Hang on a minute." I wasn't happy.

"Don't get your shorts in a twist, Michael. I was just pointing out..."

"Let's not. And you're not to drink beer. You need to go back to your place, apologize, and explain exactly what you meant."

He stood up in a huff. "Well, I thought you would at least support me."

"George, I do support you, and so does Lily. But you

can't go around saying the word 'sex' to your nurse," I told him, holding Lily against my chest as she laughed.

"Okay, I'm going. I guess I'd better apologize the minute I enter, before she slugs me with the skillet."

He walked out, and Lily and I burst out laughing. "Unbelievable."

"He's so funny." Lily said, kissing my neck.

I moved away from her slightly. "If you keep doing that, I guarantee we're going to have sex." I smiled. "I'd like to spend the rest of the evening with you in my arms on this sofa, watching a movie. Then, I'll take you to our bed, where I'll make slow, passionate love to you before holding you in my arms for the rest of the night. In the morning, I'll wake you up with kisses and make love to you again."

"Michael," she whispered, taking my face in her hands, and kissing me. When she moved away, I pulled her back, and she snuggled down.

I got the TV remote, and we started watching Titanic, Lily's favorite movie.

28

Lily

MICHAEL AND I HAD BEEN TOGETHER FOR ONLY TWENTY-five days, but I couldn't have been happier. I loved him, and although we hadn't said it out loud, I felt that he loved me, too. Sometimes, I'd catch him looking at me with so much love, but when he caught me looking back, he'd grin and say something mischievous.

Most mornings, I'd wake up in his arms. On the mornings he wasn't there, I'd wake up to the smell of coffee when he walked back through the door. I told Michael numerous times that he didn't have to make me coffee in bed every morning, but he insisted on taking care of me.

I had yet to wake up before him so I could return the favor. More than once, though, I showed him my appreciation while we showered together. He had a fabulous body that I couldn't keep my hands off. He said his toned abs were from playing rugby with his brothers.

Michael had gotten over his jealousy of seeing me socialize with Lucien. I think he realized that Lucien treated me like a little sister. That was good because Lucien had quickly become my best friend, aside from Michael.

"Ms. Redmond?"

I jumped up. "Yes." I'd forgotten for a few minutes that I was sitting in the doctor's office. I told Michael that I was going shopping for his mother's birthday present while he was in a meeting across town. What I didn't want him to know yet was that my menstrual cycle was five days late. I'd never been late in my life. Always four weeks to the day.

"Please take a seat, Ms. Redmond. I'm Doctor Julia Forrester. How can I help you today?"

I took a deep breath. "I think I might be pregnant," I blurted out.

She smiled. "I see. Well, we should do a pregnancy test." She stood up and handed me a white stick. "Do you know what to do with this?"

"Pee on the stick."

"Yes, the bathroom is just outside my door, to your right. Once you've finished, just put the lid back on and come back in here."

"Okay."

I walked to the bathroom on wobbly legs and got down to business. I was excited about the possibility of carrying Michael's child, but I was also terrified that he wouldn't be happy if I was pregnant. I couldn't imagine that, but since we hadn't talked about having children, I honestly had no idea how he would feel about being a father.

When I was with David, the thought of children never crossed my mind because I knew he couldn't have any, though he insisted on using condoms anyway. Now, the possibility that I might be able to have a child and start the family I had always secretly craved filled me with joy.

I looked down at the stick. Positive. Oh boy! I must have been sitting in the bathroom for more than five minutes because the nurse knocked on the door to see if I was okay.

After straightening my clothes, I nervously made my way back to the doctor's office.

The doctor took one look at me, took the stick from my hand, and led me to the bed on the other side of the room.

"Do I have your consent to perform an internal scan so we can see what's going on?"

All I could manage was a nod. I'd expected the result to be positive, but it was still shocking to have it confirmed.

"I'll just pull this curtain around." Please remove

everything from the waist down. Lie back on the bed, relax, and try to be as comfortable as possible. Cover up with this blanket," Doctor Forrester told me.

As I undressed, I couldn't stop thinking about Michael and how he would react. I prayed the news would be welcome.

After getting comfortable on the bed and covering myself with the blanket, I tried to calm down. This was nerve-racking, and I really wished Michael had been with me.

"Are you ready, Lily?" Doctor Forrester asked.

Ready or not, I replied, "Yes."

The doctor appeared around the curtain with the nurse who had shown me into the room. The nurse moved forward and held my hand while Dr. Forrester positioned my legs for the internal scan.

I felt slight discomfort when the head of the probe was pushed inside me, but I forgot all about it when Doctor Forrester pointed to the bean on the screen.

"That's your baby, Lily." I started to cry. "Would you like me to print a picture so you can show the father?" I nodded, unable to find my voice. I was going to have Michael's baby. I couldn't wait to tell him. He loved me. I knew he did. Maybe if I told him first, he would find the courage to tell me, too. Was that the problem? Was he afraid to tell me? I hoped that was all it was.

I left the doctor's office with a prescription for prenatal vitamins and a smile on my face. Was I happy that I was pregnant? Yes. I was bursting with happiness. But was I terrified of telling Michael that I was pregnant with his child? Yes. We'd never discussed having children. We never used protection when we made love. I'd never considered going back on the pill, and Michael never used a condom, so it wasn't surprising that I was pregnant.

The office wasn't too far away, so I decided to walk. Then I could stop in a boutique and buy his mother a birthday present. I thought about how happy Pippa would be to finally have a grandchild. She had confided in me that she really wanted one, although a shadow crossed her face when she admitted it. She'd had enough of her sons being "man whores," as she called them. I laughed when she said that and commented that they couldn't be that bad. Then it was her turn to laugh and say they were worse.

I didn't know how to respond, so I changed the subject.

I was pregnant. I was pregnant. Maybe if I said it enough times, it would feel real. I couldn't wait to have a big belly with our baby inside it. I wanted to go shopping with Michael for everything the baby would need.

I stood outside the boutique, pushed the door open, and stepped inside. I began browsing the jewelry display to select something for Pippa.

Michael

I sat in the large chair in the lounge, a whiskey in hand for courage, and watched the clouds break up and move away through the window.

I was glad today was almost over. I had a huge surprise for Lily—if I didn't back out at the last minute, that is. I was nervous as hell.

This morning, I told Lily that I had a last-minute meeting with a company across town and wouldn't be back for a couple of hours. She'd been distracted and asked if she could take an hour or two to go shopping for my mother's birthday. I kissed her and told her it was fine, and that I'd see her later.

Every time I thought about Lily, my heart quivered. She was my whole world, and I planned to find the courage to tell her just how much she meant to me.

This morning, my business meeting had been a trip to the jewelers, where I purchased a stunning platinum engagement ring. The diamond wasn't too big—Lily wasn't the flashy type—but the cluster of small diamonds around the slightly larger one really made the ring stand out. All I had left to do was find the courage to propose and tell her how much I loved her. I was nervous as hell.

"Michael, are you all right?" she asked as she walked into the room.

I held my hand out to her. She walked straight over to me, slid her fingers through mine, and sat on my lap. I pulled her close and nuzzled her neck. She always smelled delicious—like my woman.

She lifted her face to mine, placing light kisses around my lips before sealing her mouth to mine. She turned and straddled my thighs, fusing our tongues together. I abruptly put my drink down on the table beside the chair and put my hands on the back of Lily's head, deepening the kiss.

Lily began to wriggle around on top of my cock, which had hardened the moment our mouths met. I moved my hands down to her hips and thighs, then slid them up inside her dress to her ass. Fuck! She wasn't wearing panties. I was done for.

She smiled against my mouth. "Surprise." She moved her hips slightly, undid my zipper, and reached inside for my happy cock. I was on the brink of an orgasm every time she touched me. She rubbed the head with her thumb, then lifted and impaled herself on my excited shaft.

I was balls-deep inside her, and nothing had ever felt better. She wriggled closer, and my eyes rolled back in pleasure. I could have come inside Lily without moving because I was so excited to be surrounded by her heated sex.

She had changed into a sundress as soon as we came home, so she slid the straps down her arms while I pulled the dress down to her waist. Her breasts were magnificent. Large and perfect. I bent her back slightly over my arm and put my mouth to one of her breasts. Her nipples were rock hard as I licked and suckled them, rolling the other one between my fingers.

Her breasts were sensitive to my touch; she was more aroused now than before. Her sex quivered around me, and her wetness coated my groin. My cock jerked in excitement.

"Michael, help me move," she said, trying to move her hips. I gritted my teeth and tried to conjure an unpleasant scenario to prolong the experience for her. However, she was able to move and touch the tip of my penis. Our breathing was labored, and my balls were heavy. She slammed back down on me, and I lost it. I grabbed her hips and ground her into me as I came. Then, Lily started to orgasm around me. She was so tight, and her vagina contracting around me always managed to make my orgasm last longer than with anyone else.

Even as she collapsed against my chest, her vagina fluttered along my penis, keeping me hard.

"I love having you inside me."

She was going to kill me. "Lily," I said warningly.

I could feel her grin against my neck where she was buried. "Your dick is so thick and long, with a huge head. Just thinking about having you inside my pussy or my mouth makes me wet." My dick jerked inside her. "Mmm, and when you come in my mouth, it makes me feel powerful knowing that I make you lose control like that. Sometimes you flood my mouth, and I must finish you off with my hand, which is hot because I get to watch you. It's such a turn-on watching you come."

"Fuck, will you stop talking?"

She started to laugh while squeezing her inner muscles, clamping down on my cock.

"Stop. Go upstairs, put on your yoga pants and a T-shirt with underwear. Then, we're going to have a nice meal out on the back deck. Afterwards, we'll go to bed, and I'll make love to you."

"Sounds good."

I helped her stand up and watched her walk out of the room to change while I shoved my cock back into my jeans. Then, I headed for the kitchen to check on the potatoes.

The salad was all chopped. I'd just finished setting the table when Lily appeared in the doorway, looking odd.

"Are you okay?" I asked.

She just stood and watched me. "I'm pregnant," she blurted out.

I wasn't sure I'd heard her correctly. "What?"

She seemed to gather her courage. "I went to the

doctor's this morning. I'm pregnant. We're going to have a baby in about eight months." She smiled.

Her words made my heart race. I never expected to hear what Lily said, but I did, and it broke my heart. How could she have done that to me? I should have told her that I couldn't have children. Then, at the very least, she wouldn't be standing in front of me, announcing her pregnancy. It couldn't be mine, so it must be someone else's child. Everything was a mess, and I needed to leave before I did something I'd regret.

"I'm going out. Don't be here when I get back," I said, barely able to speak.

Her face fell. "Michael, I understand it wasn't intentional, but please don't leave me. I love you," she said in a terrified voice. I turned away from her and began to leave. I froze when I heard the words I desperately wanted to hear. But I couldn't be with her right now.

"Just leave, and don't come back," I told her.

I turned and walked out, leaving Lily in tears in the kitchen, and my whole world fell apart.

29

Lily

"LILY, PLEASE TALK TO ME. I CAN'T HELP YOU IF YOU don't tell me what's wrong." Lucien had been asking me this question ever since he picked me up from Michael's house after Michael left me in tears.

I couldn't speak. I cried all over Lucien, unable to stop the tears. One minute, everything was wonderful, and I was overjoyed. The next, Michael told me to leave. I had assumed that he loved me and would embrace our child. When I told him I was pregnant, his entire demeanor changed. I had no idea what to do, so I called my friend Lucien to pick me up. I was still sobbing all over him. I needed to tell him; maybe he would know why Michael had acted the way he did.

After a slight adjustment, I was out of his arms and

sitting upright in the chair. I brushed away my tears and blew my nose. I turned to Lucien. "I told Michael that I'm pregnant." His eyes widened in surprise. "I love him, Lucien." I started crying again. "When I told him, he said he was going out and that I had to be gone when he got back. Why would he say that to me? I thought he loved me too. He's never said it, but the way he looks at me makes me think he does." I took hold of Lucien's hands. "Do you know why he acted like he did?" Lucien turned away but kept hold of my hands. "Lucien, please. If you know, please tell me."

He pulled me back into his arms and stroked my back as I cried. "How far along are you?" Lucien asked.

"Close to five weeks, but I conceived about three weeks ago." They date the pregnancy from the first day of your last period. Lucien, if you knew what was going on, would you tell me?" I asked him.

"Lily, please don't ask me that."

I sat up. "You do know," I accused.

"I'm not actually sure. I have an idea, but I need to talk to Michael first."

"I feel sick," I groaned.

Lucien jumped up from his chair and carried me to the bathroom just in time for me to throw up. When I was finished, I stayed on the bathroom floor in a heap, crying.

"Do you think you'll be all right if I carry you through to the bedroom?"

I nodded.

He picked me up and carried me to his bedroom, where he laid me on the bed. He covered me with a fleece blanket, then walked back to the bathroom. He returned with a washcloth.

He sat on the edge of the bed and wiped my face while I watched him. He was a great guy.

"Thank you for taking care of me." I didn't know who else to call. Maybe I shouldn't have called you because you're Michael's brother," I said, my voice catching, "but I needed you." Tears welled up in my eyes again.

"Lily, we're friends, okay? I'm glad you called me. I really am. At first, you scared me when I saw you. I thought something had happened to Michael."

"I'm sorry."

"You don't need to keep apologizing. Lily, can I ask you something without you screaming at me?"

I moaned. "Okay, I promise no bodily harm."

He took a deep breath and met my eyes. "You've lived with Michael now..."

"Twenty-five days," I interrupted.

"Twenty-five days. Is there any chance you could be further along than three weeks?"

I shook my head. "No, I conceived about three weeks ago, but I'm five weeks pregnant."

"All right. Sorry, you've already told me that. Is there any chance David got you pregnant?"

Why was he asking me these questions? "You don't believe me, do you? That this is Michael's baby?"

"I…"

"Don't say anything. David had a vasectomy four years ago. There's a disease that runs in his family that can harm an unborn child, so he didn't want to put anyone through what his parents went through twice after he was born. He was particular about it, insisting that I use the pill and that he uses a condom. I ran out of the pill and didn't bother to replace it. The only other man I've had sex with is Michael, and we never used protection. Does that answer your question?"

"Sort of," he replied.

I just looked at him. What did he mean by "sort of"? That wasn't an answer. "Yes" or "no" would have been more appropriate.

"Listen, Lily. I need to find Michael and make sure he's okay. I texted my mom, and she's on her way to stay with you." I panicked. "It's okay. She'll look after you. But I don't want to leave you here alone, okay?"

"I guess."

"Try to rest. If you need anything, I'll be outside until my mom gets here."

"All right. Tell him I love him. Ask him to come talk to me in the morning, please. I need to know why he reacted the way he did."

"Don't you want to talk to him tonight?"

I shook my head. "No, I need to rest and think. I'm

not sure I can handle seeing him tonight. He broke my heart, Lucien. Nothing has ever hurt as much, yet I still love him." I started crying again.

"I know you do. I'll tell him to wait until tomorrow to come talk to you."

"Thank you."

Lucien hugged me before walking out of the room and shutting the door. I cried myself to sleep.

Michael

Lily had left. I told her to go, and she did. Why didn't she wait for me to come back? Because I told her to. I was an idiot. I loved her. I still loved her. How could she do this to me? I really thought she loved me. Could I live with knowing that the child she was carrying wasn't mine? I wasn't sure.

For the first time since I was a young boy, I felt like crying. She'd looked nervous but happy when she blurted out that she was pregnant. When she saw my anger, her face fell; her tears started to fall.

I assumed she'd been unfaithful, like Viv, but what if she'd gotten pregnant before moving in with me? Could I accept her baby if he were the father? Maybe! If he were the father, that would mean she hadn't been unfaithful. We would have a child together. We could raise the child together and maybe let him see the child once a week. Okay, I liked the idea. But who am I kidding? It would break my heart to see her breastfeed someone else's child.

"Michael."

"Lucien."

My brother was standing in the doorway of the living room, and he looked angry.

"Brother, what brings you to my abode?"

"The woman you love," he replied.

I should have known she would run to Lucien; they were friends. He was the only friend she had made since moving in with me.

"You're an ass, Michael. How could you kick her out like that?" he asked, walking closer and sitting opposite me.

"She's pregnant."

"I'm aware of that, but I still can't get my head around you are kicking the pregnant woman you love out of her home."

"She. Is. Pregnant."

"Talk to me, brother, because I left a very distressed and sick woman who loves you in my hotel room with Mom."

"Oh, fuck. Why did you have to get Mom involved? What do you mean she's sick?"

"Because I needed to check on you, and I couldn't do

that with how upset Lily is. I didn't want to leave her alone."

It hurt knowing she was so upset because of me. "Is she really that bad?" I asked, hoping he was exaggerating.

"Yes, I had to hold her hair back while she threw up in the toilet. Then, I carried her to bed, and she cried herself to sleep."

I wiped away a few tears that had leaked out.

"Michael, I know you love her, and I can see how much this hurts you. Why didn't you tell her?"

"I thought she would leave me."

"So, you let her tell you she was pregnant, and then you kicked her out anyway?" Lucien said. I really wish he would just shut up.

"How pregnant is she?" I asked, knowing that at least then I would know if the baby was his or someone else's.

"She's about five weeks along. The doctor said she conceived about three weeks ago."

It isn't his. She was just like Viv. God, I trusted her. I gave her my heart. I told her that I knew she was nothing like Viv, and I meant it.

I leaned forward and buried my head in my hands as the tears flowed. They wouldn't stop.

"Michael, you assume Lily was unfaithful, but when was she supposed to have done so? Think about it. Since she moved in with you, she has either been with you, in the office, or having coffee with me. As far as I know, she's never gone anywhere alone."

I heard him and was perplexed. What he said was true. She was always with him or me.

"I can see the wheels spinning, and I swear to God that if you say what just flashed across your face, I will hit you. You know me better than that. You know Lily better than that, too."

"Sorry," I mumbled. What he said was true.

"Are you sure the results you got back then were accurate? Do you always have sex without a condom?"

I grabbed some tissues, wiped my face, and exhaled. "I thought they were. I never used protection with Viv throughout our marriage. I stopped having sex with her the moment I found out she had been unfaithful. I never considered using a condom with Lily. To me, she was my woman. I didn't need to."

"Do you still have the paperwork somewhere?"

"No, I never saw them. Viv told me the results."

His eyes widened. "You, my brother, are a fucking idiot. How could you believe that bitch without seeing evidence?"

He was right. Had I completely ruined my relationship with Lily because I'd believed Viv? I sat back and contemplated what we had just discussed. Could Lucien be right? Viv had lied about many things, but I never expected her to lie about something so serious.

Once I had calmed down, I realized that I was a jerk, a particularly insensitive one at that. Lily had my heart like no one else ever had. I trusted her. If I'd been thinking straight when she made the announcement, I hoped I would have reacted differently.

There was no way Lily would have had an affair, which could only mean that I was the father. I felt my eyes well with tears. All these years, I'd thought I would never be able to father a child—and I had. I destroyed Lily when I told her to leave. I was a bastard. I needed to make things right.

"Michael, you need to take another test. I'll arrange it tomorrow," Lucien said. I'd forgotten he was still in the room.

"No."

"What do you mean, 'no'? There's a heartbroken woman you love in my hotel room. She needs to know why you reacted the way you did. You need to know the truth. So yes, I will make you an appointment, and you will keep it."

"I do know the truth," I said. He raised an eyebrow in curiosity. "Lily would never have been unfaithful to me. When she told me she was pregnant, I didn't believe it could be mine. I saw red and spoke without thinking first. I adore her so much, Lucien, that it scares me. I know Viv lied to me. I know deep down that I am the father of Lily's child." I struck my chest where my heart was. "A test will just confirm what I already know, and I need Lily to believe me regardless. I need her to know that I genuinely trust her. I believe her, even without a piece of paper stating the truth. Do you understand?"

He stood and smiled at me. "Yeah, I do. It's about time. You need to come with me to the hotel in the morning and tell her. She needs to hear it from you."

"I know. Let's go." I started to walk out of the room.

"Not yet." He looked uncomfortable. "Lily wanted me to ask you to talk to her in the morning and explain why you reacted the way you did. She just wants to be alone tonight."

"Lucien, I need to talk to her now."

"I promised her, Michael. Please don't make me break my promise."

I was stunned. How could he expect me to wait until morning? "I don't like this."

"I know you don't. You broke her heart, Michael. Leave her to sleep. She could use the rest. I'll have you there first thing in the morning."

"I guess." I ran my hands through my hair as I walked back to the cabinet holding the whiskey and retrieved the ring I'd left there earlier when I poured myself a much-needed drink.

"I went shopping at the jeweler's this morning. I bought her an engagement ring." I opened the small black box and showed Lucien. He whistled.

"That's Lily. She'll love it once you've spent a long time groveling on your knees."

"I hope she loves it. I'll spend the rest of my life groveling if that's what it takes."

30

Lily

I OPENED MY EYES AND REMEMBERED EVERYTHING THAT had happened the night before. Tears welled in my eyes, and before I could stop them, I started sobbing again.

"Lily, please stop crying. You're breaking my heart."

I cried even harder.

"Now, now, honey. Come here. Let me hold you."

I turned over and found myself wrapped in Pippa's arms. She patted my back.

After about ten minutes, I started to calm down, moved away from her, and sat up. On unsteady legs, I made my way to the bathroom.

"I'm just going to take a quick shower. I won't be long."

I shut the door, stripped, and got into the shower. I

needed a shower, but it was partly an excuse. I wasn't sure what to say to Michael's mom. I badly wanted to know why he behaved the way he did. I knew he struggled with trust, but all I wanted was to be back home with him, his arms around me, assuring me that everything would be fine.

I washed my hair with Lucien's shampoo, then washed my body. I smoothed my hand over my stomach, which sheltered our child.

Determined not to cry again, I turned off the shower and climbed out. I took my time drying off and found Lucien's robe behind the door. I quickly put it on and wrapped a towel around my hair.

When I walked out of the bathroom, I realized that I hadn't brought any clothes with me. Looking at the bed, I found a pair of leggings and a T-shirt, which I presumed Pippa had brought me.

I dressed quickly and walked into the living room to find Pippa sitting at the table by the window, eating breakfast.

"Do you feel better?" she asked.

I tried not to cry again. "A bit." I walked over to the table and took a seat across from her.

"I wasn't sure what you like to eat, so I ordered a few things." She stood up. "Let me pour you a coffee." My stomach rebelled.

"I think I'll stick to the orange juice but thank you."

She looked at me funny and took her seat again

while I slowly sipped the juice. My stomach growled, making Pippa laugh.

"What would you like to eat, Lily?"

"I'll just have the fruit for now, please."

She passed me a bowl containing strawberries, melon, grapes, and orange slices, and it slid down my throat rather well, considering the huge lump that was stuck there.

"Lily," she said in a questioning voice. "Michael can be an idiot at times. I don't know what happened between you two, but I want you to know that in his thirty-six years, he's never been in love until now. He was badly hurt by what Viv did to him. Has he talked about her?"

I nodded.

"She was a wicked woman. He married her thinking with his dick instead of his head and heart."

I laughed, stunned that she would say "dick."

"Viv never touched his heart, and no one else has either. I'm guessing it's something Michael has done that made you run to Lucien. But please be patient with him while he works everything out."

"I'm pregnant," I blurted out.

She was stunned. "You are?"

"Yes. The doctor thinks I conceived about three weeks ago." My eyes welled up with tears again. I told Michael, and within seconds, he ordered me out of his house. Why would he do that? I think Lucien knows, but he wanted to speak with Michael first. Do you understand why?"

Pippa had tears on her cheeks. "Are you sure that's how far along you are?"

I looked at her strangely. First, Lucien asked me this question, and now their mother. Why? I was starting to get annoyed.

"Yes, I'm sure. Or rather, the doctor was sure after giving me an ultrasound." I stood up and started pacing. "David had a vasectomy four years ago, and I haven't slept with him since I met Michael. The only person I've slept with is Michael. Why did both you and Lucien ask me that question? Please tell me, Pippa."

She shook her head. "You need to talk to Michael."

Then it hit me. I knew why. "He thinks he can't have children. I'm right, aren't I?"

Pippa just nodded.

"Why, though? Why would he think that? Surely, telling him that I'm pregnant would make him happy rather than angry."

I didn't finish, as a thought struck me. Did he think I'd been unfaithful to him?

I felt the color drain from my face as I sat back down abruptly. I felt sick to my stomach. How could he even think that?

Pippa just looked at me with an odd expression. "He thinks I've been unfaithful to him, doesn't he?"

"Maybe," she whispered.

"How could he think that? I love him. I've only ever slept with two men in my life: David and Michael."

I stood up and stormed to the bedroom to find my purse. If Michael thought I'd been unfaithful, he was going to hear about it. I started to cry heavily, burying my face in a pillow on the bed.

"Lily," Pippa whispered. I felt her climb onto the bed with me. She pulled me into her arms. Being held by a mom overwhelmed me, and the tears fell even faster.

"How could he think that? I never looked at another guy when I was with David until Michael came along." I sniffled. "He's all I want. I never gave David my heart, but I gave it to Michael. I can't believe..."

I couldn't talk anymore because of my tears.

Michael

On the way to the hotel, I prayed that Lily would accept my apology and explanation, something I hadn't done in a long time. I was the world's biggest idiot for acting the way I did. Yes, I'd been burned in the past, but I knew Lily well enough to know that she wouldn't do anything like I'd first imagined.

When she blurted out that she was pregnant, I was so shocked that I couldn't think straight. I reacted by thinking the worst, but then last night, when Lucien asked questions, I came to my senses.

I had the engagement ring in my pocket and was prepared to beg if necessary. Losing her wasn't an option.

Lucien kept looking at me out of the corner of his eye. It started to give me a complex. I knew I didn't look my best. Unable to sleep last night, I sat in the "cave" with the television on—I couldn't tell you what I was watching—and thought about Lily. I thought back over the past twenty-five days and how fulfilled my life had been.

"Michael, I think you should have shaved before leaving this morning," Lucien said.

"All I want to do is be with Lily. If I'd shaved, it would have taken even longer to leave. I need to see her. Hold her. I need to tell her what a fucking idiot I am and hope she forgives me because I really don't know what I'll do if she refuses. Do you think she'll refuse to listen to me and accept my apology?"

Lucien parked the car, then turned to look at me. "I don't think she'll give up on you. But if she's upset after what you said to her, then all I can say is you deserve it. Come on, let's go."

We both climbed out of the car and made our way into the hotel. We got a few stares in the lobby, but I didn't care. Lucien shoved me into the elevator, and that's when I caught sight of myself.

"Fuck." I ran my hands through my hair, trying to straighten it. There was no hope for my wrinkled shirt. The jeans weren't too bad. You could always rely on denim.

Outside the room, I was terrified. Whatever I said in there would either strengthen or destroy my relationship with Lily.

I raised my hand to knock when Lucien used his key card to open the door. "I told Mom I'd let myself in when I got back. She might be in the bedroom with Lily."

He pushed the door open, but there was no Lily in the room. Lucien pointed to a door to the left. "The bedrooms are through there." I stood there, unable to move. Lucien sighed. "Michael, Mom probably knows I'm back. Get in there and talk to Lily."

My brother shoved me toward the bedroom door, and I knocked before I could turn tail.

The door opened slightly, and my mom stepped out.

"She cried herself to sleep. What's really going on, Michael?" She placed my face between her hands, kissed my cheek, and hugged me tightly. Then, she let me go and stared at me. "I don't believe there's been anyone else since she met you. She's too heartbroken."

I wiped a stray tear away. "There hasn't been. I knew that when she told me about the baby. I just heard the word 'pregnant' and didn't think. I love her mom so much." Good God, I was so close to breaking down. Could I be any more pathetic?

Mom opened the bedroom door for me. I hesitated at the threshold before carefully walking in. Lily was lying on the bed with her eyes closed. Worry lines creased her forehead, and she had dark circles under her eyes. I winced with guilt, knowing that I had caused them. Despite her worry, she was the most breathtaking woman I'd ever seen.

I just wanted to climb onto the bed with her, hold her, and tell her how much I loved her and how sorry I was.

"Michael?"

"Yeah," I croaked. "It's me, babe."

She sat up on the bed, looking sexy as hell. I sat on the edge of the bed next to her.

She moved closer to me.

"God, Lily. I don't know where to start." I caressed her face, and she melted into my palm. She turned her face and kissed my palm. That kiss filled my heart with hope. Maybe all wasn't lost. I sure as hell hoped it wasn't. "Will you listen to what I have to say before you ask anything?"

She sat back on the bed and nodded.

"Oh, boy." I moved closer to her, took her hands in mine, and looked her in the eye. "Before I do, I need you to know that I love you with all my heart." Tears started to leak from her eyes. I couldn't hold back my tears anymore. "To hell with this."

I stood up, climbed onto the bed, and wrapped her in my arms. We melted against each other while she sobbed. I lay down on the bed and pulled her back into my arms.

"I'm so sorry, Lily. You have no idea how sorry I am. I was a bastard to you. I spoke first without thinking. I need to tell you why," I said. She looked up at me and probably saw that my face was covered in tears.

"I know why," she whispered.

"You do?"

"I figured it out, and I can't believe you thought I'd been with someone else while I was with you. That's what I can't get over. Please make me understand."

I tucked her head under my chin, held her tight, and fought back my own tears.

"Viv wanted to have a baby. We tried for a while and nothing happened, so she arranged to have these tests done. A few days later, I discovered she'd been having an affair. Not just one, but several. I didn't sleep with her again after that. When we received the results, she said that I was the problem. I was an idiot and believed her. All this time, I thought I would never be able to have a...

I couldn't finish." She held me tight, lifted her face to mine, and kissed my tears away.

"Lily, I'll spend the rest of my life making it up to you. Please forgive me for how I reacted before. When you first told me you were pregnant, I was so hurt that I lashed out at you. I was hurt, so I lashed out at you. It took Lucien talking to me to realize just how much of a bastard I was, and to see what Viv did."

She kissed my eyes. She kissed my nose. She kissed my lips. "You hurt me, Michael. I thought my heart was breaking, but I love you. Knowing what you thought explains why you reacted the way you did. You were upset, and I understand that. But how could you think I would be with someone else when I have you? You're all I want and need."

"Yeah, I thought that. I guess my hang-up goes deep. Yesterday, I wasn't in a meeting. I went to the jewelers. I planned on asking you to marry me last night until I messed everything up."

"You were?" She was stunned. "Do you still want to ask me?" She smiled at me, and then her grin spread wider.

I climbed off the bed and knelt on one knee. She moved to sit in front of me. "Lily, I'm the biggest idiot around, but no one will ever love you as much as I do. I promise to never be such a jerk again, and to always love you and our children. You and our family will always come first. Will you marry me?"

She cried. "I love you so much, Michael. Yes, I'll marry you." She threw her arms around my neck, and our momentum sent us both tumbling to the floor.

31

Lily

I WAS LYING IN MICHAEL'S ARMS ON THE FLOOR, AND I never wanted to leave them. I understood why he'd reacted the way he did. It still hurt, but not as much. I loved him too much to let it come between us. I just held on to him.

We laughed, and then I looked into his eyes, my mood turning serious. "Michael, I love you. You're the only one I want. I understand your hang-up because of what Viv did to you, but I can't live with you mistrusting me because of her."

"Lily, last night, when I thought I'd lost you, I realized what I'd done. I realized that I trust you. I don't need to remember what Viv did because I have the chance to make new memories with you."

"You've turned me to mush," I said, then sealed my mouth to Michael's. He opened his mouth and sucked my tongue into his. I wrapped my arms around his neck and held on tight. He really was my world.

His hands were on my T-shirt seconds before he pulled it over my head. "Michael, we can't. Not here."

Lucien has taken Mom out for breakfast." He grinned.

I quickly stood up, took off my leggings, and climbed onto the bed.

"Fuck." Michael jumped up from the floor, took off his clothes, and crawled onto the huge bed behind me. I got on all fours, spreading my legs so he could see straight between my thighs.

He held my legs apart, licking between them before shoving his tongue into me. I moaned.

"Your pussy is soaked." He put his mouth back on me. "Your clit is swollen." He sucked it into his mouth. "Put your face on the bed and keep your ass in the air." I did as I was told. He spread my legs wider and used his finger. He rubbed between my pussy lips, spreading my arousal up between my buttocks.

I couldn't stay still, writhing under the onslaught of his fingers and mouth. My breasts rubbed against the bed while Michael had his mouth between my thighs. I felt like I was experiencing sensory overload.

I cried out as I came hard with his tongue inside me and his fingers rubbing my clit. He didn't let up, and I could feel myself heading toward another climax when he moved from behind me, rolled me onto my back, and continued.

We were both breathing heavily. My pussy was so wet, and Michael's cock was huge and leaking with arousal.

"I want you to taste yourself on me." He slammed his mouth down on mine, giving me the most erotic kiss of my life. It went on and on while he rubbed his dick against my hip.

He pulled away, grabbed the belt from the robe I'd left on the chair by the bed, and tied my hands together. He looked at me and grinned. "Your turn." He kissed me, then tied my right wrist to the headboard and followed with my left.

When I was all tied up, he sat back and admired his handiwork. "You're beautiful," he said. He moved in, starting with a quick kiss on my lips. Then he moved on to licking my neck and nibbling my ear, sending tingles all the way to my core.

As my breathing sped up, he moved down my body, caressing one of my breasts gently and playing with my nipple. He took my other breast into his mouth and massaged my nipple with his tongue.

"You taste good," he told me. I moaned and tried to touch him. "Behave. I'm going to love you well."

He licked down my stomach to my pubic bone while

caressing my sides, hips, and thighs. I felt like I was about to combust internally.

"Your pussy is so sweet. It's always wet and pulsing."

"Only for you," I shouted when he put his mouth between my legs and kissed me as if it were my mouth.

He moved up my body, using his knees to gently push my legs apart and allow himself to slide directly into me. I arched my back in pleasure as he began moving in and out of me slowly and deliberately. With each thrust, I felt myself getting closer and closer to the edge of ecstasy. He moved his legs to the outside of mine and pushed them closer together. The pleasure became intense.

"I love you, Lily. So much." He kissed me and slowly moved his hips. He pulled his penis out until only the tip remained inside me, and then slowly entered me again. I threw my head back and arched my back. He groaned. "Fuck, that felt good. Do it again."

I arched my back off the bed, tightening my sex even more. I watched Michael through hooded eyes. He gritted his teeth and rolled his eyes in pleasure.

He clamped his mouth on my breast, sucking my nipple into his mouth. Then he used his tongue to rub it against the roof of his mouth.

We both breathed heavily. "I can't stop."

"Don't," I replied.

Michael started thrusting in and out of me. I felt him swell, and then my orgasm hit. I screamed and came hard while Michael cursed above me, covering the walls of my vagina with his thick semen. Thinking about his cock shooting its load inside me set me off again.

"Please," I said. I wasn't sure what I was asking for, but my second orgasm wouldn't stop.

"Jesus, Lily, I've never come so fucking hard until I met you. My cock's still shooting." He groaned, and with one slight thrust, he collapsed on top of me.

I could still feel him twitching inside me. Michael slid free, untied me, and rolled onto his side, pulling me with him.

"I love you, and I hope you know how much. I'm going to spend the rest of my life telling you, so you better get used to it now."

I smiled against his naked chest. "I do know. I love you, too. You better never doubt it again because if you do, there won't be any makeup sex. In fact, there won't be any sex for six months. So, if you mess up again, I expect a vibrator as a 'sorry' present."

He roared with laughter, which was my intention.

Michael

I woke up with Lily in my arms and had no intention of moving. She was still upset that I'd thought she'd been with someone else because of her pregnancy. I was an idiot, willing to spend the rest of my life begging for forgiveness if she stayed with me.

After making love to her in Lucien's hotel room—which made me cringe when I realized it—we dressed, and Lucien drove us back to our home. I spent the rest of the day making sure Lily was well taken care of.

Lucien promised to explain to Mom what had been going on and our conclusion that Viv had lied to me. Why I accepted what she told me all those years ago without following up, I really couldn't say. All I knew was that I thought I'd never be able to father a child, but I had with Lily.

"What are you thinking about with that serious look on your face?"

I hadn't realized she was awake. "I was thinking about what a jerk I was, how close I came to losing you, and that I'm going to spend the rest of my life making it up to you."

She had tears in her eyes. "Michael, you don't need to spend the rest of your life making it up to me. I love you, and I know how sorry you are. I understand where you're coming from. Yes, you hurt me, and you hurt me badly. I'm not going to deny that. But I love you, and I know you love me. If you don't do anything like that again, we'll be fine. Please stop worrying that I'm going to leave you because of it. I won't." She smiled at me through her tears. "It would kill me to leave you. Don't you know that?"

Now she had me in tears. "I love you so damn much." I pulled her tightly into my arms and held on while trying to control my emotions. She really did crush me.

I pulled back slightly. "We need to get dressed. Lucien is downstairs. He probably wants to make sure you're okay."

"All right." She looked at me, holding my face in her hands. "I want you to take another test."

I couldn't have been more stunned.

"Michael, I know this baby is yours because I know who I've slept with. But all these years, you've believed you couldn't father a child. For me and for this relation-ship to move forward, it's important for you to hear from the doctor that your little swimmers are good."

"I don't want to do that. Believe me when I say that I know you weren't with anyone else, and this child is yours. I need you to believe me without the test getting in the way. Do you understand where I'm coming from?"

She smiled at me. "Yes, but you're still having the test done. I sent Lucien a text and asked him to set it up for you. Don't be angry with me, but it's important to me that you take the test. I believe you when you say this child is yours. I really do. But this test is getting done today."

I wasn't sure whether to be angry or not. I hated

being forced to do something I didn't want to do, but Lily was adamant that this was what she wanted.

"Besides, think how hot it will be...me going down on you in the doctor's office. Mmm, a real turn-on."

I couldn't believe my ears. "Lily, there is absolutely no way you are coming with me to the doctor's office if I must do this. I can't believe you'd want to come and watch me masturbate into a pot."

She sat up and looked pissed. "Let's get something straight. I'm going with you, and there won't be any masturbation." She grinned. "I plan on giving you a blowjob, but I'll pull away as you come so that it hits the pot instead of my throat."

God, this was going to be embarrassing. "Let's get dressed and discuss this on the way there."

She climbed out of bed and got dressed. "Nothing to discuss," she said, quickly slipping her flip-flops onto her feet. She opened the top drawer of the dresser and walked back over to me.

"The doctor took this picture when she did an ultrasound. It only shows a blob, but it's our baby." She held the picture out to me.

I took it from her and sat back down on the bed rather heavily. I could hardly see through the tears running down my face. She sat on my lap, wrapping her arms around my neck.

"I love you, Michael."

"I love you, too. Thank you for giving me everything

I've ever wanted: A woman to love and who loves me as much as I love her and a child."

"Come on. Let's go see Lucien and get this morning over with."

She stood up, gave me a quick kiss, and walked out of the bedroom.

I put on jeans and a T-shirt, then walked downstairs to find her drinking coffee with Lucien at the table.

"Lily, I thought we agreed on one coffee a day."

"We did, but my other one is practically untouched in the bedroom."

I ran my hands through my hair when I noticed Lucien smirking. "What are you smirking at?"

He tried not to laugh. "Nothing."

"Boys! Pregnant lady here. Please play nice," said Lily, looking sexy as hell in her denim shorts and pink T-shirt with her long curls trailing loosely down her back.

"I was just telling Lucien that I'm going with you this morning."

I groaned and sank into the chair across from my brother. "Lucien, please talk her out of this."

He roared with laughter. "No chance. This is going to make one hell of a story when we finally have another boys' night."

I just sat and scowled at him. "I'm glad my situation is so funny."

He sobered up. "You know damn well I don't find

your situation funny. What I find funny is Lily wanting to go and, ah, help." He started laughing again.

"Fuck," I said. I turned to look at Lily, who was still standing to the side, looking unsure, but trying to hide her laughter. "Come here, babe."

She walked over to me, laughing. I reached out to her, pulled her onto my lap, and said, "If you really want to come with me and help, we'd better get going. Do you want something to eat first?"

"No, we can have breakfast once the deed's done."

"Okay."

I looked at Lucien, who quickly stopped laughing and jumped to his feet to follow us out of the house.

32

Lily

As Lucien parked outside the doctor's office, I couldn't help but feel nervous. I'd told Michael that I was going to bring him to orgasm, but I was anxious about it. I hoped I was doing the right thing by making him take this test. I believed him when he said he knew this baby was his, but I needed proper results from the experts.

"Lily, are you coming?"

I smirked and climbed into Michael's waiting arms. "No, but you will be soon," I whispered.

Lucien heard and froze. "I think I'll wait in the car." He climbed back in, and we both laughed.

Michael took my hand and led me inside the build-

328

ing, where we found the doctor talking to his receptionist.

"You must be Michael McKenzie." The doctor held his hand out to Michael. "I'm Doctor Stephen Rowl."

He held his hand out to me. "I'm Lily Redmond."

"She's my fiancée," Michael stated. I pinched his butt.

He smiled and led us down a corridor, stopping outside a door.

"If you want to go in there and lock the door, everything you need is inside." When you're ready, just leave the pot in the room. I'll call you in a few days with the results," Dr. Rowl told us, hiding his amusement behind his hand—probably because I was with Michael. I bet they didn't get many fiancées or girlfriends accompanying their guy to an appointment to masturbate.

Michael quickly ushered me into the room and locked the door. I turned to look at him, and he was bright red with embarrassment.

"God." He put his head in his hands. "You owe me big time for letting you come with me. That was embarrassing as hell."

I smirked and dropped to the floor in front of him. "I want to play now."

"Lily." He pulled me up. "You can play, but first, we need to find a pot."

He was right. I moved out of his arms and walked around the small room. There was a television with a

DVD player, about ten erotic DVDs, a table with pots and lubricants, and a hospital bed with fresh linens.

Michael came up behind me, placed his hands on my hips, and started kissing my neck. "I think we have too many clothes on," he whispered.

I stepped out of his arms, quickly removed my clothes, and stood before him naked. I watched as he looked at my breasts, moved slowly down my body, and then back up to my face.

His breathing had become uneven. His eyes were full of lust.

"Take your clothes off, Michael, and sit on the chair." He cocked an eyebrow at my request. "We're going to play." I grinned at his shocked expression. "Hurry up."

He quickly stripped out of his jeans and T-shirt and sank into the chair. I licked my lips. He made me wet with just one look. I walked over to him, bent my head, and swiped my tongue over the head of his erect penis. "You taste good."

"Lily," he growled in warning.

"Hold on to the side of the chair and don't move your hands."

"Fuck."

I smiled up at him as I knelt in front of him, pushing his legs apart so I could move in between them. Boy, what a view! His erection twitched, the tip glistening. His balls looked heavy. I looked up and met his lust-filled eyes. "This isn't going to last long, Lily," he whispered.

I leaned forward and lightly bit the inside of his thigh. He sucked in a breath. I smoothed my hands along the tops of his thighs as I nibbled his other thigh. When I reached his testicles, I sucked one into my mouth. Michael arched off the chair and cursed. After swiping it a few times with my tongue, I released it and went for the other one.

"Lily, hell. You're killing me."

I released him. "Not yet!" I licked up his precum, then ran my hands up his abs to his nipples and shoulders. I cupped his face and pulled him down to meet my lips. "Taste yourself on me."

He growled and slammed his lips down onto mine. I put my hands on his shoulders to steady myself. One touch of his lips, and I went into sensory overload. I pulled away and bent down to his erect penis.

I massaged the head with my tongue, then took him into my mouth. Michael's whole body quivered with need. I massaged his balls with my hand and tightened my hold around his shaft while swallowing him deeper.

"Pot," he croaked, pushing my head away.

I quickly grabbed the pot and held his dick as he ejaculated into it. When I thought there was enough, I put my mouth back on him and sucked. He cursed and nearly bolted out of the chair.

After cleaning him up, I sat back on my heels and looked up at him.

He was totally satisfied. "You are amazing. Amazing," he said. His eyes sparkled, and before I knew it, he lifted me off the floor and into his arms.

He kissed me, causing my toes to curl, and placed me on the edge of the bed. "Lie back. It's your turn."

I dropped back onto the bed while he knelt on the floor with my legs over his shoulders.

"You're so wet." He licked me. "So sweet." He flicked my clit with his tongue. "You're mine." He spread me open with his fingers. "I'm going to eat your pussy." He dove in, flicking his tongue in and out of my sex while rubbing my clit. I was so close. "Play with your nipples. Let me watch you."

God, he was amazing at this! Michael sucked my clit into his mouth and slid two fingers into me, while I reached up and began twisting my nipples with my thumb and fingers. I met his gaze and came all over his mouth.

Michael

It was Sunday morning, two weeks after I'd nearly

destroyed what Lily and I had. She was snuggled in bed beside me, and I'd never been happier.

At Lily's insistence, we took the "little" test at the doctor's office. It probably took much longer than usual thanks to Lily's mouth and my desire to please my woman.

The doctor smirked when we left the room—no wonder; Lily was flushed to high heaven. I got her out of there quickly, and four days later, the doctor called to tell me my little swimmers were above average. Lily celebrated by giving me a blowjob while I was talking to Lucien on the phone.

I bit back a groan. "Michael, you're rock hard. What are you thinking about?"

"You giving me a blowjob at the doctor's office, and me returning the favor by eating your pussy. Then I remembered you sucking me off to celebrate while I was on the phone."

She laughed. "That was hot. You had to keep talking instead of moaning and groaning while I pleasured you. Then, when you came, you dropped the phone." She moved down between my legs.

"I think we need to do something here." She smirked and kissed the tip. "Have I told you how much I love your dick?"

She threw the covers off us and smoothed her hand over me. "You're so long. So wide. So hard. I love the crown and how it fits in my mouth." She sucked the head into her mouth. "I love how you leak precum when I have you so excited." She sucked me in again. "I love how you twitch when I lick along this vein with my tongue." She licked me. "I love how you quiver when I do this." She gripped my shaft with one hand, massaged one of my balls with the other, and sucked the other ball into her mouth. I nearly shot off the bed.

"Fuck, Lily. Come up here," I panted.

She looked at me. I shoved some pillows behind my head and helped her straddle my face. With her pussy in my face, I wasn't going to last long.

"Lily, you look so fucking hot. I'm going to eat your pussy while you suck me off." She moaned, and I groaned.

Lily wrapped her mouth around me and started sliding her mouth up and down my shaft. Leaning closer, she lowered her arms across my groin for support and started to play with my balls.

I licked her pussy lips, sliding my tongue into her while kissing her as though her mouth were locked to mine. I took hold of her hips to keep her still. My breathing was heavy, and my cock was in heaven. I could feel Lily's breasts against my stomach. Her nipples were rock hard and dug into me.

I shoved a finger into her while sucking her clit. She was close, but not quite there.

She pulled her mouth away from my cock, turned

her head to look at me, and sucked her finger into her mouth.

Oh, fuck, I wouldn't survive this!

She turned back around, taking me deeper into her mouth, while I used my tongue to fuck her and my fingers to play with her clit. I used her arousal to wet my finger.

She massaged my balls, then moved downwards. As she started to rub against my ass, I did the same to her. She moaned deeply, and the vibration traveled along my entire body.

She took me down her throat while shoving a finger in my ass. I came while shoving my finger in Lily's ass. She screamed around my cock as we both climaxed in powerful bursts of pleasure.

Lily collapsed, resting her head on my balls. If I'd had the breath, I would have laughed. I leaned forward and kissed her pussy. Then, I moved her legs to one side and pulled her up into my arms.

Her eyes sparkled.

"I've never had anyone nod off on my balls before," I told her. She started to laugh, which turned into a full-on belly laugh.

"I wasn't asleep, you ass. I was admiring what was mine." She smirked.

"Good answer. Christ, if I hear any more of that, I won't be able to walk. Hell, I'll probably walk around with a permanent erection. One memory of this at the most inopportune moment, and everyone will know what you do to me."

"Then it's fortunate that we work together, so I can lock your office door and lend a hand."

"Mmm, one of my favorite fantasies," I told her, grinning.

"You do realize it's going to be hard for me to sit outside your office and work while you're inside having erotic fantasies about what you can do to me."

"Please, don't mention hard."

"You can't be hard again...so soon!"

I laughed. "Love, I only have to think about you, and I'm in this condition." I took her face in my hands and caressed it. "Will you marry me soon, Lily? I love you with all my heart."

She climbed on top of me, took my face in her hands, and kissed me. "Yes, I'll marry you soon. I love you and can't wait to be your wife."

THE END
Continued in The Wedding Novella

DEAR READER

Thank you for reading *Playing with the Boss,* and thank you for your reviews! It's really appreciated.

Sign up with your email to be alerted on new releases, sales and events.

http://lexibuchanan.net

MCKENZIE
BROTHERS
HOLDINGS

OTHER BOOKS BY AUTHOR

Hawke's Ridge

Maddox · Colton (2026)

Den Hollows

One of Six · Two of Six (2026)

Den of Filth (New MC Series 2025)

Reckless Wilder (2026)

Fifth Realm Series (Romantasy)

Quiver of Chaos · Wings & Arrows (2026)

Standalone Romantasy

Persephone Unchained

Tallulah James Mystery

Dead and a Murder or Two · Dead and the Wedding Crashers · Dead and a Deadly Deed · Dead and a Best Friend

Boston Bay Vikings

Camden · Bennett · Ethan · Sutton · Carter · Bryson · Ivan · Theo · Noah · Knox · Jericho · Roman

Boston Bay Vikings Minor League

Lake · Rhodes · Nikoli · Dario · Madden · Bradford

Single Titles

Butterflies and Darkness · Come Back to Me · Indecent Villain · Lawful · Love Stryker · Tears in the Rain · Whispers of Yesterday

Holiday Season

Holiday Kisses in the Snow · Jingle Bells

Romantic Suspense Series

Twenty Eight Days · The Next Victim (2025)

Blossom Creek

Christmas at Emelia's · A Rake in Blossom Creek · Heatwave in Blossom Creek · Secret Love in Blossom Creek · Mischief in Blossom Creek · Runaway Bride in Blossom Creek · Naughty & Nice in Blossom Creek

Bad Boy Rockers

My Brother's Girl · Past Sins · My Best Friend's Sister · Never Let Go · Saving Jace · Silent Night (Novella)

Kincaid Sisters

Meant to be Mine · You Were Always Mine · Will You be Mine

McKenzie Brothers

Playing with the Boss · A McKenzie Wedding (Novella) · Playing with Fire · Playing with Desire · Playing with Trouble · Playing with their Hearts · A McKenzie Christmas (Novella)

De La Fuente Family (McKenzie Spinoff)

Love in Montana · Love in Purgatory · Love in Bloom · Love in Country · Love in Flame · Love in Game · Love in Education

McKenzie Cousins

(McKenzie Spinoff)

Baby Makes Three · A Business Decision · Secret Kisses · Kissing Cousins · If Only · Princess & the Puck · A Bakers Delight · A Cowboy for Christmas · A Secret Affair · One Christmas · The Pregnant Professor · It Started with a Kiss

Novella's

Educate Me · One Dance · Pure

ABOUT THE AUTHOR

While Lexi is the author of the chick lit series, Tallulah James Mystery, and the fantasy/romance series, The Fifth Realm, she is also the author of over seventy novels. Based in Ireland, this British author has been writing since 2013.

Follow on social media:

Website: http://lexibuchanan.net
Email: authorlexibuchanan@gmail.com

facebook.com/lexibuchananauthor
x.com/AuthorLexi
instagram.com/authorlexib
bookbub.com/author/lexi-buchanan
amazon.com/Lexi-Buchanan/e/B009SPA94U